SHOOT OR DIE

Evan lunged for the gun. As he moved, one of the outlaws glanced back and saw him.

From the corner of his eye, Evan saw the man reaching for a pistol. He concentrated on scooping up his own weapon and rolling to the side, bringing the Colt level as he came to a stop. The owlhoot hesitated as his own gun cleared leather, and Evan could almost read the man's mind. The outlaw had just realized that if he fired, he would send a warning to the gang's intended victims.

Evan didn't have to worry about that.

Books by James Reasoner

Wind River
Thunder Wagon
Wolf Shadow
Medicine Creek
Dark Trail
Judgment Day
The Wilderness Road
The Hunted

Published by HarperPaperbacks

THE HUNTED

James Reasoner

HarperPaperbacks
A Division of HarperCollinsPublishers

![HarperPaperbacks logo] **HarperPaperbacks**
A Division of HarperCollinsPublishers
10 East 53rd Street, New York, N.Y. 10022-5299

This is a work of fiction. The characters, incidents, and
dialogues are products of the author's imagination and are not to
be construed as real. Any resemblance to actual events or
persons, living or dead, is entirely coincidental.

ISBN 0-06-101145-2

Cover illustration by Rick McCollum

First HarperPaperbacks printing: May 1997

Printed in the United States of America

Visit HarperPaperbacks on the World Wide Web at
http://www.harpercollins.com/paperbacks

❖ 10 9 8 7 6 5 4 3 2 1

For Robert J. Randisi,
a good friend
who once took a chance on an old cowboy.
Thanks, Bob.

Special thanks to L. J. Washburn,
uncredited collaborator on this
and many other books.
You make it all possible, Livia.

THE HUNTED

1

One foot in front of the other. Evan Littleton had been doing that for what seemed like an eternity. The muscles in his legs throbbed painfully, but his feet were beyond that. They were numb, and when he paused and looked behind him, he saw dark spots in the dust of the road where blood from broken blisters had seeped through the holes in his boots. As he watched, the flecks of moisture were sucked up by the thirsty Texas soil.

Still and all, he told himself, this beat a Yankee prison camp all to pieces.

With a sigh, he trudged on. A few minutes later, the road topped the crest of a long ridge, and Evan looked down into the valley in front of him. A thrill of recognition went through him. There was the Colorado River, winding through rocky hills dotted with post oak and cedar. More times during the past four years than Evan liked to think about, he had been sure he would never see the river that flowed through his homeland again.

But there was the Colorado, and the ferry that ran across the stream, and beyond—still out of sight but so close, relatively speaking, that he felt as if he could reach out and touch it—his home. Evan closed his eyes and covered them with a hand. A shudder of emotion ran through him.

Tall and whip-thin before the deprivations of the prison camp, Evan was even more gaunt now. His long hair and drooping mustache were streaked with gray. He was almost forty years old, but he supposed he looked older than that. There were deep trenches in the darkly tanned cheeks below the blue eyes. He wore a floppy-brimmed straw hat that he had found on a road over in the piney woods of East Texas. Once it might have been the fancy headgear of a wealthy planter, but now it had holes chewed in the brim and crown. Still, it kept the sun off Evan's head. The coat that protected him against the autumn winds was also a castoff. Under the coat was a homespun shirt he had been given by a farm wife down close to Austin as payment for some wood he had chopped. He knew she had taken pity on him, and though that galled him, he hadn't refused the shirt, nor the hot meal or the night's sleep in the farm couple's barn. The uniform pants that flapped around his legs were Confederate issue, once butternut gray but now faded almost to white, as were the boots that were little more than chunks of leather held together by a few frayed threads.

No gun, of course. The Yankees hadn't been just about to arm the hordes of Rebel prisoners they were forced to turn loose after Robert E. Lee and

Ulysses S. Grant had gotten together at Appomattox Court House and put an end to the War for the Southern Confederacy.

Months has passed since then, and Evan had been making his way home all that time. He had been packed onto a train with hundreds of other released prisoners, taken to Atlanta, and turned loose. That had been fine for those Georgia boys, but Evan faced a long walk back to the hills of Central Texas. Alabama, Mississippi, Louisiana . . . he had spent the summer crossing them, finally reaching the Sabine River and standing on Texas soil again in late August. For a short time, *that* had felt like home, but of course it wasn't. He had moved on almost right away, always working his way west.

Evan glanced up at the sun. Not yet noon, he judged. He might make it to Richland Springs today. San Saba was closer, and the last he'd heard, he had some cousins there who might offer him a place to stay. But that would be a little out of the way, and Evan couldn't stand the thought of anything delaying him even an hour from his reunion with his family.

An image of Lynette and the children floated in his mind, drawing him on as it had all these past months. Thad and Dinah, Billy and Penelope—*not* Penny, he recalled with a tired smile; she had hated the nickname even at the age of six, which was how old she had been when he went off to war—and Rockly and little Fulton, the baby of the family. All of them would be waiting to greet him when he came walking up to the farmhouse. The thought of that moment, that one special moment, had kept him going, had given him the strength to survive not only the years in the prison camp but also the long trek home after the war.

Caught up in his reverie, Evan almost didn't hear the pounding of hoofbeats behind him in time.

"Out of the way, you blasted scarecrow!" The shout reached his ears an instant after the thunder of galloping horses. Evan jerked around and saw the animals almost on top of him. He flung himself to the side, his tiredness forgotten as instincts took over.

He landed hard on his shoulder and rolled into the bar ditch alongside the road. The riders swept past him, the hooves of the horses kicking up a choking cloud of dust. Evan had already determined from the condition of the road that it had been a dry, dusty summer and fall in this part of Texas, which was nothing unusual. He had been a Texan all his life and knew there was always either too much rain or not enough.

Coughing and hacking from the dust he'd breathed in, Evan raised himself onto his knees and peered after the riders. There were three of them, and the tails of their long coats flapped behind them as they rode hard toward the ferry landing. Evan hadn't gotten a good look at any of them, but he figured he wouldn't have recognized them anyway. Texas was full of strangers these days. Reconstruction wasn't quite as oppressive a force here as it was in the other former

Confederate states, but it was bad enough. Evan had already learned to avoid the hated State Police, which was manned largely by Yankees and turncoat Texans.

He stood up and tried to brush some of the dust off his coat and trousers. It wouldn't do to think too much about the war and its outcome. Slavery had never really been much of an issue in this part of the country; Evan, like most of the other pioneers on the western frontier of Texas, had never had any sympathy for the practice. But he was a firm believer in states' rights, and that was why he had marched off to join the cause.

And the only thing he had accomplished by doing that was to lose four years of his life, four years away from his farm and family, years that he could never get back.

With a snort of disgust, he swallowed his bitterness—and some more road dust—and started walking down the hill toward the river again. The riders had disappeared where the road ran through a grove of post oaks.

As he approached the ferry landing a few minutes later, Evan heard loud, angry voices. There was something familiar about the one that said, "You'd better do as we tell you, old man!" Evan frowned and decided the voice belonged to the same man who had shouted at him to get out of the road, just before the riders almost trampled him.

Evan walked through the sun-dappled shade under the oaks and saw that the three riders had dismounted and were standing next to the ferry landing, which was a short pier extending into the river on stout pilings. There was an identical landing on the other side of the Colorado. Also on this side of the broad stream was the cabin where old Jonas Russell, the operator of the ferry, lived with his grandson.

Jonas was standing next to the windlass that his team of mules turned to pull the ferry along the thick ropes stretched from one side of the river to the other. Evan recognized him immediately. That long white beard was pretty distinctive, and Jonas looked as if he hadn't really changed much in the four years Evan had been gone. Evan wished he could say the same about himself, but it wasn't true. After everything he had gone through, he was afraid that he would never again truly be the man he had been.

Standing beside Jonas was a boy in his early teens. That would be Terrance, Evan thought, the old man's grandson. But there was another child, a smaller boy, peeking out from behind Jonas, and Evan wondered fleetingly who that might be. Some kid Jonas had taken in, more than likely; the ferryman was well known in these parts for his generosity.

Jonas wasn't feeling generous at the moment, though. That much was obvious. He glared at the three men in black hats and long coats and said, "I ain't ferryin' no Yankees acrost this river just so's they can get up to mischief. You got no business over there." He spat, dribbling tobacco juice in his beard and adding to the stains already there. "You got no business anywhere in Texas, far as I'm concerned."

"You can make noises like an unreconstructed Rebel some other time, old man," said one of the strangers. Evan felt certain now that they were members of the State Police, and that assumption was confirmed as the man went on, "We can go anywhere we want, and you know it. We're the law around here now."

Jonas spat again. "You want to get to the other side of the river, you can swim them horses you prob'ly stole from good Texans."

One of the other men brushed back his long coat and reached for the gun on his hip. "This old fool's interfering with the law. We can deal with him however we want."

Evan saw the gesture, knew how this situation could easily turn deadly. He swallowed, well aware that he could duck into the trees and wait unnoticed until it was all over, one way or the other. But instead he lifted his voice and called, "Howdy, Jonas! How you doin', you old moss-back?"

The three Yankees stiffened and turned their heads to see who was behind them. They relaxed visibly when they saw it was only Evan, the same ragged, gaunt man they had nearly ridden down a few minutes earlier. It was clear they didn't consider him any sort of threat.

Evan's gaze studied them quickly. They were all cut from the same cloth: tall, broad-shouldered, handsomely arrogant. Their clothes were expensive, and so were the pistols that rode on their hips. Evan glanced at their horses, saw the fine saddles and the polished wooden stocks of rifles protruding from saddle boots. Only the best for the State Police, he thought.

"Do I know you, mister?" Jonas said, no recognition in his eyes as he looked at Evan. That came as no surprise; Jonas hadn't known Evan very well, just as an occasional customer for the ferry, and Evan knew how much he had changed.

"It's Evan Littleton. I'm back from the war at last, Jonas."

One of the men took a step toward him. "You looking for trouble, Reb? You armed?"

Evan held up his hands, palms out, and nervously backed up a step. "No, sir. No, sir, I ain't looking for trouble. Don't have no gun, neither. Don't want one."

The State Policeman grunted. "Glad to see not all of you Rebs are fools. Move along, mister, unless you have business here."

"No, sir, no business." Evan scuffed one of his worn boots in the dusty road. "Jonas, I was wonderin' . . . if I could have a bite to eat?"

"Go on in the cabin," Jonas said, his quavery old voice touched with disgust. "There's some leftover biscuits on the stove, and you might find a little coffee in the bottom of the pot."

Evan just muttered something meaningless and shuffled toward the log cabin near the landing. The Yankees weren't paying any attention to him anymore. They went back to trying to browbeat Jonas into ferrying them across the river.

Evan stepped into the cabin, let the door swing

shut behind him, and looked around quickly. A rifle he recognized as one of those newfangled Henry repeaters hung on pegs over the door. Evan reached up and took it down, worked the lever to see if it was loaded. It was. He found a Walker Colt, also loaded, in the top drawer of Jonas's old rolltop desk. Evan started to tuck the revolver into the waistband of his trousers, but he stopped when he realized the gun was so heavy it would just pull his pants down. With a grim smile on his face, he held the Colt in his right hand and tucked the Henry under his left arm, so that he would have a hand free to open the door.

A curse and the sound of a blow came from outside. Terrance Russell shouted angrily. Evan opened the door and stepped through it into the sunlight.

Jonas was on the ground, one of the men standing over him with clenched fists. The other two had drawn their guns. The little boy, who looked to be about five years old, was being held back by Terrance. The youngster was mad as a baby bobcat, Evan saw. The man who had obviously just knocked Jonas down drew back his foot, ready to kick the old man in the head.

Evan leveled the Colt and said in a loud, clear voice, "Do it and I'll blow your head off."

It was amazing how good he felt, how the months of weariness had fallen away from him, just because he had the smooth walnut grips of a gun in his hand again.

The three men jerked their heads around, surprised and furious that someone else would dare to challenge them. The two who had their guns out began to twist their bodies, clearly intending to bring the weapons to bear on Evan.

"I wouldn't," Evan said. "This Colt has five shots in it, and I can empty it by the time you boys turn around." He hefted the rifle in his left hand. "If that's not enough, this Henry's got fifteen shells in its magazine, and I can put each and every one of 'em right where I want it faster than you can blink your eyes." That last was a lie; he had never even fired a Henry. But the Colt . . . well, that was another matter.

The man who had been about to kick Jonas stepped away from the ferryman. He turned a hard stare toward Evan and said, "Mister, are you sure you know what you're doing? You know who we are?"

"I know enough about you," Evan replied. "I've seen plenty just like you in the past few months, riding roughshod over folks and making their lives miserable, all in the name of some misbegotten Reconstruction. I've seen enough carpetbaggers and thieves like you to last me a lifetime."

"You're in a lot of trouble, Reb. You made a mistake when you said your name. I'm not likely to forget it. Even if you run us off today, we'll come back and hunt you down."

A grin stretched across Evan's face. "Then I reckon the thing to do would be to kill you now, so you can't bother me later on."

He saw them pale as he watched them over the barrel of the Colt. He wasn't really trying to push them into a gunfight . . . or maybe he was.

Suddenly, the image of his family flashed into his mind again. He couldn't allow the memories of the wild old days to goad him into bringing down such trouble on the heads of his loved ones.

"Look," he went on quickly, "you may not believe it, but I don't want a fight. Why don't you boys put your guns up, get on those horses, and turn around and ride back to Austin or wherever you came from? Nobody gets hurt."

"It's too late for that—"

One of the other men reached out and laid a hand on the arm of the man who was speaking. "Forget it, Mike. The Reb's right. We'll go patrol somewhere else, and nobody has to die." He holstered his pistol as he tried to talk sense to his companion. The other man who had drawn a gun slid the weapon back into its holster, too.

The one called Mike, who was practically quivering with rage, still stared at Evan for a long moment. Finally, he gave a curt nod. "All right," he said. "But I won't forget this, Littleton. You ever cross me again, I'll kill you." He looked down at Jonas. "And the next time we ride up here, old man, you better do like we say."

Jonas got to his feet, struggling to regain some of his lost dignity. "One of these days, we'll boot you Yankees out of here. Things'll be different then."

"Don't count on it," Mike said with a harsh laugh. He stepped over to his horse, swung up into the saddle. The other two followed suit. They wheeled their mounts around, dug their spurs cruelly into the flanks of the horses, and galloped off to the east, raising another cloud of dust as they went out of sight.

Evan didn't ease down the hammer of the Colt and lower the gun until the three men were well and truly gone. He had made some new enemies today, and he knew it. But he had spent years surrounded by enemies, in constant fear for his life, and as long as his family was safe, he didn't care much about any threat to him.

Jonas hurried over to him and slapped him on the back, saying excitedly, "Whoo-eee! You sure put the fear o' God into them Yankees. Might've been smarter for you to stay out of it, but I got to admit I sure was happy to see you step out of that cabin armed for bear. Hoped that was what you was up to when you acted so scared of them fellas."

"I reckon I was a little scared," Evan admitted. He handed the rifle and the revolver to Jonas. "But I learned in that Yankee prison camp not to show it. That was about the worst thing you could do."

"Prison camp," repeated Jonas. "Heard about them places. Reckon you must be a lucky man to've made it out alive."

"Yeah," said Evan. "Lucky."

2

"**C**ome on inside and set a spell," Jonas invited. "There really are some leftover biscuits and coffee from breakfast."

"Thanks, but I ought to be on my way." Evan gestured at the ferry. "I don't have any money, but if I could get a ride across the river . . ."

Jonas laughed. "Don't you worry 'bout that. After the way you saved my bacon from them Yankee carpetbaggers, I'll ferry you back an' forth acrost this river any time you want. I'd sure like to sit down and break bread with you first, though."

Evan wasn't anxious to be delayed any more than he already had been, but since he was asking a favor of the old man, he supposed the least he could do would be to accept the offered hospitality. He nodded and said, "All right."

"Glad to hear it! Come on in." Jonas turned to the two boys and went on, "Terrance, you and the Gunderson boy keep an eye out and come a-runnin' if you see them Yankees comin' back this way."

Terrance nodded. "Sure, Grandpap."

Evan looked at the two youngsters as they ran off a short distance down the road. He frowned. "Gunderson, did you say? Some of my neighbors are named Gunderson."

"You mean over toward Richland Springs?"

"That's right."

Jonas stroked his long white beard as he led Evan into the shadowy interior of the cabin. "Couldn't recollect if you was one of the Richland Springs Littletons, or part of the bunch from down San Saba way."

"They're cousins of mine," Evan explained. "My farm's about two miles this side of Richland Springs."

Jonas nodded and motioned for Evan to sit down on one of the benches at the rough-hewn table in the center of the cabin's only room. "I see folks come an' go on the ferry, but I can't keep up with 'em. Only reason I know about the Gundersons is because Lars left that boy here."

"Abandoned him?" Evan asked in surprise. He couldn't imagine doing such a thing.

"Lars's wife died," Jonas said as he took a plate of biscuits and placed them on the table. He put a tin cup in front of Evan and poured thick black coffee into it from the pot that had been sitting on the cast iron stove. "That ol' Swede figgered he couldn't raise a child by hisself. And he was tired of livin' on the frontier, 'specially after his missus passed away, so he decided to go back over to East Texas where he come from in the first place. Begged me to take in the boy when he came through here." Jonas sat down opposite Evan and sipped from his own cup of coffee. "Don't reckon I really needed another mouth to feed. This ferry don't bring in *that* much money, 'specially nowadays, what with the Yankees ruinin' everything. But I never could say no to helpin' out a kid."

Evan picked up one of the biscuits and gnawed off a hunk of it, glad that he still had pretty good teeth. Jonas Russell's biscuits were so hard, Evan figured they could be skipped along the surface of the river, just like rocks. But he had learned in the camp never to miss an opportunity to eat. Another chance might not come along for a while.

"War's been over for a good spell," Jonas said. "You just now gettin' back?"

"Had to walk from Atlanta. It took a while."

"I reckon it would. We never got much war news in these parts, but I heard tell there ain't much left of Atlanta. One o' them Yankee generals burned it down or somethin'."

"That's what happened, all right," Evan said. "Sherman came right through there on his way to the sea. Didn't leave much standing. They're rebuilding it now." He hadn't learned about Sherman's savage march until after the war. The prison camp and the Texas frontier had one thing in common—it took a long time for news to reach anyone in either place.

For the next fifteen minutes, Evan chewed on the hard, dry biscuits, washing them down with the coffee, and between swallows he answered

Jonas's questions about the war. Evan was hardly an expert, since he had spent half the time he had been gone behind the walls of the camp after being captured at Antietam, but he did the best he could to tell the old man what had happened. It was a pretty sad story, to Evan's way of thinking. He didn't see how even the Yankees could be glad about what had befallen the country during those long and bloody years.

He was just about to stand up, thank Jonas for the food, and push on, when the door of the cabin opened and the two boys came hurrying in. Jonas slapped a palm on the table and roared, "Them Yankees ain't tryin' to sneak up on us, are they?"

"No, Grandpap," replied Terrance. Evan noticed that the youngster's pants were wet, and the smaller boy's clothes were soaked. "Fulton here sort of fell in the river, and I had to wade in and fish him out."

"Well, get them wet clothes off, boy," Jonas said. "You'll catch your death of the grippe if you don't."

Evan's fingers had tightened on the handle of the tin cup at the mention of the younger boy's name. He had a son named Fulton, the baby of the family, who had been barely three months old when Evan had gone off to war. But Jonas had said that this boy was a Gunderson . . .

Fulton turned his back and pulled his wet, homespun shirt over his head.

Evan stared at the large purple birthmark squarely in the center of the boy's back.

His mind shot back to those last weeks before he had left the farm. As clearly as if it had been the day before, he remembered the birthmark on the back of his infant son. Lynette had fussed over it, upset that anything had marred the beauty of one of her children, but Evan had assured her that Fulton was still handsome as could be. No one was ever going to notice that birthmark.

But Evan noticed it now, and the tin cup clattered on the table as it overturned, knocked over by his hand as he got hurriedly to his feet.

Jonas looked at him in surprise. "What's the matter with you, Littleton? You look like you done seen a haint."

Evan pointed at Fulton and said, "I thought you said this boy was a Gunderson." His voice shook a little.

"Far as I know, he is. 'Twas Lars Gunderson who left him here, no doubt about that."

Evan stepped quickly around the table, ignoring the startled looks Jonas and Terrance gave him. He grabbed Fulton's shoulders and spun the youngster around, leaning over to stare into his wide eyes.

Lynette's eyes were staring back at him, Evan realized. And Fulton's nose, as well as the line of his jaw, was familiar, too. Evan had seen similar features reflected back at him every time he saw himself in a looking glass.

There was no doubt in his mind. He was looking into the face of his youngest son.

"Here now!" Jonas said, standing up. "What are you doin', Littleton, grabbin' that kid like that?

I'm grateful for what you did earlier, but I won't stand for no trouble—"

"This . . . this is my son." Evan managed to choke out the words. His voice strengthened a little as he added, "I'm the boy's father."

"What in blazes are you talkin' about? Lars Gunderson left him here, I tell you, and asked me to take him in."

"Maybe so, but I know my own boy." Evan's certainty grew. True, it had been four years, and Fulton had been a baby the last time Evan had seen him. That was why Evan had not recognized him right away. He had never expected to find his son here. Fulton should have been on the farm, some twenty miles west.

"Mister?" Fulton asked in a thin, frightened voice. "Are you sayin' you're my pa?"

Evan went down on one knee so that he could look into the boy's eyes again. "That's right," he said. "I'm your pa. But what happened to your ma? Where's all your brothers and sisters?"

Tears welled up in Fulton's eyes and trickled down his cheeks. "My ma's dead," he said, "and everybody else is gone."

A sensation like the kick of a mule hit Evan in the middle of his chest. Lynette . . . *dead*? It couldn't be, it just couldn't. He swallowed hard and asked, "What happened? Did she get sick?"

Fulton nodded. "A fever came and took her."

"When?"

"A long, long time ago. Maybe a year?"

"The boy's mixed up," Jonas said gruffly. "He's thinkin' about the Gunderson woman. She took sick and died, just like I told you. That was eight or nine months ago. Lars tried to make it for a little while 'fore he pulled up stakes and left. That's what the boy's thinkin' about."

Evan put his hands on the child's shoulders again. "What about it, Fulton? Is that the way it was? Is Gunderson your last name?"

"No . . . my name's Fulton Littleton."

Evan looked up in a mixture of sorrow and triumph. "You see?" he said to Jonas. "I told you the boy's my son."

"Well, I'll swan!" Jonas tugged on his beard and said to Fulton, "How come you never told me you wasn't a Gunderson, boy?"

Fulton shook his head blankly. "Nobody ever asked me."

Evan let out a strangled laugh and pulled Fulton into his arms, hugging him tightly. After a minute, the boy said, "You're . . . you're squeezin' me to death, mister—I mean, Pa."

Evan loosened his grip on the child and realized how cold Fulton's skin was. The youngster still needed to dry off and get into some dry clothes. Evan let go of him and said, "You finish getting out of those wet clothes, like Mr. Russell told you to. Then we'll talk some more."

"All right," Fulton said with a nod.

Evan straightened and looked over at Jonas. "Walk outside with me?"

Jonas nodded and said, "Yeah. We got some figgerin' to do."

The two men left the cabin and walked toward the ferry landing. With his gaze fixed on the river,

Evan said, "My wife must have died, and the Gundersons took in Fulton."

"That's what it looks like, all right," agreed Jonas. "I'm mighty sorry 'bout your loss, Littleton. Then I reckon Miz Gunderson passed away, too, and that left your boy with Lars. I wish that Swede had *told* me all this when he left the younker here."

Evan took a deep breath. "Well, we've figured it out. Now I've got to find out what happened to the rest of my children. Fulton's got three brothers and two sisters."

"Could be they're still around Richland Springs somewhere," Jonas suggested. "They're prob'ly stayin' with some other neighbors." The old man shrugged. "Times is hard. Most folks couldn't afford to take in more'n one or two extra kids. Could be they're scattered all over the county."

Evan had to close his eyes for a moment as he tried to come to grips with all the unexpected discoveries he had made in the past few minutes. His wife was gone—the pain of that was just starting to set in—and his children might have been scattered to God knows where. He had to get home as quickly as possible. He opened his eyes and turned to Jonas. "Is there anywhere around here I could borrow a horse?"

"I was just thinkin' the same thing," the old man said. "I ain't got no horses, but you can have the loan of one of my mules. I got a couple of spares." Jonas chuckled. "He won't be very comfortable ridin', but he'll get you to Richland Springs faster'n you can get there on foot."

Evan nodded and said solemnly, "I'm much obliged. Can I . . . leave Fulton here until I find out what . . . what happened?"

"Sure. The boy helps out around the place, and he ain't no trouble. Me an' Terrance'll be glad to keep on watchin' him for you."

"Thanks." Evan looked toward the cabin. "I guess I'd better go tell him."

It wasn't going to be easy, saying good-bye so soon after he had been reunited with his son.

But this time it wasn't going to be for four years. Evan swore that with every fiber of his being.

He didn't have to go all the way to Richland Springs to find out what had happened to his family. Around the middle of the afternoon, he rode up to the farm of a family named Brackett. They had been friends of his and Lynette's before the war.

"My God!" Andrew Brackett exclaimed as he came out of his cabin and saw the gaunt, ragged figure dismounting awkwardly from the back of a mule. "Evan Littleton? Is that you?"

"It's me, Andy," Evan said as he held out a hand toward his old friend. Brackett grasped it and returned the firm handshake.

"It's like shaking hands with a ghost," Brackett said. "Everybody around here had given you up for dead, Evan. We thought you'd been killed in the war, like—" He stopped short.

"Like all the other fellas who didn't come back?" Evan shook his head. "I was in a Yankee prison camp.

There were plenty of times I figured I might as well be dead, but I hung on and they finally let me out after the South surrendered. Been trying to get back here ever since."

From the doorway of the cabin, Elizabeth Brackett called, "Who is it, Andy?" Evan glanced at her, saw the children clustered around her skirts, and his heart just about broke at the reminder of all he had lost without even being aware of it until now.

"It's . . . Evan Littleton," Brackett told his wife. He took hold of Evan's arm. "Come on inside. Beth's got coffee on, and you can stay to supper."

Evan wasn't interested in coffee or food, but his ingrained politeness made him nod his appreciation and take off his battered old hat as Brackett tugged him toward the cabin. They went inside.

"I'm so sorry about Lynette, Evan," Beth said as he sat down at the table.

"I don't really know what happened," Evan said. "I found my boy Fulton staying at old Jonas Russell's ferry over the Colorado. He said his mama got sick and died."

"That's right," Brackett said with a sympathetic nod. "For what it's worth, I don't think she suffered much. The fever came on her sudden-like, and she was gone by the next day. Lars Gunderson and I, we buried her on that knoll overlooking your place."

One of Evan's hands clenched into a fist, and he brought it up and tapped it lightly on his beard-stubbled chin for a minute before he was able to say, "That's good. I'm much obliged, Andy. Lynette loved to walk up on that hill and look around over the place. I reckon it's where she'd want to be."

Beth came over to him and put a hand on his shoulder. "What was Fulton doing at the ferry? I thought Lars took the boy with him when he started back to East Texas."

"He got as far as the ferry and talked old Jonas into taking Fulton in. I guess Lars was pretty busted up about Elsa dying."

Brackett nodded. "She passed away about three months after Lynette did. I tell you, Evan, we've had more than our share of tragedy around here lately."

"I reckon everybody has, since that damn war started!" Evan grimaced and looked up at Beth. "Begging your pardon for my language, that is."

She smiled down at him. "It's all right, Evan. If anybody's got a right to curse that war, it's you."

Evan swallowed and nodded, then looked across the table at Brackett and asked, "Andy . . . where are the rest of my children?"

The uneasy look on Brackett's face as the man hesitated in answering made Evan squirm inside. Finally, Brackett said, "Well . . . folks had to take them in. Some people named Ashmore took Dinah. Don't reckon you know 'em, since they came here after you left for the war. Billy and Penny went with the Cartmills, and Rockly was taken in by Frank and Suellen Wilson."

"What about Thad?" Evan asked, unable to keep a trace of anger out of his voice. "He's a man full-grown by now. Why didn't he keep the family together? He could've kept the farm going if he'd tried."

Brackett and Beth looked at each other, and Evan suddenly knew he wasn't going to like the answer to the question. Beth's eyes were shining with tears.

"There's no way to soften this, Evan," Brackett said. "Thad went off and joined the Confederate Army after the word came that you had disappeared in the war and probably been killed. He never came back. He was at . . . Gettysburg. That's the last anybody ever heard of him."

Even inside the prison camp, they had heard about the massive battle at Gettysburg. Casualties had been terrible on both sides. If Thad had fallen in that battle, he was probably lying even now in a mass grave somewhere in the hills of Pennsylvania . . .

"No!" The shout came from Evan's mouth, and his clenched fists banged down on the table before he really knew what he was doing. "It's not fair! It's not fair!" He knew he was frightening the Brackett children, but he couldn't stop himself. He slumped forward, his head falling onto his arms, the sobs that he had been holding in for hours finally erupting from him.

He was barely aware of Brackett taking hold of his shoulders and lifting him. He felt the cool smoothness of an earthen jug being pressed into his hands and lifted to his mouth. Raw fire coursed between his lips and down his throat. The whiskey hit his belly and exploded like a cannon shot. He swallowed again, sucking down more of the stuff.

The liquor must have burned a hole in his pain and grief, letting it drain away. After a few minutes, he took a deep, shuddering breath and managed to say, "Thanks, Andy. I . . . I reckon I'd better go round up my kids now."

"Evan . . . you haven't heard all of it."

Evan stared at the man, wondering what could be left. What remained of his life to be devastated?

"A lot of people have been pulling up stakes around here and leaving," Brackett went on miserably. "Lars Gunderson wasn't the only one. Most of 'em have gone west, hoping to get away from the carpetbaggers. We've been lucky and they haven't bothered us, but it's probably just a matter of time."

"What are you trying to tell me, Andy?"

"The Ashmores and the Cartmills and the Wilsons . . . they're gone. They took their kids, and your kids, and left. I couldn't even start to tell you where any of 'em might be now."

A man should never tell himself that things can't get any worse, Evan thought. Things could *always* get worse.

"I'll find them," he heard himself saying. "I don't care how long it takes or how far I have to go, I'll find those kids, each and every one of them." He put his hands on the table and pushed himself to his feet, revitalized a little by the whiskey and the sense of purpose that were both flowing through him. "I'll go by the place, maybe some of the horses are still there—"

Brackett reached out and put a hand on his arm. "It won't do you any good to go there, Evan.

It's not your farm anymore. Somebody else has taken it over."

"Somebody else?" Evan repeated roughly. "Who?"

Brackett glanced at his wife, and both of them seemed nervous. He looked at Evan again and said, "Carpetbaggers. The Yankees have got your farm, Evan . . ."

3

Evan reined the horse to a stop. He had left Jonas Russell's mule at the Brackett place and borrowed this better mount from Andrew Brackett. It was a rangy, mouse-colored dun with a dark stripe down the center of its back, and it had capered around and snapped at Evan several times during the ride over here, as if to show its high spirits and dislike of him. The horse stood quietly now, however. Evan sat trembling in the saddle as he looked at what had once been his home.

The place hadn't changed much. The cabin sat at the base of a small hill, near a trickle of water lined with oaks and cottonwoods. The creek wasn't much of a stream, but it was spring-fed and never ran dry. Beyond the double-roomed cabin with the dogtrot in the middle, Evan could see a corner of the barn and the corral. Fields stretched to the north and south, paralleling the line of low hills. Some of them had been cultivated recently, perhaps for winter wheat. The doors of the barn were open, and he heard the ringing of a hammer on an anvil, another sign that the farm was occupied.

Evan lifted his eyes toward the hill behind the cabin. According to Andrew Brackett, Lynette rested up there, under the oaks whose green leaves were turning brown and orange with the coming of autumn. For a moment, he felt a fierce tugging inside his chest, as if Lynette was trying to pull him to her. He closed his eyes, shuddered, then lowered his head and hunched his shoulders against a fresh gust of chilly wind. He heeled the dun into a walk and rode toward the cabin, the reins in his left hand, his right going to the pistol holstered on his hip.

Brackett hadn't wanted to loan it to him, hadn't wanted to loan him the horse either, for that matter. But the mood Evan was in, he might have stolen both of them if Brackett hadn't gone along with the requests, and Brackett must have sensed that. Evan had ridden away with Andrew and Beth watching him, their expressions a mixture of disapproval and pity.

"Don't worry," Evan had twisted around in the saddle to call to them. "Anybody asks, I'll tell 'em I stole the dun, so nobody'll blame you for helping me."

That had been a little unfair, and he regretted the harsh words now. But at the time, he hadn't been in any mood to be careful of other folks' feelings. His own were too shattered by what he had learned.

Nor could he have said what he hoped to accomplish by coming here. His family was gone, and the time would have been better spent in getting on the trail of his children. All he knew was that he couldn't ride on without stopping by here for a look at the home place.

As he approached the cabin, the door of the room on the right opened and a man stepped outside. The man was carrying a rifle, and he made no bones about the way the barrel was pointing in Evan's general direction. "Hello," he said curtly. "Can I help you?"

No mistaking the accent—Yankee, through and through. Evan had heard enough of them during the war to figure that the man might have come originally from Massachusetts. Not that Evan cared. Anywhere north of the Mason-Dixon line was the same.

Roughly, Evan pulled the dun to a stop. "Who might you be?" he asked.

The man frowned. He was stocky, a little below medium height, with thinning brown hair. "My name is Abner Crane," he said. "I thought it wasn't considered polite in these parts to ask a man his name or where he was from—at least not without drinking some coffee with him first."

"I don't want coffee," said Evan.

"I'm afraid I don't have any whiskey."

"I want my farm back!" Evan burst out suddenly, unable to restrain himself any longer. "I want my land, and my family, and my . . . my wife."

Abner Crane's high forehead creased in a frown. He had taken a half step back at the violence of Evan's reaction, but his grip on the rifle was still firm. "Your name wouldn't be Littleton, would it?"

"I'm Evan Littleton, all right." Evan's voice was like the rasp of a file.

"Well, I'm sorry, Mr. Littleton. I was told that you were dead, that you had died in the rebellion. My brothers and I bought this farm from the county for the back taxes that were owed on it."

"Stole it, you mean," Evan ripped out.

Stubbornly, Crane shook his head. "No, sir. It was all legal and aboveboard. I'm an honest man—"

"Honest man who don't mind coming in and taking over what's not his just because some bunch of carpetbaggers say it's all right."

"I won't stand here and argue with you. I . . . heard about your wife, and I'm sorry for your loss. But if you've come to make trouble, I have to ask you to leave. You're not welcome here."

Evan's right arm trembled with the need to reach for the pistol on his hip. Even if Crane had jacked a round into the chamber of the rifle before stepping out of the cabin, it would take him a second to lift the weapon and fire. Was a time when all Evan needed to shade another man was half a second . . .

"Problem out here, Abner?"

The new voice came from the corner of the cabin. Evan's eyes darted toward the sound, saw a tall, broad-shouldered man with a neatly trimmed black beard. The man had a shotgun in his hands, both barrels pointed toward Evan.

"This is Mr. Evan Littleton, Lucius. He used to own our farm."

"Littleton, eh?" said Lucius Crane. "We've

heard stories about you, mister. The old-timers around here seem to think you're some kind of ring-tailed wonder." He made a small motion with the barrels of the shotgun. "You don't look like much now."

"I was in a Yankee prison camp," Evan said.

"Then you have our sympathies," Abner Crane said, "but I repeat, you are not welcome here. Now, are you leaving?"

Evan drew a deep breath. They would have him in a crossfire if they started shooting, and with that greener pointed at him, he had no doubt that he would be blown out of the saddle. He might get a single shot off before he was killed, but that was all.

And his children were still out there somewhere. All but Thad, he reminded himself bitterly.

"I don't care whether you believe me or not, but I didn't come here to cause trouble. I'm not staying, either. I just . . . wanted to see the place again before I rode on."

Abner relaxed visibly. "Oh. Well, that's different. I don't suppose I can blame you for wanting that."

His brother Lucius was still alert and ready for trouble, however. "You've had your look," snapped Lucius.

Slowly, Evan nodded. "Reckon I have." He lifted his right hand, which still trembled a little, and pointed toward the hill. "My wife's buried up there. I'd like to ride up and pay my respects."

"Of course. You'll find the grave undisturbed,"

said Abner. "In fact, I've kept the weeds down as best I can."

Evan felt a fresh surge of resentment at the knowledge that a Yankee had been caring for Lynette's grave. He didn't say anything, just pulled the dun's head to the side and prodded it into a trot that carried him around the cabin. He could feel the eyes of the Crane brothers watching him as he rode between the cabin and the barn and started up the hill.

Someone had carried a large rock to the top of the hill and placed it on the grave as a makeshift headstone. Lynette's name had been chiseled into the rock, along with the dates 1827–1864. Evan swung down from the saddle, letting the dun's reins trail on the ground. He knelt beside the stone and reached out to touch the chiseled letters, sliding his fingertips along them. Even losing their leaves, the oaks cast quite a bit of shade, and it was cool, almost chilly on the hilltop. Wind stirred in the branches of the trees. Evan rested his palm flat against the rock. It was cold, not a trace of heat in it.

"I'm . . . sorry, Lynette," he choked out, not knowing what to say but feeling the need to say *something*. "I never should have . . . never should have gone off that way to the war. Might've been different if I'd stayed."

How things might have been changed, he could not have said. He was no doctor; when the violent fever had seized his wife, he wouldn't have been able to do any more for her than anybody else. But at least he would have been here to keep the family together. Thad wouldn't have gone off to die in the war, the rest of the children wouldn't have been scattered, and the Yankees never would have gotten the farm. Well, he might not have been able to do anything about that last, he thought. All over the remnants of the Confederacy, the Northern carpetbaggers and Reconstructionists were doing whatever they pleased, taking whatever they wanted, and nobody had been able to rein them in yet.

Hoofbeats drifted to Evan's ears on the breeze. He stood up and turned his head, looking down the hill to see three men riding up to the cabin. They were familiar somehow, and a moment later Evan bit back a curse as he recognized them. He had last seen them over the barrel of a gun as they rode away from Russell's ferry.

"I got to go, Lynette," he said as he turned back to the grave. "But I promise you, I'll find the kids and bring 'em back here. We'll all be together again. I swear it."

With that, he clapped the battered old hat back on his head, caught up the dun's reins, and stepped into the saddle.

Indecision tore at him. Should he ride down there and confront the three State Policemen again? If he did, there might well be gunplay, and the odds would be heavily against him. But if he didn't, it would seem mighty like running away, and Evan didn't like that idea, either.

A final glance at the rock marking his wife's grave made up his mind for him. He had made a solemn promise to Lynette, and if he got himself killed, he wouldn't be able to keep it. His kids were out there somewhere, and they needed him.

A yell came from down below, and from the corner of his eye, he saw the three riders pounding up the hill toward him. The Cranes had told the State Policemen that he was up here, and they still had a bone to pick with him.

Evan drove the run-down heels of his boots into the flanks of the dun and sent it in a gallop down the far side of the hill.

He leaned forward over the neck of his horse, the wind plucking at his ragged coat. With one hand, he held his hat on. The dun had sand and plenty of bottom. It ran free and easy, its stride eating up the ground. When Evan reached the bottom of the slope, he glanced back and saw his pursuers topping the hill. He winced, knowing that the hooves of the horses had cut right across Lynette's grave.

One more score to be evened someday—but not today.

Back on flat ground to the west of the hills, the dun's pace increased even more. The three State Police riders were stubborn, though. Every time Evan looked back, they were hanging there, unable to close the gap but not falling behind any, either. They planned to run him into the ground, and if their horses were fresh, they might be able to do just that. From this distance, he couldn't tell if the carpetbaggers were riding the same mounts as they had been earlier in the day or not. They could have swapped horses since then.

Evan urged more speed out of the dun. The

horse might not like him much, but it was willing to run its heart out for him. He spoke softly to it, in that special wordless communication between horse and rider. The dun responded, stretching out and practically flying over the ground.

Something buzzed past Evan's head. He looked back to see that the riders had pulled up and dismounted, and now all three men were aiming rifles at him. In the bright sunlight, he couldn't see the muzzle flashes, but as another bullet whined past him, he knew they were firing.

Anger welled up inside him. They had no right to be shooting at him. He hadn't done anything except keep them from hurting old Jonas at the ferry.

But that was enough, he realized. He had thwarted their will, stood in their way, and their kind of man couldn't stand that. They had to annihilate everybody who blocked their path, even for an instant. Otherwise their power, the only thing that was truly precious to them, was threatened.

He glanced back again, saw the rifle slugs kicking up dust behind him now. He was getting out of range of the weapons, and pretty soon the State Policemen would have to give up. Evan resisted the urge to laugh. He hadn't won, not really. He was the one fleeing for his life, and those Yankees were still back there, ready to cause more mischief and make life miserable for his fellow Texans. And he still had no idea where his children were.

No, he hadn't won a thing. Not a single, blessed thing . . .

4

Evan rode into the town of Brady late the next morning. He had bypassed Richland Springs entirely, despite the fact that there were people there he knew, old friends who would have been glad to see him or at least know he was still alive. But he had already put Andrew and Elizabeth Brackett in danger simply by accepting their hospitality. He didn't want to be responsible for bringing down trouble on the head of anyone else.

He had left the Brackett farm with the understanding that it might be a while before he got back. Andrew wouldn't be expecting the return of the dun or the old revolver anytime soon. Which was good, Evan thought, because he had no idea how long it would take him to track down his children.

Brady was almost due west of Richland Springs, the first settlement of any size in the direction that had been taken by the Ashmores, the Cartmills, and the Wilsons when they had left their farms, taking the Littleton youngsters with them. Maybe he would be lucky, Evan thought as he ambled up to the town square on the dun. Maybe he would find that all three families had settled here. He might be reunited with his surviving children before the sun set on another day.

The thought of Lynette's and Thad's deaths had gnawed at him during the night. He had made a cold camp, eating the ham and biscuits Beth Brackett had knotted up for him in a towsack, then rolling up in the blanket Andrew had tied on behind the dun's saddle. The Bracketts had been mighty good to him. After everything he had gone through these past years, just having a horse and a saddle and a gun made him feel like a rich man. If it hadn't been for the deaths of his wife and eldest son and the disappearance of his other children, he would have enjoyed riding over these rolling Texas hills. It would have been good to be home.

Instead, *home* was a word that left a bitter taste in his mouth. With luck, he would find his children . . . but he could never put things completely right again.

Nestled in rocky, wooded hills, Brady was a busy place. Quite a few wagons were parked on the street around a couple of general stores. People both afoot and on horseback filled the square. Evan frowned and thought hard, trying to recollect if this was Saturday. That would explain things. This was ranching country, the flatter farmland having been left behind around Richland Springs, and the cattlemen and their families would come into town on Saturday to pick up supplies and do any other business that needed to be done. Must be, decided Evan. The only other thing that would bring this many people into the settlement would be—

He stopped short, pulling the dun roughly to a halt, as he saw the gallows on the other side of the square.

He had just been thinking that it would require a hanging to draw this big a crowd, and sure enough, that was what was going on. The gallows was empty at the moment, three hangropes dangling unoccupied over the trapdoors below them. Evan tensed at the sight. He had seen men hanged in the Yankee prison camp, troublemakers who wouldn't or couldn't adapt to that hellish way of life. He would never forget the frantic kicking at the air of the unlucky ones whose necks didn't break cleanly when they dropped through the trap.

Well, whoever was getting their necks stretched, it was no business of his. He angled the dun toward the nearest of the general stores and brought the horse to a stop at a crowded hitch rack. It took only a moment to dismount and loop the reins around the rack. Then he stepped up onto the porch, pausing to let a couple of women walk past him. He murmured, "Ladies," and touched a finger to the ragged brim of his hat. They looked at him curiously but didn't say anything.

He supposed he looked a sight, all right. A scarecrow, one of those State Policemen had called him, and the fella hadn't been far wrong. He wished he had some money so that he could get some better clothes, maybe clean up a mite, even take a bath at a barber shop. His kids might not want to claim him as their pa if he showed up looking like this.

Money was one thing he was plumb out of, he reflected, and he didn't want to waste the time hunting up a real job so that he could earn some. All he really needed were some supplies for his journey, and he hoped to barter for them by doing a few chores for the storekeeper. He hoped that the man might have heard something about the Ashmores or the Cartmills or the Wilsons, too.

Evan stepped into the cavernous building.

Like most frontier stores, this one stocked a little bit of everything a pioneer family might need, from farm implements to patent medicines to bolts of brightly colored cloth, from bags of sugar to kegs of nails, from barrels of pickles to bottles of ink. Everything was stacked on shelves that ran in aisles from the front to the back of the building, where there was a long counter behind which the store clerks could take orders and tote up bills. Men and women browsed in the aisles, while kids congregated around a glass-fronted display case on the left-hand wall. That was where the candy was to be found, and nearly a dozen pairs of eyes gazed avidly through the glass at the sweets on the other side. Quite a few people were standing at the counter, being waited on by a trio of white-aproned clerks. Evan saw a calendar on the wall, with dates crossed off by strokes with a piece of charcoal. All the days had been marked off until a Saturday in late October. In all likelihood, that would be today, Evan thought.

A Saturday *and* a hanging . . . no wonder Brady was full this morning.

And yet, as Evan made his way toward the rear of the store, he was struck by something odd about the atmosphere in the place. The kids at the candy counter were laughing and talking, but the adults weren't. An air of gloom hung over the aisles, with none of the gossiping and backslapping and visiting that usually went on whenever families accustomed to an isolated existence got together in town. It was almost like being at a funeral, he thought. The only sounds were the scraping of feet and the low, droning voices of the clerks as they read back the orders they had been given.

Evan had seen a few hangings besides the ones he had witnessed in the prison camp. Usually, such occasions were surprisingly festive. They had a somber undertone, to be sure, but overall, folks were generally glad for even such a grim excuse to get together for a while.

Could be the people of Brady didn't agree with this hanging that was about to take place.

It was still no business of his, Evan told himself as he stepped up to the counter. He studied the three clerks, trying to tell if one of them might be the owner of the store. He eliminated the pimply faced youngster right away, and a slow-moving, gray-haired old-timer didn't strike Evan as the type to be the proprietor, either.

That left a jowly, broad-shouldered man in his forties, and Evan waited until that individual had finished waiting on a customer before asking, "Talk to you a minute, mister?"

The clerk's dark eyes played suspiciously over Evan. The gent could probably guess within a few pennies just how much a potential customer had in his pockets, Evan thought. "What can I do for you?" the man asked.

"You the owner of this place?"

"That's right. I'm Cyrus Finch. And I don't give handouts."

"Don't expect any. I'm looking for an odd job or two, enough to earn me some supplies."

"Drifter, eh?" Cyrus Finch's expression hardened even more as he looked at the filthy gray pants Evan wore. The faded yellow stripe down the legs was barely visible, but that was enough for Finch. "I was a Union man myself," he said. "Like I told you, I don't give handouts . . . especially to Rebel trash."

Evan stiffened but held on to his temper. From his voice, it was clear that Finch was a Texan, not a Yankee carpetbagger, but not everybody in Texas had supported the Confederacy, not by a long shot. Now that the war was over and the North had won, men like Finch could afford to gloat. And as long as people had to have supplies, and his prices were good, his business wouldn't even suffer from his attitude. Evan guessed that most folks were so cash-poor these days that they would put up with Finch's Yankee sympathies as long as he gave them credit and didn't press them too often to pay off their bills.

"Anything I take from here, I'll earn," said Evan. "I'm a hard worker, and I'll do just about anything that's honest. But if you don't want to hire me, mister, I'll just go look elsewhere." He started to turn away from the counter.

"Hold on," said Finch. "You Rebs are too blasted prickly. I've got some work for you, if you want it. Pay's a good meal and a week's worth of provisions."

That was exactly what Evan wanted. He nodded curtly and said, "I'll take it."

A sly grin played around Finch's wide mouth. "Don't you want to know what the job is?"

"Don't rightly care."

"Good. I own the livery stable next door, too. The stalls haven't been mucked out in a long time. You'd best get to it."

If Finch expected Evan to grimace, or turn his nose up, or walk out, he was disappointed. Evan had cleaned out his own barn more times than he could count. It wasn't a pleasant job, but he could do it.

"I reckon you've got a pitchfork and a shovel over there?"

"The hostler'll show you where everything's at. Come on back over here when you're finished. Just wipe your boots first."

Evan nodded again, and once more Finch stopped him as he started to turn away. "Guess you're sorry you'll miss the hangin'."

"Don't know anything about it," said Evan. "I just rode into town."

"The State Police are hanging some outlaws. Ever hear of Harry Stubbs?"

Evan shook his head, answering the question honestly.

"Stubbs and his gang've been raiding around here for months, but the State Police finally caught him, along with two of his boys. They'll be dancing on air in another . . ." Finch dug a watch out of his pocket and flipped open the turnip's case to check the time. "Half hour or so," he finished as he put the watch away.

"None of my business," Evan said.

A man who had been standing by giving his order to one of the other clerks turned toward Evan and Finch. "If you ask me, the real crime is the hanging," he said angrily.

"Harry Stubbs is a murderer," said Finch. "Everybody knows that."

"The State Police are the murderers," replied the customer, who looked to be a rancher, from his boots and high-crowned hat. "They're the ones runnin' roughshod over the common folks. Harry was just tryin' to get back at 'em for the way they've been treatin' good honest Texans."

"Talk like that'll get *you* hung, Orr," warned Finch. "It ain't nothing but treason and sedition."

"Call it what you want, it's still the truth," insisted the man called Orr.

Evan didn't want any part of this argument. He didn't like the State Police any more than the next man and less than most, he supposed, but now that he knew he had to find what was left of his family, he couldn't afford to get involved, as he had back there at the ferry the day before. He just wanted to clean out those livery stalls for Finch, collect his pay, and be moving on. He left Orr and Finch arguing about the impending hanging.

At least he knew why there was an air of gloom lingering over the town, he thought as he went next door to the stable, leading the dun. Chances were, most of the people in Brady had supported the Confederacy, and they would take the side of the so-called outlaw Harry Stubbs over his State Police captors. Evan wondered how many of the lawmen were in town; had to be a pretty good number of them, he decided, for them to go ahead with the hanging in the face of such strong public opposition.

The hostler at the livery was a young man with a decided resemblance to Cyrus Finch. The storekeeper's son, Evan guessed. He showed Evan where the shovel and the pitchfork were kept in the tack room, then smiled gleefully. "I been tellin' my pa we need to get some of you Rebs to do the dirty work around here. Glad to see he finally took my advice."

That confirmed Evan's supposition about the young man's relation to Finch, and told him as well that the hostler was also a Union sympathizer, just like his father. Sternly, Evan told himself not to let that bother him. He had a job to do, and that was all that mattered.

Despite the season, this was hot work, and Evan soon took off the tattered old coat, hanging it on a nail in one of the stalls. Using the shovel, the pitchfork, and a wheelbarrow he found behind the livery barn, he began cleaning the soiled hay from the stalls and replacing it with fresh hay from the loft. His long captivity had taken a toll on his strength, and he had not regained all of it during the long trek from Atlanta. He had been at the chore for less than half an hour before his muscles began to burn with fatigue.

Ignore it, he told himself. Concentrate instead on the children he had to find . . .

He was in the loft, forking up a load of fresh hay, when he heard hoofbeats below on the hard-packed dirt of the barn's wide central aisle. The hostler's voice, high-pitched with sudden alarm, said, "What do you want?"

"Just stand still, sonny, and you won't get hurt," replied a man's voice, harsh and guttural. "Tom, get them doors shut."

"Hold on there, you can't do that—"

Evan had already frozen at the sense of wrongness that had suddenly invaded the place, filling the air as surely as did the smell of manure. So he clearly heard the metallic clicking sound that he recognized as the hammer of a gun being eared back.

"Go ahead, Tom," ordered the stranger's voice. "Junior here ain't goin' to stop you. Are you, junior?"

Using the sound of the man's voice to cover any faint sounds he might make, Evan moved to the edge of the loft. He could look down now and see three men on horseback, all of them wearing wide-brimmed hats and long dusters. At first Evan thought they might be more of the State Police, but the hostler's next words, spoken in a voice that trembled nervously, told him different.

"You owlhoots can't get away with this. The State Police caught your boss Stubbs, and they'll catch you, too."

One of the riders laughed. Horses shifted, and Evan heard the big main doors at the front of the barn being drawn closed. There were at least four men down there besides young Finch, maybe more. From the sound of it, they were the rest of Harry Stubbs' outlaw gang.

Evan had no idea what they were doing here, but he figured they couldn't be up to any good. At least not the way the State Police and other Union sympathizers might think. Evan wasn't sure how the rest of the citizens in Brady and the surrounding vicinity would feel about the matter.

"What time is it, Nate?" That was the rough-voiced man again.

"Nigh on to eleven," replied one of the other riders after a moment's pause to check a watch. "They ought to be bringing Harry and Broadus and Dunston out of the jail any minute now."

"All right. Saddle up the best horses you can find in this place. We have to be ready to move."

Evan understood now, and so did young Finch. The hostler exclaimed, "Y-you're goin' to try to rescue Stubbs and his boys!" Evan couldn't see the young man, but he could hear the fright in his voice.

"Yeah, and if you know what's good for you, you'll go back in that tack room and stay there until it's all over," said the rough-voiced man. He spat.

"We ain't lookin' to kill anybody today unless it's some of those State Police. But if there's anything I hate worse than Yankees, it's Texans who ought to know better'n to side with 'em . . ."

The threat was clear, and Evan knew the outlaw meant it. He stood absolutely still, not wanting to draw attention to himself. That stillness was a trick he had mastered during the long months in the prison camp. Not being noticed in a place like that was one way of staying alive.

The riders had their backs to him, but if they turned around and looked up, they couldn't miss seeing him in the loft. Evan hoped that wouldn't come about, because whatever happened today, he didn't want any part of it. He wished the outlaws would just go on about their business.

"I can see 'em!" came an excited voice from the front of the barn. Must be the one called Tom, Evan thought, who had closed the doors but probably left a crack to peek through. The barn was fairly close to the waiting gallows. As soon as the prisoners were brought there, the outlaws in the livery stable could rush out on horseback, leading mounts for Stubbs and the other two prisoners, and snatch them right out of the hands of the State Police. The plan had a good chance of success, Evan decided. The outlaws would have the advantage of surprise on their side, and probably nobody in town would lift a finger to help the State Police.

But he was wrong about that, Evan saw as the riders crowded closer to the front of the barn. Below him, young Finch darted out of the tack room and into view, and in his hand was a pistol. His face was pale with fear, but he lifted the gun anyway, and Evan could almost read the thoughts inside the youngster's head. The boy thought he could stop the outlaws and be a hero. More than likely, all he would accomplish would be to get himself killed.

Without even thinking about what he was doing, Evan dumped the load of hay from the pitchfork that he still held poised in his hands.

The heavy clump of hay thudded into young Finch's head and drove him to his knees. At the same time, his finger jerked on the trigger of the gun. The revolver blasted, but the bullet slammed harmlessly into the ground. That didn't stop the riders from wheeling their horses around, startled by the sudden explosion. Reflexes honed by a life on the run made pistols leap into their hands. In a matter of seconds, they would fire instinctively, and their slugs would cut the young hostler to ribbons.

Still unsure why he was doing this, Evan leaped from the loft and crashed into the half-stunned figure below him. That impact might have been enough to knock young Finch completely unconscious, but Evan drove a fist into the side of the young man's head just to make sure. Then he shouted, "Don't shoot!"

"What in blazes—" The rough-voiced man was staring at Evan over the barrel of a leveled Colt. "Who're you, mister?"

"Just somebody who doesn't want to see a kid get killed," said Evan, and in that moment, he knew he was telling the truth. He didn't like young Finch, didn't have a bit of use for a Union sympathizer, but Thad had been only a year or two younger than this boy when he marched off to die. Evan forced that thought out of his head as he scrambled to his feet and went on, "Whatever you came here to do, you'd better get on with it. Folks probably heard that shot."

"You're right," the outlaw said grimly. Even now, curious shouts could be heard outside. The element of surprise was gone. "I'm not ridin' out into a hail of Yankee lead," declared the rough-voiced man, whose face, Evan now saw, was every bit as seamed and leathery as it should have been to match the sound. His thumb pulled back the hammer of the Colt, cocking it as he pointed it at Evan. "You lead the way."

The muzzle of that gun seemed as big around as a rain barrel, and for a second as he stared into the darkness of it, Evan didn't comprehend what the outlaw had just said. "What?"

"Mount up. You're goin' out of here first."

Evan's eyes went to the horse he had borrowed from Andrew Brackett. The dun was tethered to a post a few yards away. "I'm not one of you," Evan said desperately. "I'm no outlaw."

"Those Yankee police won't know that. The plan's already ruined, but maybe we can salvage it. You lead the way, and if you ride hard and fast enough, you'll distract 'em—and maybe even live to tell about it."

"Blast it, I helped you!" said Evan, angered by the unfairness of it. "You can't just shoot me!"

The outlaw's lips drew back from his teeth in a grimace, and Evan knew that was exactly what was going to happen in about two seconds if he didn't do what he was told.

He turned to the dun, jerked loose the reins, and swung up into the saddle. Then, as two of the riders shoved the stable doors open, he prodded the dun into a lunging gallop that carried him out into bright sunshine, startled yells, and the sudden popping of gunshots.

5

For a few seconds, Evan was too confused to be scared. People were everywhere, some of them running toward the livery stable, some of them scurrying away from it as fast as possible, as if sensing just how much trouble was about to burst out of it. The most vivid impression to etch itself into his brain, however, was the sight of the three men standing on the gallows, black hoods over their heads. The hangropes had not yet been put in place, but it was clear that within another few minutes, the hooded men would have plunged through the trapdoors to their death.

The men being hanged weren't the only ones on the gallows. Four others stood around them. Two of these men held shotguns, one clutched a Henry rifle, and the other man was lifting a revolver in his hand. They all wore dusters, making it difficult to tell them from the outlaws who were even now galloping out of the livery barn behind Evan. Evan figured the heavily armed men for members of the State Police, and in addition to the four on the gallows, there were several more standing in front of the platform. They were loaded for bear, just like their cohorts. In fact, they were already shooting at something, noise and flame geysering from the muzzles of their rifles.

Him, Evan realized. They were shooting at *him.*

He veered the dun hard to the left, through a wide gap that had opened up in the crowd. He didn't want to trample anybody, nor did he want any of the lead the State Police were throwing at him to hit an innocent person. It was enough that bad luck—and his own impulsiveness—had gotten him into this mess.

Even before the war, he had known what it was like to have slugs singing around his head. Once heard, it was a sound never forgotten. He crouched low in the saddle, leaning forward over the dun's neck, and called softly to it, "Run, you jughead, run!"

The idea of stopping and trying to trade shots with the lawmen never occurred to him. He was outnumbered badly, of course, and again, he didn't want any innocents caught in the crossfire. Getting away from Brady seemed like the best idea.

There went the job for Cyrus Finch and the supplies he was supposed to be paid, Evan thought. There was nothing that could be done about it now.

Brady wasn't a big town. He reached the western edges of it in a matter of moments. Behind him, more guns were booming and people were yelling and screaming. The members of Stubbs' gang were carrying out their plan, he thought, and trying to rescue the boss outlaw. Evan couldn't bring himself to wish them luck, no matter how much he might hate the State Police. Stubbs' gravel-voiced *segundo* had ruined Evan's own plans.

The last of the houses on the outskirts of the settlement flashed behind him, and the dun was galloping freely down the dirt road. Evan glanced back over his shoulder to see if there was any pursuit. Somewhat to his surprise, he didn't see anybody coming after him. But there was still a confused knot of people around the town square, over which hung a gray haze of gunsmoke. The State Police were too occupied at the moment to come chasing after him, he decided. That was a bit of good fortune at last.

He slowed the dun to a ground-eating trot and took stock of himself. No pains other than the weariness that had already set in from cleaning out the stalls in the livery barn. No blood staining his shirt or pants. His jacket was gone, left hanging on a nail in the stable, but it appeared that was the only thing he had lost. He had been worried that a slug might have creased him during the confusion without him even noticing the wound. That didn't seem to be the case.

Evan heaved a sigh of relief. He was disgusted at the day's turn of events . . . but they could have been a lot worse.

He found himself riding west along a narrow stream that he knew had to be Brady Creek. A man who farmed for a living generally stayed pretty close to home, but Evan hadn't always been a farmer. He had ridden through these parts once or twice, but it had been years since he had been west of Brady. He kept the dun at a steady trot, and as he rode he scrubbed his free hand over his face, the gesture one of weariness and disappointment. He hadn't even had a chance to ask Cyrus Finch if the storekeeper knew anything about the three families for which he was searching.

Well, there were homesteads around here, he told himself. He would stop at the first spread he came to and ask if anyone there had heard of the Ashmores, the Cartmills, or the Wilsons. Folks were usually hospitable, too, so he would probably be invited to stay for dinner, maybe even offered a job. He could still salvage the situation, Evan told himself.

When he had ridden for an hour, he figured there wasn't much chance of any pursuit from the settlement catching up to him now, so he pulled the dun back to a walk. Still, habit made him glance over his shoulder every few minutes, and less than a quarter of an hour had passed when he saw a dust cloud beginning to boil up.

Riders were coming—and coming fast. A State Police posse from Brady? Evan bit back a curse as he realized that was the most likely explanation.

"Hate to do it to you, hoss," he said to the dun, "but you're going to have to run again." He jabbed the heels of his boots into the horse's flanks.

The dun leaped forward. Evan veered away

from the creek, reasoning that the pursuers, whoever they were, might follow the stream. He rode over a stretch of rocky ground, hoping that would kill his trail. It might not, if the posse had a good tracker with them, but it was worth a try.

When he looked back a few minutes later, Evan saw that his maneuver hadn't worked. The pall of dust still hung in the air, but now it had turned toward him. And it was closer, too, indicating that the pursuers' mounts were fresher than his. Evan felt desperation growing inside him. It seemed that everything he attempted was doomed to failure. He started looking around for a cluster of rocks or some other place he could fort up and make a stand.

With only the pistol he had borrowed from Andrew Brackett and a handful of extra cartridges, he couldn't make much of a fight. But he wouldn't let the State Police drag him back to Brady and put a hangrope around his neck. Better to go down from a bullet than that.

Spotting a grove of post oaks growing closely together, Evan made for it. The trees would provide as much cover as he could hope for, and it was just possible he might be able to hide among them and throw off the pursuit that way. As he reached the trees, he pulled the dun to a stop and swung down quickly from the saddle. Holding tightly to the reins, he led the horse into the thicket.

The dun balked at entering the prickly underbrush that grew between the trees, but Evan tugged stubbornly until the horse followed him.

He ignored the scratches as brambles clawed at him and tore his already ragged clothes. The brush closed in around man and horse, and Evan put his back against the rough bark of a tree trunk. He wished they were live oaks instead of post oaks, because the leaves had already started to fall off with the onset of autumn, leaving gaps through which the pursuers might spot him. Breathing deeply, he held the dun's reins with his left hand and rested the right on the butt of the gun at his hip.

After a few moments, the sound of rapid hoofbeats came to his ears. He listened intently as the riders drew closer, trying to judge their actions by the sounds. They didn't seem to be slowing down. Evan dropped to a crouch, edged around the tree trunk, and risked parting the brush a little so that he could peer out.

The horsemen were passing by about fifty yards away, riding fast enough so that their long dusters billowed out behind them. At first glance, Evan couldn't tell if they were State Police—or the outlaw gang led by Harry Stubbs. Lawman and criminal dressed alike, and in the eyes of many Texans, the carpetbagger badge-toters were worse than any homegrown outlaws. Under other circumstances, Evan might have spent some time pondering the irony of that, but not now. Now he just held his breath and hoped the men would ride on by, whoever they were.

State Police, he decided after a moment. He didn't recognize any of them from the livery barn, and all of the men wore broad-brimmed black hats, a style favored by the lawmen. He put their number at about a dozen. If he had to put up a fight, there was no way he could hold them off.

But evidently, it wasn't going to come to that. The riders were heading past the grove of oaks without slowing down. Evan straightened and put a hand on the dun's nose, warning it to keep quiet. The last member of the posse rode past, and Evan heaved a sigh of relief.

After the State Police were gone, he waited there for another ten or fifteen minutes, just to make certain they weren't going to double back unexpectedly. Then he turned and clawed his way out the other side of the thicket, unsure where he was going to go or what he was going to do next. With that posse roaming the countryside, he was going to have to be even more careful than before. After what had happened back in Brady, the State Police probably wouldn't believe him if he told them he wasn't part of the Stubbs gang. They would assume he had been part of the raid from the beginning, since he had led the outlaws out of the barn, and they would react accordingly: a bullet in the head or a rope thrown over the stout branch of a tree. Evan grimaced at that thought as he led the dun out of the brush.

And stopped short at the sight of the riders facing him, grouped in a half circle so that they had him pinned against the trees.

Instinctively, Evan's hand moved toward the gun on his hip. His fingers had just brushed the smooth walnut grips when one of the riders said quickly, "No need for that, mister. You're among friends."

Evan froze. He had taken the riders for the members of the State Police posse he had just seen, but now he realized that was wrong. These men wore dusters, and some of them sported black hats, but they weren't carpetbagger lawmen. Several of them had familiar faces, including the one who spoke in tones as rough as a washboard.

"Stand easy, mister. We don't mean you any harm."

The first man who had spoken edged his horse forward. He had a cocky grin on his face, and his hat was pushed back from a thatch of rumpled, fiery-red hair. He said, "If it wasn't for you, friend, I'd be dangling from the end of a rope by now. So I owe you my life, and Harry Stubbs pays his debts."

Evan glanced around. There were six of the men, which meant that at least one of them was missing. Relaxing a bit, since it was obvious they didn't mean to shoot him, he asked, "What happened back there in town?"

"That distraction of yours did the trick," replied the redheaded Harry Stubbs. "Those Yankees were so busy shooting at you that the boys were able to ride right up to them before they knew what was going on."

The gravel-voiced man, who sat his horse to Stubbs' left, added, "Our pard Broadus stopped a slug, but we were able to grab Harry and Dunston. Lit a shuck out of there slick as you please."

"A posse full of State Police rode past here just a few minutes ago," Evan pointed out.

Stubbs chuckled. "We can run rings around those Yankees, friend. These are our stomping grounds, not theirs. What's your name?"

"Evan . . . Evan Littleton."

Stubbs' easy grin disappeared abruptly, replaced by a frown. "No relation to the marshal down at San Saba, or that son of his who used to ride with the Rangers, are you?"

"Distant relations, that's all. Haven't seen any of that bunch in years." Evan didn't add that he hadn't seen much of anybody in this part of the country for years because of the war and his long imprisonment.

The grin came back to Stubbs' wide mouth. "Well, you can choose your friends, but you can't choose your relatives, I always say." He dismounted and stepped toward Evan, hand outstretched. "Glad to meet you, Evan Littleton. Like I said, I'm in your debt."

Evan shook hands with the outlaw.

"Come along with us," Stubbs went on. "We've got plenty of supplies, so an extra man won't be any burden."

Evan hesitated, then shook his head. "Reckon I'd better not."

"Afraid that folks'll think you're a desperado, like the rest of us?"

That was exactly what Evan was worried about, but he just shrugged, not wanting to anger these men.

"There's no point in worrying about that," said

Stubbs. "I've got news for you, Evan: After what happened back there in Brady, folks *already* think you're one of us."

Evan couldn't deny the logic of Stubbs' statement. The same thought had already occurred to him, which was one reason he had hidden from the posse, rather than face them and try to make them believe the truth. "Maybe you're right," he admitted, "but I've got things to do."

"Which way are you heading? Maybe we can at least ride together for a while."

Evan frowned in thought. He never had gotten the chance to ask anybody from around here about those he sought. Stubbs claimed to know these parts so well; maybe he would know if any of the families Evan was looking for had settled nearby.

"You know anybody named Ashmore, or Cartmill, or Wilson?" Evan asked, ignoring Stubbs' question for the moment.

Stubbs glanced around at his blank-faced men, then looked quizzically at Evan. "Never heard of any of 'em, and it seems like neither have the boys."

Evan tried not to sigh in disappointment. "Then I reckon I'll be heading west again," he said.

"Just so happens, we're headed that way, too. Ride with us for a few days. It'd sure make me feel better about that debt I owe you if you'd accept our hospitality for a while."

Maybe that wouldn't hurt anything, Evan thought. Harry Stubbs was a charmer, no doubt about that. Some good food and good company sounded mighty appealing at the moment. Evan hadn't had much of either of those things for a long time.

"All right," he said with a nod. "I'm much obliged for the offer, Mr. Stubbs."

"Harry," the outlaw insisted. "Call me Harry." He stepped back to his horse. "We'd better get moving, just in case those Yankees decide to ride back this way. Most of the time they can't find their hoss's rump with both hands, but shoot, even a Yankee can get lucky ever' now and then."

Evan put his foot in the stirrup and swung up onto the dun as Stubbs mounted. The outlaw leader turned his horse, motioned Evan up beside him, then urged his horse into a trot. The other members of the gang fell in behind them, except for the gravel-voiced man, who moved up on Evan's other side.

"Name's Drummond," he introduced himself with a curt nod. "Sorry if I spooked you back there in Brady. Once that boy started wavin' a gun around and you jumped him, we had to make the best of things. Wasn't time for nothin' else."

"That's all right," Evan said, though he was still bitterly disappointed in how everything had turned out. But like the outlaws, he was just going to have to make the best of the situation.

"You did just fine," Drummond went on. "Them carpetbagger lawmen didn't know what was goin' on." He chuckled, the sound like the rasp of a file. Several of the other men joined in the laughter.

Evan made himself grin. These outlaws seemed to have accepted him as one of them.

And, God help him, in the eyes of the law, he *was* one of them now.

Evan Littleton, desperado.

God help him, he thought again.

6

Harry Stubbs was right about knowing this part of the country. He led Evan and the other men along trails that were barely there, winding through the rocky hills and finding a way along gullies that seemed completely choked with brush on first glance. Evan would have hated to be the lawman who had to try to track down Stubbs in this rugged maze. He wondered how Stubbs and the other two outlaws had come to be caught in the first place. Must have been pure bad luck, he thought.

They didn't stop for a noonday meal, eating jerky and cold biscuits while in the saddle instead, washing down the simple fare with water from canteens. The food tasted good to Evan, who hadn't eaten since the night before.

"What brings you out here to this part of Texas?" asked Stubbs as he rode alongside Evan while they ate. "Looking for somebody, aren't you?"

"What makes you say that?"

"Those folks you asked me about . . . what were their names again?"

"Ashmore, Cartmill, and Wilson," Evan said.

"You've got some reason to be looking for them," said Stubbs. "You don't strike me as the sort of fella who does anything idly." His pale blue eyes looked intently at Evan. "I'd say you were in the war, went through some hard times."

"You could say that, all right."

"And these families you're looking for, they've got something that belongs to you."

Evan glanced sharply at him. "What do you mean by that?"

"You've had things taken away from you in the past. You're not going to stand for it anymore."

Evan's mouth tightened into a grim line as he thought about Lynette and Thad and all the lost years. Yeah, he had had things taken away from him, all right, but it was none of this outlaw's business.

After a moment of tense silence, Stubbs broke the mood by chuckling. "You'd think a gent like me with secrets of his own would know better than to go prying into somebody else's affairs. Sorry, Evan. No offense meant."

"None taken," Evan said honestly. He wasn't offended. He just wasn't prepared to share his pain with anybody else, especially not some carefree desperado like Harry Stubbs.

Still, he had to admit that Stubbs was a perceptive man. The outlaw had seemed to see right through to the heart of him.

The wind died down and the weather warmed a bit during the afternoon, and Evan was grateful for that change after the chilly breezes of the past few days. By nightfall, Stubbs had led them to a cave in the side of a craggy hill. The entrance was concealed by boulders and could be seen only if somebody knew exactly where to look—which Stubbs did. From the familiarity with the place that all six of the other men displayed, Evan figured the gang had used it as a hideout in the past.

"We'll spend the night here," announced Stubbs as he led the way into the cave. "You're welcome to join us, Evan. You won't find a better place in these parts. It's almost like being in a fancy hotel in San Antonio."

Evan doubted that, although he had no real way of comparing, since he had never *been* in a fancy hotel in San Antonio or anywhere else. A couple of the men got a fire going on the floor of the cave, and as the yellow glow from the flames spread, Evan could see that the hollowed-out place in the side of the hill was about twenty feet wide and twice that deep. The arching ceiling rose some fifteen feet above his head. The smoke from the fire climbed to the ceiling and dispersed there, and Evan figured it had to be escaping through a number of small cracks that led to the surface. That would make it difficult to spot, even if someone was looking for such a telltale sign. Dark, sooty circles on the stone floor of the cave told him this wasn't the first campfire to be built here. There was no telling how long the outlaws had been using the cave.

And they weren't the only ones who had stayed here, he discovered as he saw to his horse. Like the other men, he led his mount to the rear of the cave where some straw was piled, no doubt left over from the last time the outlaws had been here. As he was stripping off the dun's saddle, Evan noticed something on the wall. Curious, he finished unsaddling and rubbing down the horse, then went to the fire and fetched back a burning branch that he used as a makeshift torch. The flickering light fell on several crude drawings that had been sketched on the rear wall of the cave in ink of several different colors. He saw stick figures of men and horses and other animals, triangles, zigzag lines, squares, mountains, twisting lines that might represent either snakes or rivers, and symbols that meant absolutely nothing to him. As the light from the torch was dying down, Stubbs came up to Evan and said, "Indian drawings."

"Figured as much." Evan reached out with his free hand and gently touched a grouping of stick figures, two of them large and the rest small, that was probably meant to represent a family. "How old do you think they are?"

Stubbs shook his head. "No way of knowing. Indians have been around here for hundreds of years, maybe longer. Out of the weather like these drawings are, there's no telling how long they might have lasted before now."

Something about the painted scenes seemed incredibly ancient to Evan, and their age made them even more poignant. Whoever had made these drawings was probably long dead, and more than likely everyone pictured in them was dead and gone, too. The years kept rolling past, with nothing to show that a man had ever even been here . . . except what he could leave behind. Some daubs of berry juice on a rock weren't much of a legacy, thought Evan—but they beat nothing.

He turned and tossed the branch back on the fire before it could burn out. Telling himself that he brooded too much on such things, he hunkered on his heels and held his hands out to the flames to warm them.

The gravel-voiced outlaw named Drummond turned out to be the group's cook as well as Stubbs' second-in-command. He fried up a side of bacon and used the grease and some dough he took from a can wrapped in oilcloth to make flapjacks. Even before Evan had been captured by the Yankees, his troop had been on short rations, so the smell of food cooking always made him ravenously hungry. He tried not to seem too greedy as he ate, since he wasn't really a member of this outlaw band. After supper, when one of the men broke out a jug and began to pass it around, Evan took it when it came to him and swallowed a slug of the whiskey inside without thinking.

Stubbs grinned at him. "Some of that who-hit-John go down the wrong way, Evan?"

Evan wiped the back of his hand across his mouth and passed the jug on to the next man. "Yeah, I guess you could say that," he replied thinly.

Lassitude stole over him as he sat with his back leaned against the wall of the cave. The whiskey warmed his belly, which was full from supper, and the laughter and coarse gibes of the outlaws filled the air around him. It was almost like being back with his patrol during the war, he thought. He felt a sense of camaraderie that had been missing from his life since that time. Survival had been so tenuous in the prison camp that the men there had never really formed any sort of comradeship. Deep down, it was every man for himself, and everyone there had known it.

Given the way things were in Texas at the moment, maybe the life of an outlaw wasn't such a bad thing. If circumstances had been different, Evan could have considered riding with these men permanently—though how much permanence a gang of owlhoots had was anybody's guess.

But his kids were out there somewhere, just waiting for him to find them. He had to think about them, not about himself.

"Say," one of the men said abruptly from the other side of the fire, "don't I know you, mister?"

"Sure you do, Tully," said Harry Stubbs. "This here is Evan Littleton. He introduced himself to us this morning, remember?"

The outlaw called Tully shook his head. "Nope, that ain't what I mean. Seems I seen you somewheres else, Littleton. A long time ago, maybe. Where'd you say you was from?"

"I didn't," Evan said, trying not to feel offended

by the man's inquisitiveness. More than likely it was just the whiskey talking. He went on, "I'm from Richland Springs. Before that I was around Bastrop and down in South Texas."

Tully snapped his fingers and then pointed at Evan. "I knew it! I remember now. Indianola it was, a long time ago. Maybe twenty years ago. I was just a pup then, but I won't never forget how you killed those four hombres, Littleton."

Stubbs looked sharply at Evan. "Four men, Evan?" he asked softly.

Tully went on excitedly, "First gunfight I ever saw, and one of the best. You marched right out there in the street not far from the docks and took on all four of 'em. You should'a seen it, boys. Bam, bam, bam, bam!—and there was four fellas squirmin' their lives out in the dust."

Evan's breath hissed hard between his clenched teeth. "You've got it wrong," he forced himself to say, and his voice sounded strange to his ears.

Stubbornly, Tully shook his head. "No, sir, I ain't likely to forget. Seein' that made me want to be a gunman, too. 'Course, I was never nowheres near as good as you, Littleton."

"Seems we've got a famous man among us and didn't even know it," Stubbs said dryly. "Why'd they come after you, Evan? Or would you rather not talk about it?"

Any fool could see that he didn't want to talk about it, thought Evan, and Stubbs was no fool. But the outlaw leader was curious, and he was accustomed to having his curiosity satisfied. All of them were looking avidly at Evan, and he knew that he wouldn't be able to turn aside their questions.

He drew a deep breath and looked into the fire as he said, "I was ramrodding a cattle outfit from one of the ranches that was just getting started down in the Nueces country. Those four gents and I took a bunch of cows to the rendering plant in Indianola for the owner of the ranch. Only, the other fellas decided they'd rather take the money we got for the cows and spend it on themselves, instead of taking it back to the boss. I didn't figure to let 'em do that."

"So you faced them down and killed all four of them," Stubbs said with admiration in his voice.

"Four against one," Evan said with a shrug. "Wasn't time to be fancy about it."

"How'd you manage to stay alive after word got around?" asked Drummond, his rough tones echoing hollowly from the tight confines of the cave. "Didn't every kid who thought he was fast with a gun come after you?"

"They would have, if I'd given 'em time. I took the money back to the fella I worked for, married his daughter, and got out of that part of the country as fast as I could. Put my guns away and took up the plow, farmed for a while around Bastrop, then moved on to Richland Springs when the family started growing."

"Where are they now?" asked Stubbs. "Your wife and the kids?"

"My wife's dead," Evan replied flatly. "So's my

oldest boy. I . . . don't know where the others are."
He didn't add that he was searching for them.

Stubbs shook his head. "Sorry to hear about
that, Evan. You seem like a good fella. You sure
you don't want to ride with us, permanent-like?"

Again, Stubbs had the uncanny ability to seem
to know what he had been thinking earlier. Evan
shook his head and said shortly, "Can't."

"Well, that's up to you, of course. I reckon
we've got your word that you won't go telling any
lawmen about this place?"

"I got no more use for Yankee law than you
do," said Evan.

Stubbs nodded and said, "That's what I
thought." He rose smoothly to his feet and
stretched. "Don't know about you boys, but I think
I'm going to turn in. Any day that starts with being
just about to dance at the end of a hangrope is
mighty wearying."

That brought several chuckles from the other
men. Evan didn't laugh or smile. He was still half-
lost in memory.

Those had been wild times down there in
the brush country, the South Texas brasada.
And even before that, he had seemed to draw
trouble wherever he went. That gunfight in
Indianola hadn't been his first one, even though
he hadn't been much more than a kid at the
time.

But it had been his last, and for the last
twenty years—with the exception of the war—he
had lived a peaceable life.

Now, in the past two days, he had threatened

a trio of State Police, been chased by them, helped some outlaws escape from more carpetbagger lawmen and been pursued by *them*, and now he was sitting in a lonely cave with those owlhoots, being treated like one of the gang.

Things could sure change in a hurry—and usually not for the better.

7

It got cold in the cave before morning, especially since Evan didn't have a jacket anymore. Sometime during the night, while he slept, someone draped a blanket over him. He woke with it wrapped tightly around him, hugging it to him for the warmth it provided. He suspected Harry Stubbs was responsible for the kindness, but the outlaw leader didn't say anything about it, so Evan didn't, either.

Once again, Drummond prepared bacon and flapjacks, and the men ate well before setting out. Stubbs sent Tully and another man out of the cave to check the area before the rest of the gang saddled their horses. When the two scouts returned, Tully grinned and said, "No sign of star packers anywhere, Harry. We gave them sorry carpetbaggers the slip, just like always."

Stubbs nodded in satisfaction. "Good. We'll get ready to ride." He turned to Evan. "You coming along with us today, Evan?"

"You still heading west?"

"Sure. It doesn't really matter to us which direction we drift."

Somehow, Evan didn't really believe that. He had known Harry Stubbs for only a day, but it seemed to him that Stubbs was the sort of man who always had a plan of action mapped out. He was sure that the rescue from the hangman's rope back in Brady had been figured out as a contingency long before it actually became necessary.

"I guess I'll ride along," said Evan. After everything that had happened, he wasn't courting any more danger by accompanying the outlaws than he would be if he split off from them.

The men rode out of the cave a few minutes later and circled the hill in which it had been hollowed out by the forces of nature, then swung in a westerly direction again. Evan found himself riding between Stubbs and Drummond, as he had the day before.

Stubbs jerked a thumb toward a series of hills to the north and said, "Those are the Brady Mountains. Not very impressive, are they?"

"They're pretty good-sized hills to a boy from South Texas," replied Evan.

"Ever seen the Davis Mountains, out in West Texas?"

Evan shook his head.

"Those are real mountains, not like those hills. They're the tail end of the Rockies. *That's* something I'd like to see one of these days: the Rocky Mountains. And the Pacific Ocean, too." Stubbs shook his head wistfully. "All that water'd be a sight to see."

All Evan wanted to see were his kids and his homestead, the farm back in his hands again instead of belonging to those blasted carpetbagging Crane brothers. That wasn't likely to happen, though. Even if he succeeded in finding the children, they would probably have to start over somewhere else. Going back to the farm near Richland Springs would be just asking for trouble from the State Police, and he wasn't going to expose his family to more of that. They had already had their share.

The day was once again warming up nicely, with soft billows of white clouds floating overhead in the blue sky. Indian summer was setting in, Evan thought, the last spell of nice weather before the blue northers of winter began roaring down through Texas from the Panhandle. Good weather in these parts was to be enjoyed while it was there—because it wouldn't be around for long.

A little before midday, Evan spotted smoke rising in the distance ahead of them. They were riding alongside a small stream that Stubbs had identified as Maverick Creek, a tributary of Brady Creek. The terrain had smoothed out into rolling grassland, with the rocky hills behind them to the east and thicker woods to the south. This looked to Evan like it would be prime grazing country for cattle.

He lifted his hand and pointed to the thin tendril of smoke rising into the sky. "Is that a settlement up there?" he asked.

Stubbs shook his head. "A ranch, I think. There's plenty of land out here for the taking, and the carpetbaggers don't bother folks very much. Those Yankees are too scared of Indians to come this far west unless they have to. That's why I reckon we're safe from that posse now. It's long since turned back to Brady."

"Folks still have Indian trouble around here?"

Drummond answered, "The Comanch' still raid these parts every now and then. Most of 'em have gone up to the Staked Plains with one of their war chiefs called Quanah, but there's still a few of the bloodthirsty red savages around here. They stay clear of us, and we don't bother them."

"But they raid the homesteads?" asked Evan.

"Sure. What else would you expect a redskin to do?"

Evan didn't answer that. He had never had any dealings, good or bad, with Indians. He had been little more than a kid at the time of the Council House Fight, and after that, the Comanches had pretty much pulled out of South and Central Texas. He was as far west right now as he had ever been.

"We going to stop at that ranch?" he asked, turning to Stubbs. Chances were, since the settlers were Texans, they would offer their hospitality to any visitors, even outlaws. And Evan intended to ask everyone he ran across if they knew anything about the families that had taken in his children.

"Sure, we'll stop," said Stubbs. "Wouldn't be polite not to pay a call on the folks."

They rode on, drawing closer to the smoke, and the sun was just about directly overhead when they finally topped a small rise and saw a shallow valley opening up before them. Maverick Creek trickled through the center of the valley, its banks lined with cottonwoods and pecan trees. The gentle slopes of the valley were still thick with grass, despite the advancing autumn. As Evan reined in, along with the rest of the men, his breath caught in his throat for an instant at the beauty of the place. Small groups of longhorns grazed here and there, dotting the still-green landscape.

In the center of the valley, not far from the creek, was a large double cabin with a covered dogtrot in between. Instead of logs, the two sides of the cabin were constructed of beams hewn from logs, which fit together better and cut down on drafts. It was the mark of someone who cared enough to take some extra time and trouble in building a shelter for his family. Beyond the cabin were a good-sized barn and a pole corral, and even farther along the creek sat a smaller, single cabin that looked as if it had been built recently. The smoke Evan and the other men had been following came from the stone chimney of the larger cabin.

The place was bustling with activity, but not the kind that would normally be going on around a ranch, Evan thought with a frown. Several tables were sitting in front of the dogtrot, and they appeared to be heavily laden with platters of food. Half a dozen men stood around the tables, smoking pipes, and women hurried in and out of the cabin, adding more platters to the already groaning tables. Some sort of feast was about to take place, and the family had invited guests. Evan saw several saddle horses tied to a hitching post, and a couple of buckboards stood nearby.

Evidently the festivities, whatever they were, were about to get under way. A couple of the men put their pipes away and picked up fiddles, tucking the instruments under their chins and readying their bows. A moment later the strains of distant music came to Evan's ears as the men began to play.

Evan's frown deepened. The song sounded like the one folks usually played at weddings . . .

A woman in a long white dress stepped out of the cabin.

A wedding, sure enough.

"Well, boys," said Harry Stubbs, "what say we go pay our respects to the bride and groom?"

Evan glanced over at the outlaw leader and saw with a shock of surprise that Stubbs was pulling a bandanna up over the lower half of his face. The other men were doing the same. "What in blazes—" exclaimed Evan.

"You can ride with us, Evan," Stubbs said, and his voice was hard and flinty now, "or you can stay here. Either way's fine."

"You're . . . you're going to raid that ranch!"

"That's right. Everybody around here knows old Ashmore's a rich man, and it's about time he shared it with somebody else."

The name was even more of a surprise. It hit Evan like a blow in the face. Stubbs and the other outlaws had sworn they had never heard of anybody named Ashmore—and yet here they were, about to attack a ranch owned by a man of that name. They had played him for a fool, Evan thought bitterly.

But what else should he have expected, he asked himself, from a bunch of owlhoots?

"You know the Ashmores," he accused Stubbs.

"Of course. Figured when you asked about them that you planned to pay 'em a visit, too. Their oldest boy's getting hitched down there today; that's why those other folks are here. People will come from miles around for a wedding." Stubbs' face creased in a grin under the makeshift mask. "They can stand and deliver, too. More loot for us that way."

Evan stared hard at the outlaw. "Folks back in Brady seemed to think of you as some sort of hero, Stubbs."

"It's no lookout of mine what people think of me." Stubbs' voice hardened. "What'll it be, Evan? Are you with us or not?"

"I'm no thief—" Evan began, but the words were barely out of his mouth when he heard the sound of sudden movement behind him. He twisted in the saddle, saw the burly outlaw called Drummond slashing at his head with a pistol.

Sure, thought Evan as he tried desperately to jerk out of the way of the blow. They couldn't afford to leave him up here where he could sound the alarm and ruin the raid. If he wasn't going to join them, he had to be shut up.

He wasn't quite fast enough. The barrel of Drummond's pistol glanced off the side of his head. A dark curtain dropped over Evan's eyes, the blackness relieved only by a shower of red sparks that came cascading down around him. He barely felt himself fall out of the saddle and hit the ground next to the dun.

"Lemme get down and hit him again," he heard Drummond say, the words seeming to come from a thousand miles away. "I'll stove in his skull."

"Let him be." That was Stubbs, just as faint and strange-sounding as Drummond. "By the time he comes around, he won't be a danger to us anymore—and he *did* help you save my bacon back there in Brady."

Drummond growled, clearly disliking Stubbs' decision to let Evan live. Instinct told Evan that if he wanted to survive for more than a few seconds, he had better lie completely still, as if he had been knocked out cold by the pistol-whipping.

"Come on," said Stubbs. "Let's get down there before somebody notices us."

The horses moved away down the hill, the sound of their hooves like hollow thunder to Evan's ears. He had dirt in his mouth, but he didn't spit it out. He didn't move at all for several moments.

He had to stop Stubbs and the other outlaws somehow. That thought echoed in his brain more loudly than the hoofbeats of the horses. When the gang raided that wedding, there would be gunplay, that was certain. Folks would get hurt, maybe even die. And some of them could be his children, at least one of whom had been taken in by the Ashmores. The youngster was bound to still be down there with the family, about to celebrate the wedding along with everyone else.

Faintly, Evan still heard fiddle music . . .

He pulled his head up and opened his eyes. Thankfully, the blow hadn't affected his sight. A warm wet trickle on the side of his face told him the blow on the side of his head had opened up a gash that was bleeding, but he ignored the blood and the pain that throbbed in his skull. He pushed himself up with his left hand and reached for his gun with the right.

The Colt wasn't in its holster.

For an instant, Evan nearly panicked as he looked at the outlaws, who were still close by, having just started down the hill toward the ranch. He had hoped to fire a couple of shots in the air to alert the Ashmores and their wedding guests, but he might have to shout a warning instead.

Then his gaze fell on the revolver, which was lying on the ground a couple of feet away. It must have fallen out of the holster when he tumbled off the dun, he realized.

Evan lunged for the gun, and as he moved, one of the outlaws glanced back and saw him. From the corner of his eye, Evan saw the man reaching for a gun. He concentrated on his own weapon, scooping it up and rolling to the side, bringing the Colt level as he came to a stop. The owlhoot hesitated as his own gun cleared leather, and Evan could almost read the man's mind. The outlaw had just realized that if he fired, he would send a warning to the gang's intended victims.

Evan didn't have to worry about that. His thumb had looped over the hammer and eared it back as he raised the revolver. As the blade of the sight came to rest on the outlaw's duster, Evan pressed the trigger and felt the gun buck against his palm as it roared.

The slug drilled into the outlaw's body and slewed him sideways in the saddle. He dropped his gun, grabbed at the horn, but missed and fell. One foot tangled in the stirrup, and as the horse bolted, the man screamed as he was dragged over the ground.

The other outlaws were reining in and twisting around in surprise. Evan cocked the pistol and fired again, aiming into their midst. If he actually hit any of them, it would be a bonus. The main thing he was trying to do was warn the Ashmores and their guests.

In that, he had been successful, he saw as he tried to scramble to his feet. A glance toward the cabins told him that everyone was now scurrying around in response to the shots. The women were heading for the shelter of the cabins, hustling the bride in her long white gown and a group of children ahead of them. The men were drawing pistols or running to fetch rifles from their horses and buckboards. Stubbs and his gang wouldn't be able to take them by surprise now.

But Evan wouldn't live to see the outcome of the fight unless he got moving, he realized. Harry Stubbs turned a face twisted with hate toward him and yelled, "Get him!" The gun in Stubbs' fist blossomed smoke and fire.

Evan turned and ran. There were half a dozen of the outlaws, and he was no match for them. He darted from side to side to give them a harder target as he sprinted toward a couple of oaks about thirty yards away. The trees wouldn't give him much cover, but they were better than nothing.

He saw bullets kick up dust ahead of him and to one side. The outlaws were missing, but not by much. Behind him, Stubbs yelled, "Take the boys and get down there, Drummond! I'll take care of Littleton!" The drum of his horse's hooves told Evan that Stubbs was galloping after him while the rest of the gang tried to carry out the raid on the Ashmore ranch.

Guns were popping all over the place now, a steady rhythm of death and destruction. Evan heard men shout and women scream, and his feet went out from under him when he was still ten yards from the trees. He fell heavily but managed to hang on to the gun. The sound of hoofbeats was deafening. Stubbs was almost on top of him.

Evan flung himself around and saw the dark shape of the outlaw's horse looming over him. Steel-shod hooves slashed at his head. Evan rolled blindly to the side. Dust choked him and stung his eyes, and he hoped that he hadn't gotten confused and rolled toward the horse, rather than away from it. He saw hooves chewing up the ground right in front of his eyes, then that sight vanished as he kept rolling. Stubbs swept past him.

Stretched out full-length on his belly, Evan

looked up and saw Stubbs yanking on the reins and sawing on the horse's bit as he tried to haul the animal around. The horse reared up instead, spooked by all the chaos around it. Stubbs struggled to control his mount and at the same time brought the gun in his hand down in a chopping motion, aiming at Evan. He fired.

The bullet thudded into the ground beside Evan, and in that same instant, Evan pressed the trigger of his own gun. Acrid powdersmoke mixed with the dust swirling around Evan as the Colt blasted. Through the haze, he saw the bullet strike Stubbs' horse in the throat. He had been aiming for Stubbs, not the horse, but the result was almost as devastating for the outlaw leader. The horse, still reared up on its hind legs and dancing around skittishly, went over backwards as it screamed and blood spouted from its throat. Stubbs vanished, his wildly tumbling body hidden by the rolling and thrashing of the mortally wounded animal.

Slowly, shakily, Evan pushed himself to his feet and waited for the dust to settle. He held his revolver ready if he needed it. A glance down the hill told him that the settlers had met the foolhardy charge of the outlaws with a deadly welcome of gunfire. Most of the raiders were already down, and as Evan watched, the last two members of the gang, Drummond and Tully, fell in the withering hail of lead that came from the cabins and the buckboards, where some of the defenders had taken cover. The attack was over, thought Evan, as he noted how Drummond and

Tully lay motionless after landing sprawled on the ground. That left Stubbs.

Who was no longer any threat, Evan realized as he heard the thin, mewling cries that came from the huddled heap lying near the still body of the dead horse. Evan walked slowly toward the injured man, keeping his gun trained on Stubbs just in case.

There was no need to worry. Blood ran from both sides of Stubbs' mouth, and his head sat at an odd angle on his neck. He was lying on his back, wet, shiny, jagged bones protruding from both legs where they had splintered like matchsticks under the massive weight of the dying horse. Stubbs' chest was caved in, too, and Evan figured that just about everything inside the man had been busted up by the fall. He didn't seem to be able to move anything except his eyes and mouth.

Evan came up beside him and felt a surprising surge of pity for the man. True, Stubbs wasn't the noble outlaw folks thought he was . . . but he *had* stopped Drummond from killing Evan. Stubbs must have been truly grateful for the help Evan had inadvertently provided during the escape from the gallows in Brady.

But regardless of that, there was no way Evan could have stood aside and watched as the raid on the Ashmore ranch endangered one or more of his children. He had done what he had to do.

Stubbs' eyes gradually focused on Evan, and he stopped wailing. "K-kill me," he pleaded in a rasping voice. "F-finish it, blast you!"

Evan frowned. "You want me to shoot you—in cold blood?"

"F-for God's sake . . . kill . . ."

The life faded from Stubbs' eyes, and more blood welled from his mouth as his head fell to the side.

Evan closed his eyes for a second as a wave of relief went through him. He was glad he hadn't been forced to decide if he could have finished off Stubbs or not.

He turned away from what was left of the desperado and looked around for his horse and his hat. The dun was grazing peacefully about halfway down the hill, as if the recently concluded battle hadn't bothered it a bit. Evan's hat, a little more battered and dusty now, was lying on the ground in the same direction, so he picked it up, brushed it off, and put it on as he walked toward the horse. The dun shied away a couple of times as Evan approached, then decided to allow him to catch hold of its dangling reins. Evan was profoundly grateful when the horse did that; he was way too tired to go chasing it all over this valley, and besides, his head still hurt where Drummond had clouted him.

Leading the dun, he walked slowly toward the buildings below. The men who had fought off the outlaws had emerged from the cabins and from behind the buckboards and were even now checking the bodies of the fallen owlhoots, rolling them over onto their backs to make sure they were dead. Arms flopped loosely as the outlaws were toed over. Death was mighty ugly, thought Evan; there was no getting around that fact.

Several men holding rifles stood and watched him coming toward them, their eyes following his every move as he slowly and cautiously holstered the Colt and then lifted both hands about to shoulder level to show that he meant no harm. For all these people knew, he was one of the bandits, so he couldn't blame them for being suspicious of him. When he was close enough, he called out, "Don't shoot, folks. I'm not looking for trouble."

But he sure had found it a lot in the past few days, he thought.

One of the defenders, a tall, husky man with a white beard, wearing a black broadcloth suit, gestured with the rifle in his hands. "You one of that bunch?" he asked as he jerked the barrel of the weapon toward the dead outlaws.

"No, sir," replied Evan. "I rode with 'em for a spell, yesterday and today, but I wasn't one of them."

"Did you know they were going to attack this ranch?" demanded the man.

"Not until they pulled their bandannas over their faces and got ready to ride down here." Evan was only about fifteen feet from the waiting men now. He stopped walking and added, "I was the one who started shooting up there so you'd know something was wrong."

The white-bearded man grunted. "Figured as much. We're obliged for the warning, stranger." He turned to his companions. "Might as well put those rifles down, boys. I reckon this man's on our side, and even if he wasn't, I don't think he's foolish enough to try anything when he's so outnumbered."

Evan summoned up a tired grin. "You're right about both of those things, mister. Would one of you gents happen to be named Ashmore?"

The question surprised the white-bearded man. "I'm John Ashmore," he said. "This is my spread. Do I know you, sir?"

Beyond John Ashmore and the other members of the reception committee, several of the women emerged from the cabin, including the bride. Some of the others seemed to be trying to hold her back, but she strode out determinedly. Evan glanced curiously toward her, seeing now that she had long, thick brown hair under the veil. He said to Ashmore, "Nope, we never met, but I've been looking for a family named Ashmore."

Suddenly, a new fear struck him. What if these were the *wrong* Ashmores?

He swallowed hard and said, "My name is Evan Littleton."

"Daddy?!"

Evan's gaze jerked back to the bride, who despite the circumstances was as young and beautiful as any girl Evan had ever seen. His heart seemed to stop in his chest as he realized he was looking at his oldest daughter.

8

"Dinah?" Evan whispered hoarsely, eyes widening in surprise.

She ran toward him, coming past Ashmore and the other men, and threw herself into his arms. Still startled, Evan embraced her instinctively. He could feel her trembling with the depth of the emotions that were coursing through her.

"Daddy . . ." she said raggedly, "we . . . we thought you were dead!"

He lifted a hand to her long hair and stroked it, letting his fingers comb through the strands as he had when she was a little girl and had climbed up in his lap every time he sat down in his rocking chair. In a way, that seemed like only yesterday.

And yet, it had been years, and much had changed. Dinah was a young woman now. Evan did some quick ciphering in his head. Dinah was fifteen, he realized. He wasn't surprised that somebody had decided to marry her. He put his hands on her shoulders and stepped back so that he could get a good look at her. She was beautiful.

One of the men came toward them with a quick, angry stride. "What's going on here?" he demanded. "Who's that old man? Hey, mister, let go of my wife!"

Dinah rounded on him and said hotly, "I ain't your wife yet, Matthew Ashmore, and I'll thank you not to talk to my father like that."

"Father?" repeated the young man, frowning in confusion.

John Ashmore gestured at Evan. "This is Evan Littleton, Matt," he said. "Seems like he's Dinah's pa." Turning to Evan, Ashmore went on, "We were told that you died in the war, Mr. Littleton."

"Nope, but I thought a few times that I'd never make it out of that Yankee prison camp alive." Evan slid an arm around Dinah's shoulders protectively, not sure why he was doing it but willing to obey his instincts for the moment. "I thank you for looking after my girl here. I was told back in Richland Springs that a family named Ashmore had taken in some of my children. Are any more of them here?"

"No, Daddy, I'm the only one," Dinah said before Ashmore had a chance to reply to Evan's question. "Billy and Penelope went with the Cartmills, and Rockly's with the Wilsons."

Evan felt a surge of relief. Luck had reunited him quickly with his eldest daughter, and she knew where the other children were. If his good fortune held, they might all be together again soon.

"Where can we find the others?" he asked.

"You know where those families settled after they left Richland Springs?"

Dinah shook her head, and Evan felt his spirits fall. "No," she said. "They headed west, like we did, and we all traveled together for a while. But then they pushed on when Mr. Ashmore decided to homestead here."

"I told you, Dinah," said Ashmore, "no need to be so formal. I'm going to be your pa, too, once you and Matt finish the ceremony."

Evan felt a prickle of irritation on the back of his neck. *He* was Dinah's father, the only one she would ever have, no matter who she married. But he supposed Ashmore was just trying to be nice to the girl, so he told himself not to get too proddy over something that didn't really mean anything.

"I'm not getting married with a bunch of dead outlaws lying around," Dinah said tartly.

Ashmore nodded. "We'll haul the bodies down to the ravine. Come on, boys."

The white-bearded rancher led his companions away from Evan and Dinah, including the bridegroom, who went reluctantly. Matt was around twenty, Evan judged, with dark hair and a handlebar mustache that he was obviously quite proud of. He kept glancing over his shoulder at Evan and Dinah as he and the other men began dragging the bodies of the dead outlaws away from the cabin.

"That boy you're marrying doesn't cotton to me very much," Evan said quietly. "The old man's his father, right?"

"That's right," Dinah said. "And here comes Matt's mother."

Mrs. Ashmore was a small, pinch-faced woman with graying brown hair. She made no secret of how upset she was as she said to Dinah, "Oh, this is terrible! To have those awful outlaws come riding down here and try to kill us all, just when you and Matt are about to get married!" She took a deep breath and seemed to calm down a little. "Well, I suppose the wedding will go on, just a little later than we intended."

Dinah put her hand on Evan's arm and said, "Mrs. Ashmore, this is my father, Evan Littleton."

The woman sniffed and frowned in disapproval as she looked at Evan, taking in his battered hat, worn-out clothes, and especially the gun holstered on his hip. "You look like a desperado yourself, Mr. Littleton. Were you part of that gang?"

"No, ma'am," Evan told her, swallowing the irritation she provoked in him. "I was riding with them, true enough, but I've already explained to your husband that I didn't have any idea they were planning to raid your ranch until the last minute. That's why I raised a ruckus to warn you."

"I see." The coolness of Mrs. Ashmore's tone made it clear she wasn't sure whether to believe him or not.

At the moment, Evan didn't care what the Ashmores or anybody else thought of him. He was just glad to be back with one of his children. He was sorry that Dinah didn't know where the others were—but he had found her, and he could find them, too, he told himself.

Dinah took hold of his arm and led him off to the side. "I want to talk to my father for a minute, Mrs. Ashmore," she said over her shoulder to her future mother-in-law. Mrs. Ashmore folded her arms over her sparse bosom and glowered. She was an unpleasant little woman, thought Evan, but some people were just that way. For Dinah's sake, he would try to get along with all the Ashmores. After all, she was going to be part of their family.

Dinah put her arms around Evan and hugged him again, resting her head on his shoulder. It was still difficult for him to believe she was as old as she was; she had still been a gawky kid when he left for the war, and now she was a young woman, about to be married. He gave a lot of credit for Dinah's poise to Lynette. Dinah's mother had raised her well, doing so under difficult circumstances, what with both her husband and her oldest son disappearing into the cauldron of war.

"I can't believe you're here, Daddy," said Dinah. "How did you find me?"

Quickly he explained to her how he had found her little brother Fulton at Jonas Russell's ferry and learned of Lynette's death. It took only a few moments to fill her in on his visit to the Brackett farm and everything he had discovered there about the fate of his wife and children, as well as how their homestead had been taken over by Yankee carpetbaggers.

"I couldn't just turn around and ride off," he said. "I had to find you and the other kids. I knew the families that had taken you in had headed west when they left Richland Springs, so I came this way, too. Good luck brought me here." He didn't go into detail about how he had fallen in with Harry Stubbs and the other outlaws. His voice catching in his throat, he went on, "Tell me about . . . your mama."

"It was over fast, Daddy, it really was," Dinah said as she hugged his arm and shivered a little. "The fever came on her and took her away in less than a day. She didn't suffer."

"Did she . . . say anything before she passed on?" Evan didn't know what he was hoping for: some sort of final message, maybe.

Dinah shook her head regretfully. "Mama was out of her head nearly the whole time," she said. "I'm sorry, Daddy."

Evan sighed. "That's all right. She knew I loved her, and I know she loved me. That's enough."

For a moment, the two of them were silent, then finally Dinah asked, "After we find the other kids, are we all going back home?"

Evan looked up in surprise. "We?" he repeated. "I thought you were getting married."

Dinah's eyes met his, and there was desperation in her gaze. "Please, Daddy," she said, "don't make me go through with this wedding!"

Evan stared at her in surprise. It was a moment before he could speak, and then he said, "You . . . you don't want to marry Matt Ashmore?"

"I hate him!" she hissed in a whisper. "Well, maybe not hate him, exactly . . . but marrying him wasn't my idea."

"Whose idea was it?"

"Oh, Matt asked me to marry him, all right,

and he's eager enough to do it, but I think it was really his mama and daddy's idea." Dinah's voice took on a tone of bitterness as she continued, "They seem to think that just because they took me in, that gives them the right to treat me like a slave! Mrs. Ashmore's got me doing all the cooking and cleaning, and I heard her tell Mr. Ashmore that they'd better get me married to Matt before somebody else comes along and takes me away."

Evan didn't know what to make of this unexpected story. It wasn't like Dinah to complain about cooking and cleaning. Hard work was a way of life on the frontier, and he remembered clearly that even when she was little, she had never shirked doing her part of the daily chores. If she was this upset, the Ashmores must have really treated her badly.

"You're sure about this?" he asked.

She met his gaze squarely. "I can show you the marks on my back where Mrs. Ashmore's taken the strap to me when I didn't do something to suit her."

The words kindled a flame of anger inside Evan. He believed the Scriptures that talked about sparing the rod and spoiling the child, but he also believed in tempering punishment with kindness. He had seen too much harshness in his own life to impose it unfairly on others, especially kids.

Dinah went on, "Mrs. Ashmore thinks they can treat me any way they want, since they took me in out of the kindness of their hearts." Her mouth twisted in a grimace. "That's what she calls it, anyway."

"And what's Matt's part in this?"

"He just does what his folks tell him." Dinah looked down at the ground, suddenly embarrassed. "And from the way he's been looking at me the past year or so, I reckon he wants to bed me, too."

Evan didn't waste time being shocked by his daughter's blunt words. Bad situations called for plain talk. And this was clearly a bad situation.

He took a deep breath and patted Dinah on the shoulder. "If you don't want to marry this boy, then you won't marry him. It's as simple as that. But we'd better tell the Ashmores, because it looks like they're waiting to get on with that marriage ceremony."

Indeed, the family and the guests were all gathered together in front of the dogtrot again. A skinny, bald-headed gent who Evan took to be the preacher was standing by himself, holding a Bible and waiting as well. The fiddle players had resined up their bows and were ready to start sawing out the Wedding March again. All that was missing was the bride.

Evan studied the gathering. Matt Ashmore stood in front of the minister. His parents were off to one side, looking impatient. Behind Matt were three other men, all of them good-sized and bearing a strong family resemblance to him. His brothers, Evan figured. A dozen other men and women, friends and neighbors of the Ashmores, stood back to watch the ceremony when it resumed, and several children fidgeted under the stern gazes of their mothers.

If there was trouble, it would come from the

Ashmore men, Evan decided. They might not take kindly to the wedding being called off so abruptly.

"We're waiting for you, Dinah," said John Ashmore. "Come along. Your father is welcome to join us, of course."

"Hurry up, girl," snapped Mrs. Ashmore. "It's bad enough those outlaws made us wait."

Evan exchanged a glance with Dinah, then stepped forward, putting himself between his daughter and the wedding party. "Sorry, folks," he said, "but I'm afraid you're going to have to wait a spell longer. There's not going to be a wedding today."

Exclamations of surprise came from several of the guests, and Matt Ashmore said angrily, "What are you talking about? Of course, there's going to be a wedding today! Get over here right now, Dinah!"

Evan shook his head. "Nope. Dinah's decided that she doesn't want to go through with this, and I reckon that's her right."

"Wait just a minute," John Ashmore said. "We're grateful for the help you gave us, Littleton, but that doesn't mean you can come in here and ruin everything we've planned—"

"That's just it," Evan cut in. "*You* planned this wedding. It was your idea, yours and your wife's and your son's. Dinah never wanted any part of it."

"That's a lie!" said Matt. "Tell him, Dinah. Tell your pa that he's wrong!"

Dinah stepped forward enough so that Matt could see her and then shook her head. "No,

Matt," she said. "I never really wanted to marry you."

Matt stared at her in disbelief for a few seconds, then his eyes narrowed. His face took on an ugly look. "Well, you're going to," he said flatly. "It's all planned out. You're going to marry me, and there's nothing you can do about it." He strode toward her, clearly intending to step around Evan, grab Dinah, and drag her back to face the preacher.

Evan moved to block Matt's way and said quietly, "I wouldn't do that, son."

"Just a blasted minute!" John Ashmore said as his other sons all stepped forward, their faces hardening. Matt was the closest to Evan, however, and he balled his fists.

"Out of my way, old man!" he shouted as he swung a roundhouse right at Evan's head.

It was just one fight after another these days, Evan reflected wearily in the split second that he had before Matt hit him. In that same eyeblink of time, he jerked to his left, so that Matt's fist whipped harmlessly past his right ear. Thrown off balance by the missed blow, Matt stumbled forward, lost his footing, and fell past Evan.

Dinah was waiting for him. She clubbed her hands together and brought them down hard on the back of Matt's neck as he fell. "Don't you hurt my daddy!" she yelled. Matt smacked face-first into the ground, driven down by his own momentum and Dinah's blow.

Matt's brothers were hurrying toward Evan, shaking off the young women who grabbed at their arms. Probably their own wives, Evan thought as he tried to figure out how to handle three burly, enraged men who were almost twenty years younger than he was.

Reaching for his gun seemed to be the only way.

But he hesitated. The Ashmores might be misguided, might even be sorry skunks to have treated Dinah the way they had, but they weren't owlhoots like Harry Stubbs and his gang had been. Evan didn't want any more gunplay. He held up his hands, empty palms extended, and began, "Hold on! Can't we talk about—"

The closest of the Ashmore brothers—if that was who they actually were—launched himself into a dive, tackling Evan around the waist. Evan felt himself being borne backward, and then he slammed into the ground with the husky young pioneer on top of him. All the breath was knocked out of Evan's body, leaving him gasping for air and unable to get any because of the man's crushing weight.

"Get him, Claude!" somebody shouted.

Evan's opponent was trying to get his hands around Evan's throat. That would be the end of the fight, Evan knew. He managed to lift his arms and smacked his fists against the young man's ears. That caused a momentary pause in the onslaught, and Evan was able to arch his back and throw the man off by putting all of his strength into one desperate heave.

Knowing that he had to get back on his feet while he had the chance, Evan scrambled up, only to run right into another fist. This punch caught him in the jaw and sent him careening backward again. He crashed into the onlookers, most of whom were shouting, and brought three of the men down in a tangle of arms and legs. Over the tumult, Evan heard a splintering sound and hoped he hadn't broken any bones. A second later, as he struggled to get up, he heard an anguished wail, followed by a man's furious voice. "My fiddle! Somebody stepped on my fiddle!"

There was no time to worry about that now. Evan regained his feet and saw a knobby-knuckled fist coming at his face. He ducked under it and threw himself forward, driving his shoulder into the chest of the man who had thrown the punch. Evan hooked a hard right into his belly, making the man's breath gust in his face. The fella had been drinking apple cider, Evan thought as he shoved the man away and turned to meet the next threat.

The wedding guests seemed to be staying out of the fight, thank goodness. Odds of four against one were overwhelming enough already. Evan knew there was no way he could win this fight; sooner or later, he would go down under the concentrated attack of the Ashmore brothers, and he wouldn't get up anytime soon. He just hoped they wouldn't stomp him to death while they were at it.

Maybe it was time to use that gun after all.

He didn't get a chance to even reach for the Colt, let alone draw the gun and fire it. A deep-throated roar slammed through the air, making Evan and his four opponents wince and then freeze as they circled him, ready to close in. He recognized the sound: Somebody had just squeezed off one barrel of a double-barreled greener.

Evan looked around for the source of the shot. To his surprise, he saw Dinah standing beside the dogtrot, a shotgun in her hands. The barrels were pointing toward the sky, but she lowered them quickly and shouted, "Leave my daddy alone! Get away from him!"

"Dinah!" Mrs. Ashmore said furiously. "Put that shotgun down this instant!"

"No, ma'am!" Dinah snapped back at her. "You'd better call off your boys, or I'll sure enough dust their britches with buckshot!"

John Ashmore took a step toward her and held out a hand. "Be reasonable, Dinah—"

She swung the greener to point at him, and he stepped back hurriedly. "Stay away from me! I'm about fed up with all you blasted Ashmores!"

Evan dragged a deep breath into his tired, aching body. "Dinah, put the shotgun down," he said. "There's way too many innocent people around here to go shooting off a scattergun."

As a matter of fact, most of the wedding guests had scurried off to what they considered a safe distance, dragging their kids with them. Only the Ashmores, Dinah, and Evan were still close to the cabin. The preacher poked his head up over one of the buckboards, saw that Dinah was still holding the shotgun, and ducked back down again.

"Daddy—" Dinah began.

"Put the gun down," Evan repeated. "Shooting somebody's not going to solve this problem."

Dinah snorted in disagreement. "It would if I shot Matt."

Under his tan, Matt Ashmore paled.

Evan grimaced and stepped over to his daughter, shouldering aside a couple of Matt's brothers. He reached out, wrapped his fingers around the barrels of the greener, and pulled it out of Dinah's grasp. She let go of it with a soft "Oh!"

Evan turned and held out the shotgun toward John Ashmore, who stepped forward and took it gingerly. "You folks have been through a lot today," Evan said. "Been a lot of surprises. So I'm not going to hold this ruckus against you. But I'm not going to let you force my daughter into getting married when she doesn't want to, either."

Now that Dinah was disarmed, the stubborn expression was coming back onto John Ashmore's face, and Evan gave a mental sigh of exhaustion. The rancher didn't look like he was going to give up, and neither would his sons.

That was when one of the wedding guests said to another in a voice loud enough for everyone to hear, "Say, I've heard of that Littleton fella! Didn't he used to be some sort of gunfighter, back before the war?"

John Ashmore's bushy white eyebrows lifted in surprise, and his gaze dropped to the holstered Colt on Evan's hip for a second before jerking back up to meet Evan's level stare. "Gunfighter?" repeated Ashmore.

People were recognizing him too blasted much

lately, thought Evan. First the outlaw called Tully, now this settler who had come to see Dinah and Matt Ashmore get married. He had always known that he could never completely live down his reputation, but folks around Richland Springs had gotten used to him, he supposed ... and during the war, a reputation as a fast gun hadn't really meant much. Now, though, it might come in handy.

"That was a long time ago," Evan said. "And it's not something I'm proud of, either."

Matt Ashmore said, "Then you *are* a pistoleer?"

Evan looked squarely at him and said, "Some have called me that."

Matt looked at Evan's gun, just like his father had, and his thoughts were obvious to Evan: *That old man could've drawn his gun and killed me any time he wanted to* ...

"Look here, Littleton," said John Ashmore, his tone mollifying now instead of arrogant, "we didn't mean to do anything Dinah doesn't want. Why, she's like our own daughter, for God's sake! If she doesn't want to marry Matt, well, then, she doesn't have to."

"Pa!" Matt said, a whine creeping into his voice.

"What are you doing, you old fool?" Mrs. Ashmore asked her husband, the words lashing him like a whip. "You know what we planned—"

"Plans don't always work out," Ashmore interrupted gruffly. "Hush, woman! I know what I'm doing."

From the look on Mrs. Ashmore's face, Evan

figured the rancher would pay for those words later—but that was none of his business, Evan told himself. All he cared about was taking his daughter and getting out of here.

He extended a hand toward Dinah. "Come on, girl. We've still got your brothers and sister to find."

With an excited smile on her face, Dinah caught hold of his hand. "You're taking me with you?"

"Well, I don't much care for the idea of leaving you here."

Hurriedly, she shook her head. "Neither do I." She squeezed his hand and went on, "I'll get out of this wedding dress and get my own clothes on."

"You have a horse?"

Dinah shook her head again.

"Well, we can ride double," Evan said. "That'll slow us down some—"

John Ashmore broke in, asking, "What was that you said about looking for your other kids, Littleton?"

"I intend to find them and make a home for all of us," Evan said.

The wedding guests had come closer, now that it was obvious there wasn't going to be any gunplay. One of the men called out, "I've got a horse your girl can have, mister. If you're looking for some more kids, you don't need anything holding you back."

Evan smiled tiredly at the man. "I'm much obliged."

"Wait just a blasted minute," said John

Ashmore. "You're on my ranch, and you *did* keep those outlaws from ambushing us and probably killing all of us. It's my hospitality you'll accept."

"John!" Mrs. Ashmore said, and Matt added angrily, "Papa!"

Ashmore ignored their scolding and stepped toward Evan, extending an empty hand. "What do you say, Littleton?"

Evan hesitated only a second, then clasped the rancher's hand firmly. "I say thanks, Ashmore," he replied fervently. "I surely do say thanks."

9

Even though John Ashmore invited them to stay for a spell, by nightfall Evan and Dinah were on their way, riding southwest. "That's the way the Cartmills and the Wilsons headed last year when I decided to stay here," Ashmore had told them. "Clive and Melinda Cartmill had your boy Billy and your girl Penny with 'em, and Frank and Suellen Wilson were looking after the littlest one, Rockly."

Evan didn't bother reminding Ashmore that there was one child even younger than Rockly. He hoped Fulton was doing all right back there at the ferry and that Jonas Russell hadn't run into any more trouble from the State Police. When he went back to fetch Fulton, he would do it quickly and try to avoid those Yankee carpetbaggers and turncoat Texans.

Dinah was riding a chestnut mare that Ashmore had provided for her, again over the objections of his wife and sons. Something had touched a spark of decency in the man, probably

Evan's determination to find his children. Ashmore was a father, too; he had likely realized how he would feel if he had been in Evan's boots.

Their saddlebags were full of supplies, another gesture on John Ashmore's part. Dinah wore a riding skirt, a simple shirt, a short jacket, and high-topped black boots. A wide-brimmed hat dangled on her back from its chin strap, leaving her dark hair loose to spill around her shoulders.

As they rode along, Evan asked his daughter, "When you were traveling with the Cartmills and the Wilsons on the way out here, did you ever hear any of 'em mention where they might decide to settle?"

"Not really," Dinah replied with a shake of her head. "Mr. and Mrs. Cartmill had never been out here in this part of Texas before, so they planned to go on until they found a place to their liking." She frowned in thought for a moment, trying to summon up a memory, then said, "I did hear Mr. Wilson say something once about having relatives in El Paso. Maybe they were going there."

"El Paso?" repeated Evan. He swallowed a groan of dismay. "El Paso's a *long* way out there, Dinah. You can't go much further and still be in Texas."

Dinah shrugged her slender shoulders. "I just know what I heard Mr. Wilson say."

"I know, I know. Didn't mean I was doubting you. It's just that it'll be a long ride if we have to go all the way to El Paso."

"At least we're together again."

Evan grinned at his daughter, feeling a

familiar tightness in his chest. He had experienced it the first time when he had seen the wrinkled little bundle of soft flesh that was his son Thad, wrapped in a blanket and lying in the protective cradle of Lynette's arms a few minutes after being born. The feeling had come to him hundreds of times since then, unexpectedly, at odd moments when he was looking at his children.

Fathers were mighty lucky, he thought, because they were the only ones who got to experience that sensation.

"Yeah, we're together," he said, "and we're going to stay that way."

A little later, after a time of companionable silence, he asked, "How was it decided which of you would go with which family?"

"You mean after Mama died?" Abruptly, Dinah caught her breath as she saw him wince. "Oh, Daddy, I'm sorry, I didn't mean—"

"It's all right," he told her with a wave of his hand. "You've had more time to mourn, to get used to the idea that your mama's not around anymore. I just found out a few days ago. But you go ahead."

"Well . . . afterwards . . . there wasn't really much choice. It was hard times around home."

Evan nodded. "I know."

"We had to stay with whoever offered to take us in. The Ashmore and the Cartmills and the Wilsons had all come to Richland Springs after the war started. They came out from East Texas."

"So the Yankees would have farther to come to

get them if the war went bad for the South," guessed Evan. Which it surely had, he added to himself, remembering the devastation he had seen throughout the former Confederacy during his long walk home. Many of his fellow Texans, the ones who had stayed home, didn't really know how lucky they had been to escape that.

"I reckon so," said Dinah. "They were a little bit more well-to-do, so they could afford to take us in. I would have rather stayed with somebody like the Bracketts, but we couldn't have done that to Andrew and Elizabeth. They had enough to do just holding their own family together without having a bunch of extra mouths to feed."

Evan felt a surge of pride. He was glad his kids had thought enough of others to reach that conclusion. But it would have been a lot easier to round them up again after his homecoming if they had all stayed where he had left them, he mused.

That had been impossible, of course, and they had done the best they could. If Thad hadn't gone off to the war and gotten himself killed . . .

Evan's jaw tightened as he forced that thought out of his head. No point in such thinking now, and besides, he couldn't blame Thad for enlisting. After all, *he* had gone off to fight for the Great and Glorious Cause, too, hadn't he? His mouth quirked bitterly.

The only cause that was truly great and glorious was loving your family and taking care of them. He knew that now.

He just hoped the knowledge hadn't come to him too late.

For the next ten days, Evan and Dinah rode west by southwest, through country that gradually grew flatter and more arid. There were few trees now, and most of the ones they saw were only scrubby mesquites. Most of this land was unclaimed, there for the taking . . . but who would want it, Evan asked himself as he rode through the increasingly bleak landscape.

The Cartmills and the Wilsons should have stopped back there where the Ashmores had settled, he decided. That was better country for ranching. Out here where the vegetation was more sparse, a man would have to control hundreds of thousands of acres in order to graze a good-sized herd. Of course, maybe that was what attracted some men to this territory: its emptiness and open spaces, the lack of people, the opportunity to build what could eventually become an empire. Captain King had done that down in South Texas, in the Coastal Bend. Others might do it here in West Texas, but in many ways, the challenge would be even greater, Evan thought.

King had not had to contend with Indians, for one thing.

Several times since leaving the Ashmore ranch, Evan had sensed that they were being watched. He had kept his eyes open, trying to locate whoever was spying on them, but so far he had been unsuccessful. Might not be anybody, he told himself. Might just be his imagination. But he had been unable to convince himself of that. He had heard stories all his life of the wild savages that roamed the West Texas plains.

Dinah was nervous, too. Evan could tell that by the way her eyes grew big and round at night when coyotes howled in the distance and owls hooted nearby. He knew she was wondering the same thing he was: Were those sounds genuine, or were they signals passed back and forth between groups of Indians who were preparing to attack their camp? After a few days, Evan started calling a halt early each day so that he could build a small fire and cook their supper before night fell. That way the flames could be extinguished before they served as a beacon for whatever—or whoever—was lurking out there in the darkness.

That made for cold camps, especially with the chilly breezes that were once again sweeping down from the north. Evan and Dinah wrapped up in their blankets and shivered through the nights.

By the time a week and a half had passed, they had not come to a settlement or even another ranch. Unable to ask anyone if they had seen the families he sought, Evan felt despair growing inside him. He had hoped to find the rest of the kids before winter set in, but it was beginning to look as if that was unlikely.

That day, Dinah reined in around midmorning and pointed at something rising in the distance. "What's that?" she asked.

Evan squinted at the long blue line, hazy with distance. After a moment, he said, "Mountains."

"Real mountains? Not hills?" Dinah had never seen real mountains.

Neither had Evan, at least not in Texas. He remembered the Smoky Mountains in Tennessee—but not fondly. He had no fond memories of *anything* he had seen during the war.

"Those must be the Davis Mountains," he said. "That outlaw Stubbs told me about them. Said they were the tail end of the Rockies."

"They don't look very big."

Evan chuckled. "They're seventy, eighty miles off, girl. I expect they'll look a mite bigger by the time we actually get to them. *If* we go that far. I haven't given up hope of finding your brothers and your sister before then."

Evan's hopes rose even more when they spotted some buildings ahead of them around noon. As they rode closer, he saw that both structures had been built of adobe. One had a corral made of mesquite poles attached to it, so Evan figured that was a barn. The other building was low and sprawling. That would be where the people who owned this place lived. The spread didn't look like much, but since it was the first sign of civilization they had seen in days, Evan was cheered considerably by it.

They hadn't reached the buildings when Dinah pointed to the south and said, "Something down there."

Evan looked and saw dust rising. It would take several horses to kick up that much dust. His jaw tightened. Without knowing who those other travelers were, he was going to assume they represented potential trouble. Practically everything *had* since he had gotten back to Texas. But he wasn't going to turn away from the isolated ranch, not without asking some questions about those whom he and Dinah sought.

After a few minutes, though, as he and Dinah approached the adobe buildings along with the cloud of dust, he relaxed. He could see now that the dust was being kicked up by a six-horse hitch pulling a stagecoach. The red and yellow Concord coach rocked and bounced on its leather thoroughbraces as the driver whipped his team into a run. Suddenly alarmed by the thought that the stagecoach might be fleeing from something, Evan turned in the saddle to look behind it. There was no pursuing dust cloud. Obviously the jehu simply enjoyed speed.

Dinah laughed as she reined in alongside Evan and watched the stagecoach. "It's really moving," she said.

"Fella better hope he doesn't lose a wheel or break an axle at that speed," said Evan. "If that coach went over, it'd be smashed to kindling."

The driver seemed to know the capability of his vehicle, however, because he gradually slowed and brought it to a halt in front of the big adobe building. "Must be a stagecoach station," Evan commented. "Maybe we can get news of your brothers and sister there." He heeled the dun into a trot again, and Dinah's chestnut followed. Quickly, they covered the last few hundred yards that separated them from the buildings.

By the time they got there, the doors of the

coach stood open, and the passengers had evidently all gone inside the station. The driver, a tall, burly man in a sheepskin coat and a high-crowned hat with the brim pushed up, was supervising the changing of the teams by two young men who had brought fresh horses out of the barn. As Evan and Dinah rode up, the driver swung to face them, and Evan noted the greener tucked under his arm. From the looks of it, the jehu served as his own shotgun guard.

"Howdy," the man called in a friendly voice. "Light and go on inside, folks. Farley's got lunch on the table, and I reckon there'll be plenty for two more pilgrims." The twang in his tone marked him as a Texan.

"Much obliged," said Evan as he and Dinah swung down from their saddles and looped their mounts' reins over a hitch rack next to a large water trough.

"Don't thank me, mister, thank Farley," said the stage driver. "This is his spread."

"The stagecoach line doesn't own it?" Evan asked curiously.

"Shoot, no. They just contract with ol' Farley to supply 'em with a change of horses a couple of times a week. Feedin' the passengers is a sideline for Farley, but just 'tween you an' me, I callate he makes just as much dinero off that as he does from the stage line." The driver stuck out a gloved hand. "Ben Thayer."

As Evan shook hands with the man, Dinah said, "Been There? That's your name?"

"No, ma'am. Last name's Thayer." He spelled it

for her, then let out a hoot of laughter. "But I reckon if you're talkin' about pert' near anywhere in this West Texas country, I sure 'nough been there, all right."

Evan felt a flicker of interest. "You know the people who live out here?"

"Sure. They're mighty few and fur between, so there ain't many to know."

"What about a family named Cartmill, or one named Wilson?"

Thayer took off his hat and used his long, blunt fingers to scratch a freckled scalp visible through thinning, rust-colored hair. "Cartmill," he repeated. "Ain't a very common name, like Wilson. Seems I've heard tell of somebody with that name. Best ask Farley inside. Likely he'll know, if anybody will."

"Thanks," Evan said with a nod. He felt an instinctive liking for this rough-hewn stagecoach driver.

Thayer slapped him on the shoulder. "Come on, let's get some grub. Them hostlers've just about got my teams changed."

He led them to the door of the station building, which was closed to block out the chilly wind. Thayer opened it, politely taking off his hat and gesturing with it for Dinah to go ahead of him.

Warmth washed over them as they stepped inside. A fire was burning cheerfully in a fireplace on the other side of the big room. A sturdy table flanked by benches occupied the center of the room, with several rocking chairs drawn up before the fire. There were no windows, only narrow slits in the wall, which told Evan the place had been designed to be easily defended against attacks. The room was lit by several lanterns that hung from the thick beams of the flat roof. Half a dozen people sat around the table, plates full of beans, bacon, and cornbread in front of them. The smell of coffee was strong in the room, and Evan's eyes found the cast iron pot sitting on the hearth. He felt an intense craving go through him. He couldn't remember the last time he had tasted real coffee.

The eyes of the stagecoach passengers seated at the table swung toward the newcomers. So did the gaze of the short, bald-headed man who was tending the pot of beans, stirring it occasionally with a long-handled spoon. Dinah was the only female in the room, and she flushed under the frank appraisal of the men. Evan saw her reaction and felt a surge of anger, but he controlled it. Dinah was his daughter, but she was also a lovely young woman, and women of any sort were probably rare out here. Men were going to look, and she would just have to get used to that. But as long as she behaved like a decent woman, she would be treated politely and with the utmost respect. In fact, the men around the table were already jerking their hats off and getting to their feet.

The bald-headed man hustled forward. "Hello," he said in a high-pitched voice. "My name is Emil Farley, and this is my place. Welcome! Have a seat, and I'll bring you some hot food."

That sounded wonderful to Evan, but he still didn't have any money. "Much obliged, Mr. Farley,

but I reckon the price is a mite out of my range—
whatever it may be. We'll settle for warming up in
front of that fire and watering our horses from
your trough, if that's all right with you."

"It most certainly is not," said Farley. "This
young lady looks like she could use a hot meal,
and I won't have it otherwise. Your . . . wife?"

"Daughter," Evan said.

That brought smiles to the faces of most of
the men. Since Dinah wasn't spoken for, they
would feel easier about talking to her, although
they would still be respectful.

"Well, like I said," Farley went on, "the two of
you just sit down and I'll bring you some food. No
charge."

"Hey, Emil," said one of the other men with a
grin, a traveling salesman judging by his suit and
derby, "is that fair? You always charge us."

"I decide what's fair around here, Mason, and
when you get as pretty as this young lady here,
maybe I won't charge you for your meals, either."

"Mason won't ever be that pretty," said
another drummer with a laugh. "Leastways, I sure
hope not!"

That brought laughter from the other men as
well. Knowing that it wouldn't be polite to argue
with Farley's hospitality, Evan and Dinah sat down
at the table, Evan being careful to position himself
between Dinah and the rest of the travelers. Three
of them were salesmen, he judged, and the other
three were wearing range clothes. They could be
anything from cowhands who were nearly stone
broke to ranch owners with hundreds of dollars in

their pockets. From his own experiences down in the Nueces country before he had settled down, he knew how hard it was to tell the difference sometimes.

"Name's Evan Littleton," he said to Farley as the stationkeeper brought plates of food from the stove and set them on the table. "This is my daughter Dinah."

"Pleased to meet you, Littleton," said Farley. "You, too, ma'am. What brings you out here to the middle of nowhere?"

Before Evan could reply, one of the salesmen said, "You can't be planning to stay. Anybody with any sense gets through this godforsaken country as fast as possible." The comment drew a glare from Farley.

"We're looking for some folks who might've passed through this way," Evan said. "Two couples, and they'd have some kids with them. Names are Cartmill and Wilson." The smells wafting up from the plate of food and the tin cup of coffee Farley placed in front of him were maddening, but Evan didn't want to dig in until he had asked the questions that had brought them here.

Ben Thayer, the stagecoach driver, was pouring his own cup of coffee at the hearth. He looked up at Evan's words and said, "I been thinkin' on that since you asked me outside, mister. Emil, ain't Cartmill the name of those folks who started a spread down on Limpia Creek last year?"

"You know, I believe you're right, Ben," replied

Farley. "And they had a couple of kids with 'em, too."

Evan leaned forward in excitement, the meal waiting for him momentarily forgotten. He and Dinah might have picked up the trail again at last. "You're sure about that?" he asked.

"Yep, now that I think about it, I'm certain that was their name. Friends of yours, Mr. Littleton?"

"You could say that." Evan didn't want to take the time or trouble to explain the convoluted circumstances that had brought him out here searching for the Cartmills.

Ben Thayer carried his coffee cup over to the table, his face grim now. "Plannin' to pay 'em a visit?"

"That's right."

Suddenly, all the men inside the stage station wore the same solemn look as Thayer. "I don't know if that would be a good idea or not," Farley said gently.

Evan's excitement turned to apprehension, and the chill that went through him had nothing to do with the weather outside. "What do you mean?" he demanded harshly.

"We've heard they already had some visitors," said Thayer. "Apaches."

10

"Apaches," Evan repeated as he stared at Emil Farley. Beside him, Dinah reached over and took hold of his hand, her fingers closing tightly over his.

One of the cowboys spoke up. "That's right. I recollect hearing the same thing. The 'Paches raided up and down Limpia Canyon last spring, and the Cartmill place was one of 'em that got hit."

Dinah asked in a tremulous voice, "Were . . . were they all killed?"

"Ma'am, I just don't know," said Farley. "Nobody from down that way has been up here in a long time. What about you, Ben? You heard anything?"

"Nope," replied the stagecoach driver. "Just that the soldiers from Fort Davis went chasin' after them Mescaleros once the raidin' was over, when it was too late to do any good. As per usual."

Evan said, "There's a fort down there in the mountains?"

"Yep. Not much of one, but I reckon it's better'n

nothin'. Got a little settlement growin' up next to it, or so I hear, and there's a dozen or so spreads scattered out through the canyons north and west of there." Thayer settled down on one of the benches and took a grateful sip of his steaming coffee. "Old Mescalero chief called Nicholas is still runnin' wild down there along with his bucks. They don't pay no never-mind to some little army post like Fort Davis."

Evan exchanged a glance with Dinah and could tell that she was thinking much the same thing as he was: Billy and Penelope and maybe even Rockly were somewhere down there in those mountains filled with hostile Indians and might even already be dead. Evan blamed himself for that, tasting the sour tang of guilt in the back of his throat. If he had never gone off to the war . . .

Not for the first time in recent weeks, Evan forced that thought from his head. Torturing himself that way wasn't going to do any good. These men didn't know for sure what had happened at the Cartmill ranch. There was only one way to find out.

He had to go down there and see for himself.

Once he had reached that decision, it made it a little easier for him to see what all he had to do. He looked over at Thayer and asked, "Your stage line doesn't go to Fort Davis, does it?"

"Shoot, no! Our route stays north of the mountains and heads on out to the Rio Grande, then follows the river up to El Paso. If the army ever settles down them Mescaleros and Lipans, could be they'll put in a spur line down to Fort

Davis. That'll make good ranchin' country . . . one o' these days, when the 'Paches are gone."

"How close do you come to the mountains?"

"Too close for comfort, sometimes," said Thayer. "I tell you, I can feel them redskin eyes just a-studyin' us from up yonder as I drive past. Reckon that's why I got in the habit of hurryin' so through these parts. But to answer your question . . . the route comes within four or five miles of the mountains. Fort Davis itself is about thirty miles on the other side."

Evan nodded. "Is there a road or a trail that leads down to the fort?"

"Well, yeah, there's a good trail, leads right down Limpia Canyon. I could show you where it starts, if that's what you mean."

"That's exactly what I mean," Evan said. "If we could follow your coach that far . . ."

"Why, sure, if you're bound and determined to do it."

"Might not be such a bad time for it," Farley put in. "With winter coming on, Nicholas and his people could have pulled up stakes and headed south across the Rio Grande, where it's warmer. But I'd still think twice about taking your daughter down there, Mr. Littleton."

Evan drank some of his coffee. "I'm not going to," he said as he lowered the cup to the table. "Dinah's going on to El Paso on the stage. I'll come up with the ticket money somehow."

Dinah stared at him, her eyes flashing angrily. "I am *not*! I'm going with you, Daddy."

Evan shook his head. "Nope, you'll be safer

going on with Mr. Thayer and the stagecoach," he said.

"We'll all look out for the little lady, right enough," Thayer said. "Might not be too proper, her travelin' with a bunch of gents who ain't related to her—"

"I won't do it," Dinah protested.

"—but it's better'n havin' her hair wind up decoratin' some Apache lance," Thayer finished bluntly. He gestured with his spoon at the plates of food in front of Evan and Dinah. "Best dig in, folks, if you're goin' to be travelin' with us for a spell. I got a schedule to keep, you know."

Dinah was still angry an hour later as she rocked back and forth on the hard wooden bench that served as a seat inside the stagecoach. Evan could tell that by the taut line of her jaw and the hard set of her mouth. She had insisted on sitting across from him, rather than beside him, and two of the drummers had been glad to make room for her. A couple of the cowboys were riding on top of the stage now to make room for the new passengers. All of the men had sworn that they wouldn't say anything about Evan and Dinah not having tickets to ride the stage. Evan was grateful for that.

But not for Dinah's attitude. He had been as glad to be reunited with her as she was, but that didn't mean they had to stay together every moment from now on. He couldn't justify dragging her down into those mountains where danger could be lurking around every bend in the trail. She had been put in harm's way enough because of him already.

Fussing with her wasn't going to do any good. He had laid down the law, told her how things were going to be, and that was that. She might as well just accept it graciously and go on, he thought. She didn't seem willing to do that at the moment, though.

Evan had gotten to know their fellow passengers in the past hour since the stage had pulled away from Farley's station. They were a pleasant enough bunch, but even the salesmen were more hardbitten than they might appear at first. A man had to be hard to survive out here, he supposed. These drummers might be smooth talkers, but they wouldn't back down from a fight and they would hold their own in a fracas, too.

Their conversation was a welcome distraction. Evan tried to concentrate on the talk, otherwise he might start thinking too much about that Apache raid on the Cartmill ranch, might remember that it was possible Billy and Penelope were already dead.

But no one at the station had known that for sure. They had heard rumors of trouble in Limpia Canyon, but that was all they were: rumors. And none of them had known exactly how much damage the Apaches had done. It was possible that his children were just fine, Evan told himself.

He would know, one way or another, in another day or two. Traveling over an unfamiliar trail, he figured it would take him that long to reach his destination.

The stagecoach ride was rough, made more so by the speed with which Ben Thayer drove the Concord over the rutted road. The dust that boiled up from the wheels and the hooves of the team seemed to get in everywhere, even though the passengers had pulled the canvas shades over the windows. The wind that whipped in the dust was cold, and Evan wished Dinah had a better coat. The jacket she wore would just have to do until she reached El Paso.

This was the first time in his life that Evan had ridden a stagecoach. He wasn't overly impressed with it as a means of transportation, but he supposed it was better than walking. He still preferred a saddle horse, however. The dun and Dinah's chestnut were tied on behind the coach. Evan wished Thayer would slow down; at this rate, by the time Evan parted company with the other travelers, the horses were going to be tired just from keeping up with the stagecoach.

Thayer was nervous about the Apaches who might be lurking in those rugged mountains to the south, and Evan couldn't blame him. The Comanches were more savage than the Apaches, he supposed—after all, the Apaches had held sway over most of Texas at one time, Evan recalled, before the Comanches had pushed them west until all that was left of their domain was this arid tip of the state—but the Apaches were still to be feared. They could fight all day, run all night, fight all day again, and live on the meagerest of rations. Evan had no personal experience with them, but he had heard plenty of stories over the years from men who had.

The road was gradually taking them closer to the mountain range that came thrusting up from the south. Dark clouds hung over the peaks, making them look even more forbidding. As the coach rolled past a long sandy valley between the road and the mountains, Evan saw more than a dozen dust devils being whipped up by the wind. He caught hold of the fluttering shade and held it so that he could look out the window at the bizarre sight. The thin, twisting columns of dust danced this way and that, and as the sun peeked through a gap in the overcast, its slanting rays picked out the dust devils and made the clouds looming over the mountains look even blacker.

If he had been a superstitious man, thought Evan, he might have likened the sight to the entrance to Hades. Good thing he wasn't superstitious, he told himself dryly as he leaned back on the hard bench seat and let the canvas curtain fall closed.

Half an hour later, the stagecoach slowed as Ben Thayer called out to his team and hauled back on the leathers. Evan was ready as the vehicle rocked to a stop. He opened the door and stepped out.

A faint trail branched off from the road and ran toward the mountains, which seemed even closer than the four or five miles Thayer had said they would be at this point. "That's the trail that'll take you down to Fort Davis," Thayer said from the box.

"It winds around a mite, but you shouldn't have too much trouble follerin' it."

"Much obliged," Evan said as he turned to the boot where his saddle was stored and began untying the canvas cover over the storage area.

Dinah put her head out through the open door. "I still want to go with you," she said.

Evan shook his head. "Answer's still no."

"What do you expect me to do when I get to El Paso?" she demanded. "I don't know anybody there. Where am I supposed to stay?"

Evan frowned. In his concern that Dinah be protected from the possible danger of the Apaches, he hadn't considered that problem.

One of the drummers looked down at Evan through the open window of the stagecoach and said, "Don't worry about that, Mr. Littleton. The boys and I will pass the hat and collect enough money for your daughter to get a room at a respectable boardinghouse in El Paso . . . with no obligation of any sort on her part, of course."

Evan looked intently at the man as the other passengers chimed in their agreement with the idea. After a moment, he nodded, convinced that the salesman meant nothing improper by the suggestion.

"I thank you, sir. Good to know that folks will still look out for one another."

The drummer grinned. "Out here, you've got to help your neighbor whenever you can, because tomorrow it may be you who needs the help."

That was sure enough true, Evan thought. While Dinah fumed and frowned, he took his saddle and blanket from the boot and got them on the dun. He cinched the saddle tight and lowered the stirrup, then turned back to the coach. Ben Thayer was glancing nervously at the mountains, and Evan knew the jehu was anxious to be on his way again. Lifting a finger to the ragged brim of his hat, Evan said, "Thanks again for all your help." While Thayer nodded acknowledgment, Evan stepped over to the door and reached up to take Dinah into his arms. For an instant, he thought she was going to pull away, but then she flung her arms around his neck and hugged him tightly.

"You be careful, Daddy," she whispered in his ear.

"I will, darlin'," he said as he stroked her hair. Then he kissed her forehead and helped her back into the coach. He shut the door behind her with a firm slam.

Thayer waited until Evan had mounted up, then he slapped the lines against the backs of the horses and hollered at them to move out. The team lurched into motion, then settled down to a steady trot. Evan watched the coach roll away, rocking back and forth as it diminished in size.

Then, his face hardening, he turned and rode south toward the mountains.

11

He had almost reached the foothills when he realized someone was following him.

Reining in, Evan turned the horse so that he could look behind him. Some instinct warned him that he was no longer alone in this vast wilderness on the edge of the mountains. The sun had disappeared once more behind the clouds, leaving behind a cold wind blowing in Evan's face. He narrowed his eyes against the wind and studied his back trail.

A moment later, he spotted the rider coming toward him.

The trail had twisted around through several gullies and low spots, and it was from one of those depressions that the rider emerged. Evan squinted even more as he tried to make out who it was. There was something familiar about the gait of the horse and the way the rider sat the saddle—

Dinah.

Evan sighed heavily as the realization of the rider's identity hit him. He had no idea how she had managed to persuade Thayer and the others to let her leave the stagecoach and come after him, but that didn't really matter now. What was important was that she was stuck out here with him, miles from any sort of civilization, and that there could be hundreds of hostile eyes watching them at this very moment.

"Blast it!" he said aloud, giving in to his frustration. Ben Thayer and the others had agreed to look after her, and yet, no sooner had he been out of sight of the stagecoach than they had abandoned the responsibility they had taken on. Dinah had to have gotten away from them quickly in order to be following this close behind him.

Evan sat there on the dun and watched her approach. His gaze darted around constantly, on the lookout for any sort of trouble that might threaten Dinah. Within ten minutes, she was close enough for him to clearly make out her features. She was smiling as she rode up to him and reined in a few moments later, but there was apprehension in her eyes as well. She knew she had gone against his wishes.

"What are you doing here?" he asked bluntly.

"What I should have done all along," she replied with a defiant toss of her head. "My place is with you, Daddy, not waiting in some boarding-house in El Paso."

"How'd you get off the stage? Thayer and those other fellas promised they'd look after you."

Her smile had a hint of devilishness in it. "I just told them that if they didn't let me come after you, I'd tell the sheriff in El Paso that they stopped the stage and molested me."

Evan's breath hissed between his clenched teeth. Dinah was plainspoken to the point of annoyance. "You really said that?"

"I sure did."

"You think a lawman would believe that Thayer and the others would be fools enough to bother a respectable young woman?"

She shrugged. "Word would get around, whether the sheriff believed me or not."

Evan knew she was right. An accusation like that would be hard to shake once it had been made. Dinah had put the men on the stagecoach between a rock and a hard place. There had been no good answers to the dilemma that had confronted them.

"So they let you go to take your chances out here with the Indians?" he said angrily, waving a hand toward the mountains looming close behind him.

"Don't be too mad at them," said Dinah. "It was all my idea."

"Yeah," Evan said. "I figure to remember that, too." He sighed. "Well, it's too late to do anything about it now. That stage is long gone. Come on; we'll get through these mountains as fast as we can and ride on down to Fort Davis. You ought to be safe there, anyway."

"I'm not worried about being safe," Dinah said as she urged the chestnut forward and fell in beside him. "I just want to find Billy and Penelope and Rockly."

"Me, too," said Evan with a nod. "Me, too . . ."

They were deep in the mountains by the time night fell. Evan had been looking for a good place to camp since late afternoon, and he finally found one as an early dusk due to the cloud cover was settling over the rugged landscape. The trail, which wound crookedly along valleys and climbed through passes, led them to a level bench dotted with pine trees. It jutted out from the shoulder of a mountain that rose almost straight up at the rear of the narrow bench. It wasn't likely anybody would come at them from that direction, judged Evan, and the other approaches to the camp were fairly easy to command. He didn't want to risk a fire, so he and Dinah gnawed some jerky and washed it down with water from their canteens. The supplies they had brought with them from the Ashmore ranch were running low, but Evan thought they had enough to last until they reached Fort Davis. That would be late the next day at the earliest, more likely the day after that.

Unless they came to the Cartmill ranch first, he reminded himself. He didn't know exactly where it was, but he held on to the hope that they would find it—and find as well that everyone on the place was in good health despite the Apache raids.

When they were done eating, Dinah wrapped herself in a blanket and huddled against him. "I thought it was always hot in Texas," she complained.

"Not at this time of year," Evan told her, "nor at this elevation. We're a lot higher up than we were in Richland Springs."

Dinah was silent for a moment, then she said quietly, "I miss the farm. I miss Mama, too."

"So do I, honey," Evan said, tightening his arm around her shoulders.

"When we find everybody, are we going back there?"

Evan hesitated. He had told her some about the trouble that had been waiting for him when he got home from the war, and she knew about the brief time he had spent with the Stubbs gang. He said, "I don't know if that would be such a good idea. Might be better to make a fresh start somewhere else."

Dinah lifted her head from his shoulder and said, "But Mama's back there."

"Not really. She's right here, in me and in you. She'll always be with us, wherever we go."

Evan felt his daughter begin to tremble as he spoke the heartfelt words. A sob escaped from her, and tears rolled down her cheeks. Evan felt his own eyes growing damp.

He kept holding her, and eventually she fell asleep. But it was long into the night before exhaustion finally claimed Evan, driving all the haunting memories into oblivion for a time.

Surprisingly, the next day dawned clear, with bright sunshine washing down over the craggy peaks and the thickly wooded slopes. Most of the trees here were evergreens, which meant that the landscape retained its vivid colors despite the advancing season. The grass in the lower valleys was still green, too. Now that he was getting his first good look at it, Evan was struck by how beautiful this country really was.

The mountains were much more majestic than the Central Texas hills to which he was accustomed. Riding through this incredible terrain, it was difficult to believe that they were still in Texas, that the state could encompass not only these peaks but the marshy plains of the Gulf coast and the thick piney woods of East Texas as well.

Dinah's eyes were wide with awe as she and Evan followed the trail that led gradually south. "I've never seen a place like this," she said in wonder.

"Neither have I," agreed Evan. "It's mighty pretty."

"I can see why the Apaches are willing to fight for it—and why families like the Cartmills want to settle here."

Evan glanced around at the vastness surrounding them. "Seems like there ought to be room enough for everybody," he said.

But he knew that wasn't the case. The war had taught him that. There was never enough room, because people were always willing to fight over any excuse. And he was as bad as anybody else, he told himself, remembering the times his hand had almost cramped with the need to reach for a gun.

He gave a little shake of his head. Somebody else could debate the right and wrong of it. He had to deal with things as they were, not as they ought to be.

The first sign of civilization they saw was a group of longhorn cattle grazing in one of the lower valleys. Evan reined in and gestured at the rangy, rawboned animals. "Those cattle must belong to somebody," he said.

"Maybe even the Cartmills," added Dinah.

"Maybe. We can hope so."

Not long after that, the trail began running alongside a tree-lined stream that bubbled and leaped over a rocky bed. That would be Limpia Creek, Evan thought. He brought the dun to a halt, swung down from the saddle, and knelt beside the creek to scoop up a handful of water. When he brought it to his lips, he found it to be crisp and cold and clean, some of the best water he had ever tasted. He grinned at Dinah and said, "Throw me your canteen, and I'll fill it up."

"Fill your own," she said as she dismounted and unhooked the strap of her canteen from the saddlehorn. She came over to the creek and knelt to drink, then unscrewed the canteen's cap and lowered it into the water.

Smiling, Evan straightened and went back to his horse. He reached for his canteen—

And froze as he saw the figure standing on a nearby hill, watching them.

The air was so crystal clear today that he could see the headband of bright cloth bound around the man's long dark hair. The watcher wore a shirt with loose, blousey sleeves, a cowhide vest, and leather leggings under a breechcloth. High-topped black cavalry boots were on his feet, and he held a rifle in his hands as his arms hung loosely at his sides. Bandoliers of ammunition crisscrossed his chest. Even at this distance, which had to be close to two hundred yards, Evan felt as if the Apache's eyes were boring directly into his.

"Dinah," he said, forcing the words out through suddenly dry lips, "finish filling up that canteen and get back on your horse."

"What's wrong, Dad—" Her question ended abruptly in a gasp, and Evan guessed she had looked back over her shoulder and seen where he was looking, then glanced that way and seen the Apache for herself.

"Don't panic," Evan went on, making an effort to keep his own voice calm. "He's a ways off, and he's not showing any signs of getting ready to use that rifle he's carrying."

"But . . . but he's watching us!" Dinah said shakily.

"Could be him and others like him have been watching us since yesterday," Evan pointed out. "This one's just chosen to show himself for some reason."

To spook them into doing something foolish, maybe? Evan considered that possibility and decided it might have merit. What would the watcher do if they finished refilling their canteens, mounted up, and rode on just as they had been doing before?

Evan recalled hearing the old men from

Richland Springs talking about Indians during their domino games on the porch of the general store. *Always do the unexpected when you're dealin' with redskins,* he remembered as being among the bits of frontier wisdom exchanged while the bones were being shook. That might be good advice now.

Slowly, deliberately, he took his canteen from the saddle and turned toward the creek with it. Dinah watched him with an expression of surprise and fear as he knelt to fill the canteen.

"What's he doing now?" asked Evan.

Dinah's gaze flicked toward the hill where the watcher waited. "Just standing there," she said, sounding somewhat amazed. "He's not really doing anything."

"Just keeping an eye on us," Evan said. He lifted the canteen from the stream and capped it. Straightening, he turned back toward the dun. Boldly, he lifted his eyes toward the hill and stared directly at the Apache as he looped the canteen's strap around the saddlehorn. "Let's go."

"We're just going to ride off?" Dinah asked dubiously.

"Yep. If that fella wants to do something about it, it's up to him."

Clearly, Dinah thought her father had lost his mind, but there was nothing she could do except follow Evan's lead. Both of them mounted up and kneed their horses into motion again. Evan didn't look back as they rode south along the creek.

But Dinah did, and after a moment, she said excitedly, "He's gone!"

"He found out what he wanted to know. He saw that we weren't going to bolt just because we saw him."

"Will he leave us alone now?"

Evan drew a deep breath. "I doubt it, but at least we bought a little time by doing something different than he expected." He pushed the dun to a slightly faster gait. "Let's put some miles behind us."

Dinah was eager to do that.

Evan had been watchful even before they had entered the mountains the day before. Now he was even more alert, every sense on edge. If he had to *smell* the Apaches to tell they were there, that was what he would do. He knew he was hopelessly outclassed in that area, however. The Apaches were renowned as trackers, and their ability to move with great stealth was unparalleled. Evan had a sinking feeling that no matter what he did, if the Apaches didn't want to be discovered until it was too late to do anything about it, that was exactly what would happen.

Time seemed to stretch out around them. It took forever to ride from one end of a valley to the other. The sun climbed leisurely in the sky overhead, its progress so maddeningly slow that Evan wanted to shout at it . . . until he realized that he had no desire to see night fall again.

As long as it was light, he could at least see the Apaches coming. Maybe.

He judged it was not quite noon when Dinah said abruptly, "Oh, my God."

Evan was riding to her left. He jerked his head

around to look at her, half-afraid he would see that she had an arrow in her back. Instead, she was staring beyond him, looking up at something to his left. He twisted in the saddle to see what had alarmed her.

There were half a dozen of them this time, trotting along a rocky ridge that was bare of vegetation. Evan saw them clearly outlined against the sky, no more than a hundred yards away. If he had had a rifle, he could have possibly picked some of them off. They must have seen that he was armed only with a pistol, he thought.

He would have given a lot for one of those newfangled Henry rifles right about now.

"They're just pacing us," he told Dinah, once again forcing himself to sound calm despite the tumult that was going on inside him. "They're not coming any closer." Movement caught his eye, and he lifted his gaze to the ridgeline on the other side of the valley they were following. More Apaches ran tirelessly there. Dinah hadn't noticed them yet, so he didn't call them to her attention.

"What are we going to do?" she asked nervously. She had to be feeling sheer terror, thought Evan, but she was controlling it well. She wasn't lacking for sand, that was for sure.

But then, she was his and Lynette's daughter, so what else would he expect from her?

"We keep riding," Evan said grimly. "As long as they're not making any move to attack us, I'm not going to provoke them."

"But . . . surely sooner or later . . ."

"We'll meet it as it comes, whatever it is."

Dinah swallowed hard, then nodded. Her face was pale but composed.

As they rode along beside Limpia Creek, Evan had the growing suspicion that they were doing just what the Apaches wanted them to do. He was starting to feel like a wild animal boxed in by hounds, being driven on blindly into a trap. That might be exactly what was happening, he thought. But he had no doubt that if he and Dinah tried to turn around and go back the way they had come, the Apaches would be on them instantly, showering them with arrows and rifle fire. Going straight ahead might be their only chance.

And they might be doomed no matter what they did.

The knowledge that he might have led his daughter to her death gnawed at his guts. At least back there on the Ashmore ranch, she would have been alive, even if she had been forced to marry Matt Ashmore. That was better than death at the hands of savages, wasn't it? Or if she had just stayed on that stagecoach bound for El Paso—

And how would she have lived in that border town if she had gone on and he had died here in these mountains? A lovely young woman, alone and friendless in a place like that? There was little doubt about how she would have wound up, Evan thought bleakly. Like so many other times over the past few years, he—and now Dinah—found themselves facing long odds, the chances for survival, let alone happiness, so slim as to be almost nonexistent.

But something inside Evan, something too

stubborn for its own good most of the time, wouldn't let him give up. He and Dinah were alive, they were mounted on good horses, and he knew how to use the gun on his hip. They had a chance.

That was all Evan asked.

A moment after that thought went through his head, he heard the distant popping of gunshots, and bloodcurdling cries ripped from the throats of the Apaches to the right and left of them. The Indians veered suddenly from the ridges and began angling toward the valley. It took Evan only an instant to realize that the Apaches were moving to cut them off from whatever was happening up ahead.

He jerked his hat off his head and slammed it down on the rump of Dinah's chestnut. "Run!" he shouted as the horse leaped forward in a gallop. At the same instant, he jammed the heels of his boots into the flanks of the dun and sent it springing ahead, too.

They were in a race now, right enough.

A race for their lives.

12

Evan jammed his hat back on his head and leaned forward over the neck of the rangy dun as it stretched its legs out and ran. Dinah's chestnut had a slight lead on him, but the gap disappeared quickly and Evan drew alongside his daughter. He had to hold the dun in a little to keep from outpacing her, in fact. There was no way he was going to let Dinah bring up the rear by herself. They were in this together, no matter how it ended.

A quick glance to right and left told him that the Apaches were closing in on them. But there was still a gap in the center of the canyon, next to the creek, and if he and Dinah could get through there before the Apaches were able to cut them off, they had a chance. The Indians were tireless runners, but they lacked the speed of the horses. Evan knew that he and Dinah could outdistance the pursuit as long as nothing happened to the horses.

Even over the pounding of hooves, he could hear the sound of the shots growing louder up ahead. Some sort of battle was going on—but Evan had no idea who the combatants were. There was little doubt in his mind that more Apaches were on one side of the fight, but who was on the other?

If they lived long enough, they would find out, he thought.

Holding tightly to the reins with his left hand, Evan reached down and drew the Colt from its holster. His thumb looped over the hammer, but he didn't pull it back. The hurricane deck of a running horse was no place for a steady aim, and he didn't want to waste bullets. He would fire at the Apaches only if he and Dinah couldn't outrun them.

Howling and yipping, the Apaches came on. Several of them carried rifles, and they were well within range of the weapons. But for some reason, they didn't stop, take a bead, and shoot Evan and Dinah out of their saddles. That wouldn't be enough sport for them, Evan sensed. The Apaches were enjoying this little game, like kids testing their speed and skill against one another.

As the Apaches drew nearer from right and left, coming closer and closer to the creek and the trail beside it, Evan finally let the dun have its head and pull out in front of the chestnut. He would meet the enemy first and sell his life dearly if need be.

But then he saw that the Apaches might have underestimated the speed of the horses. Both groups of Indians were still twenty yards from the creek, and Evan and Dinah were no more than that distance away from flashing past them. "Come on!"

he called over his shoulder to his daughter. "We can make it!"

The Apaches were beginning to realize that, too. Angry shouts came from them, and a couple of the warriors carrying rifles came to a halt and threw the weapons to their shoulders. Evan had little hope of hitting anything, but he jerked up the Colt and fired anyway, triggering two quick shots. The slugs whistled hotly past the Apaches, close enough to make both men jump and spoil their aim. Their shots went wild over Evan's head.

That left him with three shots, since the hammer had been resting on an empty chamber as it rode in the holster. He was close enough now to see that the rifles carried by the Apaches were single-shot weapons, rather than repeaters. That was a stroke of luck. He twisted in the saddle, saw one of the Indians to the left drawing a bead on him, and fired again, snapping the shot without aiming.

Fortune smiled on them again. The bullet drilled into the Apache's chest and the Indian was flung backward, arms and legs flying out to the sides. He landed in a limp sprawl that could signify nothing but death.

Then, abruptly, so quickly that Evan barely realized it was happening, he and Dinah were past them. The horses were still running flat out, and with each stride the Apaches fell farther behind.

Evan pulled the dun back again, letting Dinah catch up to him and take the lead slightly. He waved her on, yelling, "Ride! Ride!"

Gunshots thundered up ahead. The trail ran

through a gap where the valley closed in, and Evan couldn't see what lay beyond it. Whatever it was, he reasoned, had to be better than what was behind them.

With the wind of their desperate passage plucking at his hat, Evan followed Dinah through the narrow pass and around the bend in the trail that lay just beyond it. The scenery that met his eyes was unexpected, in some ways the most attractive he had ever seen, in fact, but there was no time to appreciate it, not with a horde of furious, howling Apaches on their heels.

A longer, deeper valley fell away in front of them, angling to the northwest. On the far side of the valley, nestled against the side of a mountain, was a huge white house. It was a rambling structure of adobe with a red-tiled roof and ornate wrought iron grillwork around the windows and doors. Below the house on the slope were barns and corrals. This was probably the headquarters of the ranch that claimed all those longhorns he and Dinah had seen, thought Evan.

And at the moment, it was under attack.

Flame and smoke spurted from the muzzles of at least a dozen rifles as the Apaches who held them advanced on the house. The Indians darted from cover to cover, utilizing the barns, the pens, and a couple of parked wagons for shelter as they laid siege to the house. Return fire came from slits cut into the thick adobe walls, but none of the bullets from the house found their targets. The Apaches were too quick as they darted out from cover, fired on the house, then dropped behind fresh shelter.

Evan's eyes took in all of that in a matter of seconds as he sized up the situation. Without slowing the dun, he looked along the trail that led down the near slope, ran alongside the creek for several hundred yards, then branched and climbed along a tree-lined lane to the ranch house. If he and Dinah could reach the house, they would be safe—at least for the moment.

"Make for the house!" he shouted over the clamor of hooves. Dinah was already nodding, her thoughts clearly running along the same lines as his. She leaned forward tensely, trying to urge more speed out of the chestnut.

Evan twisted his neck and looked behind them. The Apaches who had funneled them into this valley were still back there, running doggedly after them. The Indians had fallen too far behind to be a real danger now, however, so Evan slid his Colt back in its holster. He still had two shots, and he and Dinah might need them if they were to break through the line of Apaches now advancing on the big white house.

The attack on the ranch was occupying all the attention of the Apaches in front of them. As Evan and Dinah reached the place where the narrow lane branched off from the main trail and started up the slope toward the house, the sound of their horses' hoofbeats finally penetrated to the Apaches. A couple of them spun around and saw the riders coming. The rifles in their hands came up.

Turning their backs on the house exposed them to the gunfire coming from it, however. As one of the Apaches tried to draw a bead on the galloping figures, he was suddenly thrown forward. Evan saw blood spurt from the man's chest where the bullet that had struck him from behind burst out the front of his body. The Apache sprawled on his face, motionless in death.

Evan forged ahead of Dinah and angled the dun straight toward the other man who was aiming at him. The charging horse ruined the Apache's aim, and the bullet whipped harmlessly past Evan. The next instant, the Apache went down with a scream under the slashing hooves of the dun as Evan rode over him.

He threw a glance over his shoulder and saw that Dinah had stayed on the lane, as he had hoped she would. It was the shortest path to the house. The place's defenders seemed to be concentrating their fire more on providing cover for Dinah than on trying to actually hit the Apaches. For the moment, they were content to keep the Indians down, and Evan was grateful for that. Obviously, someone in the house had seen the two riders coming and realized they were potential allies.

However, Evan was separated from Dinah now, and he was pretty much on his own. He circled around one of the corrals and palmed out his revolver as an Apache crouched beside a wagon tried to draw a bead on him. Evan and the Apache fired at the same time, the roar of the single-shot rifle and the sharper crack of the pistol blending into one sound. The Apache missed completely. Evan's slug bored into the meaty upper right arm of the Apache, jerking the warrior around and driving him against the wagon. The rifle slipped from his fingers as blood welled down his arm. He went to his knees and grasped the wounded arm with his other hand. He was out of the fight, at least for a while.

From the corner of his eye, Evan saw another of the Apaches running toward him. He wheeled the dun as the Indian drew back his arm and let fly with a knife. Sunlight flickered on the blade as it spun through the air toward Evan. He ducked, felt the knife clip the brim of his hat. Then with a howl, the Apache leaped at him, jumping high in the air to slam into Evan and pull him out of the saddle.

The impact of the collision was a shock, and an even greater one stunned Evan an instant later as both he and the Apache crashed to the ground. Evan was on the bottom, and all the breath was knocked out of his lungs. He gasped for air as his vision blurred. Before he could draw breath back into his body, iron-hard fingers closed around his throat.

Blinking away the red haze that descended over his eyes, he looked up into the hate-contorted features of the Apache who was trying to choke the life out of him. The man had his left hand on Evan's throat, pinning him down, while his right groped for a weapon of some sort. The Apache's fingers wrapped around a rock the size of two fists clubbed together, and he raised it triumphantly, poised to bring it down on Evan's head, crushing the white man's skull.

Before that could happen, Evan saw the Apache's face suddenly explode in a grisly shower of blood and bone. A deafening roar assaulted Evan's ears, and he realized someone had just let loose with both barrels of a shotgun in the Apache's face. It had blown the Indian's head almost completely off. The man's body slumped to the side, the rock that had been clutched tightly in his hand slipping from nerveless fingers and thudding to the ground next to Evan's head.

Evan rolled, shoving the gruesome corpse away from him. He came up on one knee, searching for the nearest threat, and as he did so, a strong hand grasped his upper arm. "Come on!" a man's voice commanded. "We can make it to the house!"

With his rescuer's help, Evan stumbled to his feet. There was no time for more than a glance at the man who held the now empty greener in his left fist. His right hand was still on Evan's arm, steadying him. Evan saw a tall, broad-shouldered man in denim trousers and a homespun shirt. Thick brown hair curled around the man's ears and down the back of his neck. His face, still relatively young, was already tanned and creased by long hours spent in the sun and wind.

With the man urging him on, Evan ran toward the house. They were some thirty yards away from an open gate that led into a courtyard. Even as the two men raced for that sanctuary, two more Apaches leaped to intercept them.

The man with the shotgun was slightly in the lead. He met the charge of one of the Apaches by slamming the barrels of the greener into the warrior's belly. As the Apache doubled over, the man brought the stock of the weapon across the Indian's face in a slashing motion, the butt of the shotgun pulping the Apache's nose and driving him senseless to the ground.

That disposed of one threat, but the second Apache was about to plunge a long knife into the back of Evan's rescuer. Evan was about to leap forward and try to block the thrust, but he was afraid he was going to be too late.

A dark-haired boy stepped out through the open gate and fired the rifle in his hands. The bullet caught the second Apache in the side and spun him around. He slumped to the ground, unconscious and rapidly bleeding to death. The boy with the rifle worked the lever underneath the breech, jacking another cartridge into the chamber. As he threw a second shot toward the other Apaches, Evan and the man with the shotgun ran through the gate. The boy ducked inside the courtyard after them. As soon as the boy was through the opening, the man grasped a thick wooden door and slammed it shut. The boy leaned his rifle against the wall and dropped a bar across the door.

Evan was panting, but he managed to look around and say urgently, "The . . . the girl who was with me—!"

"She's inside, friend," said the man with the shotgun. "She rode around to the other side of the house, and my wife let her in. Billy and I saw that you were in trouble out there, so we figured we'd best lend a hand."

"B-Billy . . ." Evan repeated in a husky whisper. He looked at the dark-haired boy, who had picked up the rifle again. The weapon was one of the new Henry repeaters, Evan saw, his brain registering that bit of information as an aside.

He was more concerned with the fact that he was looking at another of his own children. The boy was staring at him, too, and Billy's mouth worked soundlessly a time or two before he was able to croak, "Pa?"

Evan nodded, reached out and laid his hand on Billy's shoulder. He squeezed tightly, reassuring himself that the boy was indeed real.

The man with the shotgun looked surprised, but he said, "No time for a reunion now, I'm afraid. We've killed several of those Apaches, and the ones who are left won't take it kindly."

Evan looked at him and gave him a curt nod. "Just let me reload this Colt of mine—"

"Can you handle a rifle?"

"Well enough."

"Good. We've plenty of Henrys and an abundance of ammunition for them in the house. Come on."

Evan holstered the pistol and followed Billy and the other man at a run across the courtyard toward a door leading into the house. It opened before they got there, and Evan saw a slender, coltlike girl standing there holding the door. He knew she was ten, but she looked a little older . . . especially with a rifle tucked under her arm.

Penelope.

They were both still alive! The thought sang inside Evan's head, and in his heart as well. Rockly, the youngest save for Fulton, was still unaccounted for, but the other three remaining children were all right.

For the moment, anyway. Savage whoops from outside the house reminded Evan that they were all still in deadly danger.

Penelope slammed the door behind them. Her gaze moved over Evan without recognition. That wasn't surprising; she had been only six when he left for the war, and he had changed a great deal in those four years. Billy had recognized him, but the boy was a couple of years older than his sister.

And a good-looking youngster, too, Evan saw now as he got a better look at Billy. The boy was only a few inches shorter than his father, and he already had the strong, rangy form common to Littleton men. He had handled the rifle well, coolly shooting down the Apache who had been about to bushwhack Evan's rescuer.

That thought made Evan glance at the man, who had broken open the shotgun and was reloading it. "You'd be Cartmill," said Evan, the words more of a statement than a question.

"That's right," the man said, glancing up. "My name is Clive Cartmill." He had a faint accent that marked him as something other than a native Texan. "I believe I heard Billy call you *Pa*?"

"I'm his father," Evan admitted.

"That would make you Evan Littleton. We were told that you were dead, Mr. Littleton."

"Not yet," said Evan. "And not anytime soon, if I've got anything to say about it. Where's those Henrys?"

"Penelope, fetch your father a rifle and a box of cartridges," Cartmill said to the girl.

Penelope was too busy staring at Evan. She didn't seem to hear Cartmill's command. Billy said, "I'll get the Henry," and moved past Penelope to enter another room. He looked glad for the excuse to get away for a moment.

Evan stepped closer to Penelope and said quietly, "That's right, honey. I'm your father, sure enough. And I'm mighty happy to see you again."

He held out his arms. The girl hesitated for a moment, then something inside her seemed to snap. A sob welled from her throat, and tears began to roll down her cheeks. She came forward into Evan's embrace and put her arms around his waist, hugging him tightly. "D-Daddy," she whispered brokenly.

Feeling a little awkward, as if she was some sort of doll that he might break if he wasn't careful, Evan reached up and patted her back, then stroked her long auburn hair. "It's really me," he murmured. "We're together again. I won't leave you."

Cartmill said, "This is quite touching, but as I mentioned outside, there's little time for reunions at the moment. Those savages are still to be dealt with." The steady sound of gunfire elsewhere in the house added emphasis to his words.

Evan turned his head to look at Cartmill. "And the bunch that chased us here will be joining in on the attack, too," he said. Putting his hands on Penelope's shoulders, he moved her away from him slightly and looked down into her eyes. "We'll talk later, as long as you want. Right now we've got to run off those Apaches."

She nodded, and he saw a flash of the old familiar fire in her brown eyes. She said, "Yes, sir," and turned away from him to hurry over to a rifle slit. She thrust the barrel of her Henry through the narrow opening, steadied it, and after a moment fired. The recoil shook her, but she gave with it easily, telling Evan this wasn't the first time she had fired one of the rifles. "Apache tried to come over the courtyard wall," she said without looking around as she worked the Henry's lever.

Evan and Cartmill glanced at each other, and both men had to grin for a second. There had been no fear in Penelope's voice, just a matter-of-fact statement. Cartmill said quietly, "As you may be able to guess, we've had experience fighting off those red devils before now."

Billy came hurrying back into the room, carrying a rifle and a small wooden box. He handed them to Evan and said to Cartmill, "Pablo said to tell you it looks like they're formin' up for another charge."

Cartmill nodded. "I expected as much."

Evan said, "Tell me where you want me."

"The most vulnerable spot is this courtyard. I was thinking we might go out there and meet them head-on."

"All right," Evan said with a nod.

"Penelope, you and your brother go back to
the other end of the house and help Melinda and
Pablo," Cartmill told the girl. She still stood ready
at the rifle slit, but she hadn't fired again.

Penelope turned and said, "I can stay here
with you, Clive. I'm a good shot."

"I know, sweetheart," Cartmill told her with a
smile, "but I really want you to go back with the
others." He turned to the boy, clearly hoping that
Billy would be more reasonable. "Billy—"

"I'm stayin' here," Billy said without hesitation.
"You and Pa will need somebody backin' you up . . .
in case some of those Apaches get over the wall."

Once again Evan and Cartmill looked at each
other, and Evan said, "Boy's got a point."

"I ain't a boy," said Billy, and looking at him,
Evan could see that he was right. Despite his
youth, Billy was a young man now.

"All right, take your sister's place at that rifle
slit," Cartmill said. "Penelope, do as I told you and
go back to Melinda and Pablo."

"But—"

"Do as Mr. Cartmill says, honey," Evan told her,
his tone not leaving any room for argument.

Penelope hesitated for just a moment longer,
then nodded and hurried out of the room, heading
down a long hall toward the other end of the
house. Evan watched her go and noticed several
men stationed at rifle slits along that hallway.
From time to time, one of them fired, the blast of
the rifles echoing in the corridor. The men looked
like Mexicans, and Evan figured them for Cartmill's
ranch hands.

Billy took up position at the rifle slit. Cartmill looked at Evan and said, "Ready?"

"As I'll ever be," replied Evan, his hands tightening on the rifle.

"Good," said Billy from the rifle slit, "because here they come!"

13

Cartmill threw open the door and ran into the courtyard. Evan was right behind him, pausing only long enough to close the door. The two men hurried across the open space to the adobe wall, which Evan judged to be about seven feet tall. He saw now what he had not noticed before: A short wooden platform was built along the base of the wall so that a man could stand on it and thrust his rifle over the wall to fire at attackers. He and Cartmill veered apart, heading for the platform on separate sides of the gate.

Evan could hear the shouts of the Apaches as they charged. They sounded close, too close for him to take any foolhardy chances. As he stepped up onto the platform, he placed the box of ammunition for the Henry rifle on a shallow shelf that had also been built with defense in mind. This house was old, he thought, and had doubtless been built before repeating weapons had been invented. The original occupants would have placed a couple of spare flintlock pistols on that shelf, he guessed, so that they could grab them for close work if any invaders made it over the wall.

Carefully, he took off his hat, placed it on the end of the Henry, and extended it just above the wall. A bullet tore through the hat immediately, sending it spinning off the rifle. Yips of triumph sounded on the other side of the wall.

Evan raised up, saw the startled faces of several Apaches only a few yards away, and started firing the Henry as fast as he could squeeze the trigger and work the lever.

Flame geysered from the muzzle of the rifle as it spewed lead. Two of the little cluster of Apaches fell twitching and bleeding, while the others scrambled backward for cover. From his position farther down the wall, Cartmill was raking another group of Indians with deadly fire. Evan heard the shots but didn't have time to look over and see how the rancher was doing. He was too busy drawing a bead on an Apache who crouched behind one of the wagons, aiming a rifle at *him*. The Apache fired first, and the bullet slammed into the wall only a few inches from Evan's head, throwing dust and chips of adobe into his face, stinging his eyes. Evan had already squeezed off his own shot, and as he blinked rapidly to clear his vision, he saw the Apache tumble out from behind the wagon, rolling to a halt with his head lolling in death.

The Henry rifles with their fifteen-shot magazines and the thick walls of the house made the difference. The Apaches outnumbered the ranch's defenders by more than two to one, Evan estimated, but they couldn't get close enough to overrun the house without being cut down by the deadly accurate—and seemingly never-ending—rifle fire. After fifteen minutes or so of battle, the Apaches began to withdraw, slipping back down the hill toward the creek in the center of the valley. Every time Evan got a glimpse of one of the flitting forms, he pegged a shot at it, but he didn't think he actually hit any of the Apaches during their retreat.

Cartmill stepped down off the platform and then sat on it tiredly. He was a handsome man, Evan saw, but the strain of the fighting showed in his haggard features. "They won't be back for a while," he said. "We've driven them off."

"You sound like you've done this before," said Evan as he, too, stepped down from the platform and leaned his Henry against the wall. The barrel was hot from firing.

"Too many times," Cartmill replied. "In fact, I've lost count of how many times those savages have raided us in the past year." A weary grin stretched across his face. "If I wasn't as stubborn as they are, we might have given up and pulled out by now. Their chief, a man called Nicholas, thinks that Limpia Canyon is his, you see."

"I've heard of him," Evan said. "Heard that you'd been raided before, too. In fact, the folks who told me about it weren't even sure you were still here."

"We're here, all right. And we're going to be, from now on. This ranch is ours now." Evan could hear the stubbornness Cartmill had spoken of in the man's voice.

Before they could discuss the situation any more, the door into the house opened and a woman came hurrying out. Evan looked at her, then looked at her again. She was worth a second glance.

Pale blond hair fell to her shoulders, framing a lovely face that at the moment was drawn by taut lines of worry. She wore a dark blue dress and carried one of the Henry rifles. "Clive!" she called as she hurried toward Cartmill. "Are you all right?"

Cartmill grinned as he stood up to greet her. "I'm fine, darling," he said. He took her into his arms and hugged her tightly.

The woman was Cartmill's wife, Evan thought, most likely the Melinda he had mentioned earlier. She was trailed by a tall, hatchet-faced Mexican whose expression was made even more fierce by the bullet burn on his left cheek that was oozing tiny drops of blood.

"The Apaches are gone, *patron*," he said to Cartmill. "They have pulled back beyond the creek, out of range of our rifles. But when they are ready, they will return." There was a grim note of warning in his voice.

Cartmill looked past the woman's blond head. "I know, Pablo," he said. "But when they come, we will be ready for them, as always."

Billy and Penelope hurried out of the house into the courtyard, followed by several of the Mexicans Evan had seen earlier. The men were laughing and talking, seemingly unbothered by the fact that they had just helped fight off an attack by raiders who would have slaughtered them mercilessly, given the chance. The youngsters came straight to Evan, who looked at them solemnly and said, "You two all right?"

Billy nodded curtly, and Penelope said, "We're fine."

"Where's your sister?"

As if in answer, Dinah emerged from the house. Like the others, she was carrying a rifle. Her hat was pushed back to hang behind her neck by its chin strap, and her hair was still in disarray from the wind of their frantic race with the Apaches. Evan could tell that she wasn't hurt, either, and he felt a vast sense of relief. All of them had come safely through the battle.

"I suppose it's time for some proper introductions," said Cartmill as he turned toward Evan, his arm around the blond woman's shoulders. "As I told you, I'm Clive Cartmill, and this is my wife, Melinda."

Evan nodded to Melinda Cartmill, since he wasn't wearing a hat at the moment. It was still lying on the ground where it had fallen after he had used it as a decoy to fool the Apaches. "Mighty pleased to meet you, ma'am," he said. "I'm Evan Littleton, father to these three youngsters."

Melinda stepped forward and extended a hand to him. Evan took it. Her skin was cool and smooth, and the touch of it made something deep inside him tremble a little. There was nothing romantic about the reaction; Melinda Cartmill was another man's wife and much too young for him even if she hadn't been married. But women were few and far between here on the frontier, and Evan had spent all that time in the Yankee prison camp without even *seeing* a woman. He couldn't help but be touched by her beauty.

"And I am pleased to meet you, Mr. Littleton. You have fine children, so that speaks well of you, too."

Like her husband, she had some sort of accent. Evan thought they might be British, but he didn't want to come right out and ask. It wasn't polite to be too inquisitive.

Cartmill indicated the tall, hatchet-faced Mexican. "My *segundo*, Pablo Morales."

Evan nodded to the man and said, "Howdy," received a nod in return. Pablo didn't seem very friendly, but Evan had a feeling that was just his nature, not anything personal.

"And my *vaqueros*," Cartmill added, sweeping his hand toward the other men. "Except for the ones who are standing guard to make certain the Apaches don't come lurking about again."

Pablo spat. "They are a treacherous race and can never be trusted," he said. "I know, for my father was one of them, and a more evil man never walked the face of the earth."

Evan didn't much want to know the story behind *that* comment, and he was glad when Pablo fell silent again.

"Come inside," Cartmill invited. "I have a jug of good wine in the cellar, and I think we could use a drink."

Evan followed the Cartmills inside, ushering the children ahead of them. Only, he was going to have to stop thinking of them as children, he told himself. Dinah was definitely a young woman, Billy was more man than boy, and even Penelope seemed more grown-up than she should have.

Life would do that, he reflected. While you weren't looking, it stole things like innocence and youth . . .

As they went inside, he put a hand on Billy's shoulder and asked, "Your brother Rockly's not here, too, is he?"

"No, we haven't seen him since last year." Billy pulled away slightly, just enough to dislodge Evan's hand. "He went on west with the Wilsons. They were headed for El Paso."

Just as Dinah had thought might be the case, Evan mused. The border town at the western tip of Texas had a reputation as a pretty tough place, he recalled, but at least out there Rockly wouldn't have to worry about Apaches.

Evan had noticed the way Billy pulled away from him, but he wasn't going to think about that right now, he told himself. He was just going to be grateful that the four of them were alive and together.

Now that Evan had a chance to look around inside the house, he saw how sumptuously it was appointed. There were thick rugs on the stone floors and low, heavy wooden furniture in each room. Paintings were hung on the walls, some of them pastoral scenes unlike anything around here, others portraits of stern-looking men and women. Cartmill saw Evan looking at the paintings and said with a grin, "Ancestors. There's a bit of Cartmill family history in each of those pictures. Take that old boy, for instance." He pointed to a particularly solemn-looking portrait of a man seated in a high-backed chair with a long, thick-bladed sword across his lap. "Hugh Cartmill, one of Oliver Cromwell's faithful Roundheads. He must have been a dreadful bore."

Evan didn't have the slightest idea what Cartmill was talking about, but he nodded politely anyway. "Reckon we've all got a mite of root rot in our family trees," he said.

Cartmill laughed. "Indeed. I'll fetch that jug."

He hurried out of the big room in which they had all paused. Melinda said to Dinah and Penelope, "Come along with me, girls. We had best see to preparing a meal while we can, since one never knows when those Apaches will come calling again."

Both of Evan's daughters looked as if they wanted to argue with the order, but he gave them a look and said, "Do what Miz Cartmill tells you. There'll be plenty of time for us to talk."

He hoped that was true. He and Dinah had begun to grow close again, but he sensed it might take more time with Billy and Penelope.

Melinda and the two girls left the room, heading for what Evan assumed must be a kitchen, since Melinda had said something about a meal. Billy moved over to a narrow window and peered out, his back to Evan. Evan took a deep breath and moved over beside him. "Sorry I didn't catch up to you sooner, son—" he began.

"We didn't expect to ever see you again at all," Billy said. "Everybody told us you'd been killed in the war. That was why Thad left—to get revenge on the Yankees for killing you. Then he got killed, and Ma died . . ." Billy's voice shook, and he couldn't go on.

Without thinking, Evan reached for the boy's shoulder again and said, "I'm sorry—"

Billy jerked away from his touch. "Bein' sorry's not enough!" he said as he turned toward Evan. "Why'd you have to go off and fight in that war in the first place? It wasn't none of our business! We're Texans, not Johnny Rebs!"

Evan stared into his son's hurt-filled eyes. Billy wasn't saying anything that Evan himself hadn't thought hundreds of times over the years. The boy was right: Evan should have stayed home. Thad would still be alive, more than likely, and even though he probably couldn't have saved Lynette, at least he would be together with *all* of his children, and they wouldn't be holed up in some ranch house that was under siege by Apaches.

He took a deep breath and said, "There's no way to change what's done, Billy, no matter how bad the mistakes are. All we can do is go on—"

"Here we are," Cartmill said cheerfully as he came back into the room, brandishing an earthenware jug with a cork stopper in its neck. "Made from grapes grown on our own vines. It hasn't really aged as much as it should, of course, but, well . . . strike while the iron is hot, eh?"

What he was really saying was that it was better to drink the wine now than to leave it for the Apaches, thought Evan. Despite his worry about Billy, he summoned up a tired smile and said to Cartmill, "I'll drink to that."

"I'm what they call in England a remittance man," Cartmill said frankly as they all sat around a long mahogany dining table a little later. "My father is the Earl of Linchford, and my older brother Nigel will inherit his title and all his holdings when Father passes on. Thanks to the law of primogeniture, I shall inherit nothing."

Evan swallowed the bite of steak he had been chewing. "Don't seem hardly fair to me," he said. "Over here, most folks believe in share and share alike when it comes to family."

"Just one of the many differences between your country and mine, Evan. Hard to believe we all sprang from the same stock, isn't it?"

Evan shrugged and said, "I don't know. From what I've heard, Englishmen are pert' near as stubborn as Texans. And from the looks of the fight you're putting up against those Apaches, I can believe it."

Cartmill laughed and slapped the table. Melinda smiled across at Evan and said, "Well, we're adopted Texans now, you see."

"So we have to be . . . how do you put it? Muleheaded?" asked Cartmill.

"That'll do," Evan said dryly. "Been called muleheaded a time or two myself." He took a sip of Cartmill's wine from a crystal goblet that was the fanciest drinking glass he'd ever seen. "How'd you wind up coming all the way over here from England?"

"As I said, I'm a remittance man. My family pays me to stay away from England. This seemed as good a place as any to come to. I had heard a great deal about the American West. I must say, it's every bit as lovely—and challenging—as I thought it would be."

Evan frowned. "You can't go back home if you take a notion to?"

Cartmill shook his head and said, "Not if I want the earl to continue with my yearly remittance." He gestured at their surroundings. "Which, as you can see, is quite generous. My father's funds paid for all this—and for that case of Henry rifles, which is even more important."

"You're right about that," Evan told him. "Don't think you could have held off those Apaches with single-shot rifles. I've never seen anything quite like those repeaters."

"Load one on Sunday and shoot it all week," Cartmill said with a grin. "That was what the man from the New Haven Arms Company told me when I purchased them."

Evan ate some more steak, then said, "When I heard about some new families around Richland Springs taking in my children, I figured all of you for plantation owners trying to get away from the war."

Cartmill shook his head, and Melinda said, "We were simply passing through the area and stayed for a short time to wait for better weather before traveling on west. However, when we heard about the desperate straits in which your family found itself, we simply had to help out any way we could."

"It was no problem," added Cartmill. "We had more than enough room in our wagons for two more travelers, and adequate supplies for a dozen more if need be. I believe in being prepared for any contingency."

"I can see that," Evan said. "Still, it was mighty generous of you, taking in two kids who were strangers like that."

Melinda blushed. "Well, Mr. Littleton, you see . . . Clive and I . . . we can't have children of our own, and we thought . . ."

Her husband reached over and clasped her hand as she fell silent. "We had no intention of trying to take the place of Billy and Penelope's natural parents, you understand, but since we were under the impression that neither you nor your wife were still, ah, living, we thought that perhaps . . ."

"I reckon I know what you're trying to say," Evan told them quietly. "And like I said, I appreciate it. It was mighty kind-hearted of you."

Cartmill sighed. "I'm no longer sure of that. How kind was it to bring two children into a situation such as this, where our very day-to-day existence is so precarious?"

Despite the seriousness of Cartmill's expression, Evan had to laugh. "Shoot, I reckon that's a question that's been asked by anybody who ever had a kid. Nobody knows for sure how things are going to turn out. You just do your best and deal with what comes." He looked at Billy, hoping the boy would begin to understand why he had made some of the decisions he had made in the past.

"Perhaps you're right, Evan," Cartmill said with a nod. "I hope so, at any rate. And we're here, so we're most definitely going to have to deal with it. You've lived in Texas all your life, you said. What should we do about these blasted Indians?"

Evan held up his hands, palms out. "Hold on there. I'm a Texan, but I'm no Indian fighter. Never traded shots with one until today." He looked at the silent figure seated at the far end of the table. "Pablo's the one you ought to ask. He knows those folks a lot better than I do."

"What about it, Pablo?" asked Cartmill, looking down the table at the *segundo*. "Will Nicholas and his men ever allow us to live here in peace?"

For a long moment, Pablo made no reply, and the silence stretched out enough so that Evan began to wonder if the man was going to answer at all. Then, finally, Pablo said, "Nicholas thinks of us as invaders of his land. He will not share it willingly. And yet . . . he has lost many men in his attacks on your *rancho*, *Señor* Clive, as well as in his raids on the other *ranchos* in the canyon. Even the buffalo soldiers from Fort Davis have killed some of Nicholas's men, though the Apaches have killed more of the soldiers. There may come a time . . . when Nicholas will decide that the price to keep Limpia Canyon is too high." For the first time, Evan saw a faint shadow of a smile pass across the Mexican's face. "The Rio Grande and the mountains of the Sierra Madre are not far, and Nicholas is an old man. He would do well to live out his life over there."

"You're saying there's reason to hope that if we hold out long enough, Nicholas will give up?"

"There is always hope," said Pablo.

Cartmill lifted his glass of wine. "Then here we shall stay. To the Cartmill ranch!" He grinned a dazzling grin. "Immodest though it may be, I think I shall name it the Mulehead, in honor of its owner."

Melinda laughed, a sound as clear and pure to Evan as the waters of Limpia Creek. "To the Mulehead," she said.

Evan joined in the toast . . . hoping that the Mulehead wouldn't turn out to be a graveyard for all of them.

14

Late that night, Evan and Clive Cartmill sat in the Englishman's study, drinking coffee laced with whiskey. Evan had never seen so many books in his life; the leather-bound volumes filled several bookcases in the room. He had enough schooling that he could read—some—but the idea of even attempting to read as many books as Cartmill owned seemed completely overwhelming to him.

"The *hacienda* was already here when we arrived," Cartmill was saying, "but you probably figured that out before now. I'm not certain how old the house is, but I would guess over a hundred years."

"I reckon that's right," said Evan. "Some fella from south of the Rio figured to establish a ranch up here, but the Apaches must've run him off."

"A fate that won't happen to me," Cartmill insisted. "The place was in poor repair when we found it. We put it in order—Melinda actually did most of the work—and hired a crew. We were lucky to find Pablo. He picked the other *vaqueros.*"

"You sure you can trust all of 'em?"

Cartmill laughed. "They are a rather bloodthirsty-looking bunch, aren't they? But to answer your question—yes, I trust them. I've fought side by side with all of them. They've risked their lives for me, and I've risked mine for them. That breeds trust and loyalty, on both sides."

Evan nodded, sipped his coffee, and said, "Yep, it does, all right. Saw that during the war. Didn't matter whether you had anything in common with a fella or not. Once you'd been under fire together, that was all it took to make you friends."

"Indeed."

"So . . . just how much damage have the Apaches done?"

Cartmill thought about the question for a moment before answering. "They've run off some of our horses. That's why we keep all the mounts in that small courtyard right behind the house now; we can protect it better than we ever could the barns and the corrals. We won't know how badly they've cut into our herds until next spring, when we do the annual gather. I assume they've stolen some of the cattle, but perhaps not too many. Pablo says they have little use for cattle. They prefer horse meat."

"That's what I've heard, too."

"We've lost only two men in the fighting, though quite a few of us have sustained wounds at one time or another. The original owner may have abandoned this place, but surely not because it was difficult to defend. It's a veritable fortress."

"You're lucky," Evan told the rancher. "Pablo's probably right: If you can hold off the Apaches long enough, their chief'll get tired of it and leave you alone."

"That is my sincere hope." Cartmill lifted the cup to his mouth, took a swallow of the whiskey-laced coffee, then smiled. "I'm quite impressed with your children. I already knew how special Billy and Penelope are, and Dinah seems to be a lovely, intelligent young woman as well."

"They're growing up to be good people," agreed Evan. "I give their mother most of the credit for that."

"Oh, I imagine you had *something* to do with it, Evan."

"Maybe," Evan said with a chuckle. He grew more serious as he went on, "Billy doesn't seem to want to have much to do with me right now, though."

Cartmill shrugged. "A phase. All children go through them—or so I'm told. Not having any of my own, I can't speak from experience."

"You and Melinda were starting to think of Billy and Penelope as yours."

The Englishman looked down at his cup, his face unreadable. "The fact that we're unable to have children of our own has always been a burden to Melinda," he said quietly. "Since we were told that your youngsters were orphans, we thought perhaps . . . yes, Evan, we did intend to raise them as our own. I hope that doesn't bother you."

"Like I told you before, it was a mighty nice thing to do, and I don't hold any grudges because of it, Clive."

Cartmill grinned. "I'm glad to hear that. I wouldn't want the notorious gunfighter Evan Littleton to be angry with me."

Evan winced and closed his eyes for a second. When he opened them again, he demanded, "Where'd you hear that?"

"From your son, for the most part. He said you were a famous gunman before you were married."

"Stupid was what I was," muttered Evan. "*I* never told any of the kids about that. But I reckon they heard stories . . ."

"Some of the other people around Richland Springs seemed to know something about the matter, too," Cartmill pointed out. "But they were fairly protective of your privacy. They said you wanted to put that part of your life behind you."

"That's what I've been trying to do for the better part of twenty years. Don't seem to be having much luck with it, though. That reputation just keeps following me around."

"Well, I'll speak no more of it," promised Cartmill. "Now that I know how you feel, the subject won't even be mentioned."

"Much obliged." Evan yawned and set his cup aside on a small table next to his chair. "Don't know about you, but I'm a mite tired."

"Yes, fighting Indians *is* taxing work. Everyone

else is asleep, except for the sentries, and I suggest we join them."

Evan stood up and stretched. "When do you want me to take my turn at standing watch?"

"There's no need for that. Pablo and his men are sufficient enough in number to assure that we always have plenty of guards watching out for the Apaches," Cartmill said as he stood up. He clapped a hand on Evan's arm. "Come along, I'll show you to your room. How does a full night's sleep on a feather bed sound to you?"

Evan grinned. "About as close to heaven as I'm ever likely to get."

Evan supposed it was the whiskey, or exhaustion, or a combination of the two that helped him sleep that night. All he knew was that he fell into a dreamless slumber as soon as he stretched out on the soft bed, and he didn't wake up the next morning until the sun was high in the sky and casting slanting rays through the gauzy curtains over the room's single window.

He rose, pulled on his clothes, and made his way through the halls of the big house to the kitchen, where he found Melinda Cartmill, Dinah, and Penelope hard at work preparing lunch for the crew of the newly christened Mulehead ranch. Melinda smiled a greeting at him and said, "We didn't want to disturb you, Mr. Littleton. You seemed to be sleeping so soundly, and Clive said you probably needed the rest."

Evan rubbed a hand across his jaw, which was

bristling with beard stubble. "Figured to help with the chores this morning," he said. "But I got to admit, it felt mighty good to sleep in a real bed again."

"I agree," said Dinah. "Rolling up in a blanket on the trail just isn't the same thing."

"There a place around here where I can wash up and maybe shave?" Evan asked.

"There's a well in the rear courtyard," Melinda told him. "If you'll bring me some water, I'll heat it for you on the stove."

With a grin, Evan said, "I've been washing and shaving in cold water for a long time, ma'am. Reckon it won't hurt me to do it again."

"Suit yourself. When you're done, come back in here. I saved you some biscuits and bacon from breakfast." Melinda smiled brilliantly. "You see how much of a Texan I've become? Now I prepare biscuits and bacon for breakfast, instead of bangers and mash."

Evan glanced at his daughters and saw that Dinah and Penelope didn't really have any idea what Melinda was talking about, either. Deciding it would be best to just let the matter lie, Evan went out back and found the well in the rear courtyard. The makeshift corral was there, too; the quarters were rather close for the horses confined there, but that was better than winding up as dinner for some Apache family, Evan thought. He saw Dinah's chestnut mare and the rangy lineback dun he had borrowed from the Bracketts, both of them safe and sound after yesterday's fracas with the Apaches.

It didn't take long for Evan to wash his face and scrape off the bristles with the folding razor he carried in his hip pocket. He dried his face on a rag that was lying on the low stone wall around the well, then went back inside. His stomach was starting to growl, and that leftover breakfast Melinda had promised him sounded mighty good.

"Where's your husband and the rest of the men?" he asked as he washed down the food with more coffee, minus the whiskey this time. He had seen several of the *vaqueros* standing guard around the house, but there had been no sign of Cartmill, Pablo, and the other men.

"They've gone to bring in some of the cattle that were grazing nearby," explained Melinda. "We're running a bit low on beef, and Clive thought it might be safe to drive some of the cattle back here to the house. It's unlikely the Apaches will bother us again so soon."

Evan frowned. He wished he could be as sure of that as Cartmill evidently was. But just as the old men back in Richland Springs had said it was always best to do the unexpected where Indians were concerned, they had agreed as well that Indians themselves were mighty unpredictable. They seemed to have a talent for confounding white men with their actions.

Another thought occurred to Evan, and he asked, "Where's Billy?"

"Oh, he went with Clive and Pablo."

Evan looked up sharply from the table. Melinda didn't sound concerned; she had all the faith in the world in her husband. But Evan didn't much like the idea, and he could tell from the slight frowns on the faces of his daughters that Dinah and Penelope didn't, either.

"I told Billy you might want him to stay here," said Dinah, "but he didn't listen to me."

"He never listens to anybody," put in Penelope. "You know Billy. He always thinks he knows more than anybody else."

That was just the trouble, thought Evan: He didn't know Billy. Not really. The Billy Littleton who lived here on the Mulehead was pretty much a different person from the boy he had been when Evan left for the war.

He was finished with his breakfast, so he stood up from the table. "Think I'll go take a look around," he said. "Which way did your husband go when he left, Mrs. Cartmill?"

"Down the canyon to the south," replied Melinda, and now she looked slightly concerned as well. "You don't intend to follow them, do you, Mr. Littleton? You don't think anything is wrong?"

"Probably not. I just need to get out and move around a little."

He didn't think she was overly reassured by his answer. Dinah and Penelope didn't seem to believe it, either. Without meeting their eyes, he left the kitchen and went quickly back to his bedroom, where he picked up the shell belt and the holstered Colt and buckled the rig around his waist. One of the fully loaded Henry rifles leaned against the wall in a corner of the room, and he picked it up, too.

Bypassing the kitchen, he headed for that rear

courtyard where the horses were kept. A small room just inside the *hacienda* had been converted to use as a tack room, and he found his saddle there. He carried it and a blanket outside into the courtyard, then went to the corral gate, calling to the dun in the hopes that it would come over and make things easy for him. As usual, the horse ignored him.

Evan sighed and reached for the rope latch that held the gate closed. He would have to take the halter in there and get it on the dun, then lead the horse out of the corral.

He didn't get a chance to do either of those things. Before he could open the gate, the sound of distant gunshots came floating to his ears in the cool morning air.

Evan's head jerked up in alarm. There were plenty of reasons for somebody to be shooting in these parts: Wolves, rattlesnakes, even mountain lions weren't unheard of. But a steady rattle of gunfire like what he was hearing now could mean only one thing—trouble. The sounds were coming closer, too, which meant that whoever was doing the shooting was probably being chased.

Out here, when you were running from something, it was usually Apaches, Evan thought.

Excited shouts came from the pair of *vaqueros* who were standing guard over the horses. The only way into this courtyard from outside was through a narrow opening in the thick adobe wall that was closed by a massive wooden gate. Evan sprang toward it, shouting, "Get that gate open! Now!" If Cartmill and the others were being chased back to the ranch house, they would need to get inside in a hurry.

The Mexican cowboys hesitated, then obeyed Evan's orders. He still had the Henry rifle in his hand, and he was ready to use it as he darted through the gate as soon as the *vaqueros* had it open wide enough. A path curved around from the front of the house to this rear gate. Evan followed it, running around the rambling adobe structure until he could see Limpia Canyon opening up in front of him. He looked to the south and saw spurts of gunsmoke among the trees that blocked his view of the trail. Suddenly, a group of horsemen burst into sight, emerging from those trees as they galloped wildly up the slope toward the house.

Evan's breath froze in his throat, and his heart seemed to stop in his chest. Clive Cartmill was in the lead, a high-crowned, wide-brimmed *sombrero* such as the *vaqueros* wore strapped tightly to his head. He leaned forward in the saddle, controlling his mount with his knees and his left hand— because his right arm was wrapped around Billy, and he was holding the unconscious boy tightly against his chest. At least, Evan hoped Billy was only unconscious. As limp as the youngster appeared to be, he could just as easily be dead.

That thought wrenched at Evan's guts. He shoved it away, knowing that for the time being he had to concentrate on helping the fleeing riders get back to the house safely. A group of Apaches came from the trees, and for a change, they were on horseback, too, which meant that Cartmill and his men had lost one of their advantages. They were riding too hard to slow down and return the fire of the Apaches, who all seemed to be armed with rifles today. The old chief, Nicholas, was taking his campaign against the Mulehead more seriously now, Evan realized. Cartmill and his crew had inflicted enough damage on the Apaches that they no longer regarded their raids as a game.

Evan lifted the Henry to his shoulder. He had never used one of the rifles until the day before, but he had found them to be accurate, powerful weapons. Sighting carefully past Cartmill and the fleeing *vaqueros*, he aimed at the pursuing Apaches and squeezed off a shot.

The rifle's stock bucked against his shoulder, and its loud, spiteful crack lashed against his ears. Through the gray haze of powdersmoke that floated in front of him, he saw that none of the Apaches had tumbled from their saddles. In fact, none of them even seemed to be wounded. They came on, howling and firing, as Evan worked the lever and jacked a fresh cartridge into the Henry's chamber.

The *vaqueros* who had been left at the house were joining in the fight now, firing from the windows and rifle slits of the *hacienda*. Evan knew he ought to join them, knew he was dangerously exposed out here in front of the house. But the riders were drawing closer now, and he could see the dark red stain on Billy's shirt. Until he knew just how badly his son was hurt, he wasn't going anywhere.

Evan fired again, and this time he was rewarded

by the way one of the Apaches jerked back atop his mount. The wounded man swayed back and forth for a moment, then slumped forward, holding on to his horse's mane for dear life to keep from tumbling off. Evan figured he wouldn't be much of a threat for the rest of the fight. The wounded Indian's horse was already slowing down and falling back from the others.

It was tricky, shooting past Cartmill and the other men without hitting them, but Evan placed his shots carefully. A moment later he saw another of the Apaches go flying off the back of a horse and didn't know if his shot was responsible or if one of the men in the house had brought the warrior down. It didn't really matter, of course. What was important was that the pursuit slowed as another man and then another fell to the rifle fire coming from Evan and the *vaqueros*.

Cartmill, Pablo, and the other men swept past Evan, circling the house to reach the courtyard in the rear. Evan heard a man's voice calling, "*Señor* Littleton!" and turned to see one of the *vaqueros* standing at an open door. Evan dashed toward the door as the *vaquero* fired past him, laying down covering fire for him. The Mexican sagged back and grunted in pain just as Evan reached the door. He reached for his thigh, which had just been bored through by an Apache bullet. Evan grabbed the man's arm and jerked him through the door, slamming it behind them with a kick of his foot. More slugs thudded into the thick wood but didn't penetrate it.

"*Dios mio!*" exclaimed the *vaquero* as he tried

to stem the flow of blood from his wounded leg. He clamped a hand tightly over the bullet hole.

Melinda Cartmill came running down the hall toward the door. "I'll take care of him!" she told Evan as she took hold of the Mexican's arm. As she led the wounded man away, supporting him with an arm as he limped heavily, Evan wheeled to the nearest rifle slit and poked the Henry's barrel through the opening.

One of the Apaches was close enough so that Evan's view of him filled the narrow aperture in the wall. Barely taking the time to aim, Evan fired as the Indian galloped past. The Apache was there and then gone, and Evan couldn't tell if he had hit the man or not.

There was no shortage of other targets. Apaches were still pouring out of the trees along the lane. Evan guessed this force numbered forty or fifty men, rather than the dozen and a half of the day before. That supported his earlier guess about the new seriousness with which Nicholas regarded this standoff. The old war chief wanted to put an end to the fighting in the most efficient way possible: by killing all of those he regarded as enemies.

On a small scale, this was the same as the war that had so disrupted Evan's life and nearly ended it on more than one occasion. There should have been a peaceful way to settle the differences between Nicholas and the ranchers who had moved into Limpia Canyon, but neither side was willing to give an inch. Evan felt an unexpected surge of sympathy for the Apaches. They fought because they feared losing their land . . . just as Evan and so many of the other settlers in Texas had lost their land to the Yankee carpetbaggers.

Evan's jaw clenched tightly. Such thoughts were all well and good, but they didn't change the fact that the Apaches were doing their dead level best to kill him, his kids, the Cartmills, and everybody else on this ranch. No matter what motivated their savagery, it was still wrong. Evan lined his sights on one of the marauders and squeezed off another shot.

He never saw if it hit anything, because at that moment, a giant hand reached out of nowhere and slapped him on the side of the head, so hard that he reeled backward. He felt his feet going out from under him, felt himself falling . . .

But he didn't know it when he hit the floor. By that time, utter blackness had swallowed him whole.

15

Evan had no idea how long he had been unconscious. In fact, he wasn't even aware that he had been out cold. For the first few moments of returning awareness, the sensation was sort of like what he had experienced that morning when he woke up after a full night of deep, undisturbed sleep. An almost pleasant lassitude washed through him, and he had the urge to stretch. His muscles tensed, and his head moved slightly.

That was when the pain hit him.

The intensity of the agony that filled his skull jarred a groan out of him. The sound only seemed to make things worse. He couldn't see anything, but he realized that was because his eyes were closed. Opening them loomed as too dangerous. If he tried, there was no way of knowing what would happen.

"Lie still," came a soft voice in his ear, and for a second he thought it was Lynette, come back to him somehow. Then he decided it must be a ghost, a phantom whispering to him.

"Dinah . . ." he croaked as the truth hit him.

"I'm right here," his daughter said. "Be still, Daddy. You're hurt."

Evan's eyes blinked open as his memory came back to him. It was all clear: the Apaches attacking, Cartmill and the other men fleeing from them, Billy with the red stain of blood on his shirt . . .

"Billy," Evan husked as he looked up at Dinah. Her youthful features were creased with worry. "Wh-where's Billy?"

"He's fine," she told him. "Well, maybe not exactly fine. He's got a bullet crease under his left arm that's going to be mighty sore for a few days."

Evan closed his eyes in relief. Billy was alive. Not only alive, but evidently not seriously injured. The wound had looked worse than it really was.

What about *him*, he thought. How badly was he hurt?

He opened his eyes again and somehow managed to move his right hand. As he reached up toward his head, where the source of the pain was, he said, "What . . . what happened . . ."

"You got grazed by a bullet, too," said Dinah. "We thought for a while it was a lot worse, just like Billy's wound. But Melinda cleaned it up, and once all the blood was washed off, we could tell it wasn't too bad."

"Hard to . . . dent this . . . old skull." Where the feeble attempt at humor came from, Evan didn't know. But it brought a smile to Dinah's lips, and he was glad of that.

He was lying on a bed, he realized now, and she was sitting in a chair beside him. He listened intently. No gunshots. That was good, he told himself. Since they were still alive and evidently in the *hacienda*, likely the Apache raid was over.

He asked as much through cracked lips, and Dinah nodded. "I thought they were going to get in the house and overrun us," she said bluntly, "but Mr. Cartmill and Pablo and the other men turned them back. It was quite a fight." She added proudly, "I got in a few shots myself."

"Good . . . girl . . ." Evan said. He was incredibly tired again, the weariness stealing over him so suddenly and strongly that it even blunted the pain in his head where the Apache slug had kissed him. His eyelids lowered.

"Not yet," Dinah said. "You can go back to sleep, but not until you've had some water."

She held a dipper to his mouth, and he discovered he was as thirsty as he was tired. He gulped down the cold, clear water from the well, then sank once more onto the pillow that someone had placed underneath his head.

"Rest now," Dinah told him quietly. "I'll be right here."

"You're sure . . . Billy's all right?"

"I'm sure."

"What about . . . you and . . . Penelope?"

"Not a scratch on either one of us."

"Good . . ." Evan felt himself drifting off again. He let himself go willingly this time.

When he woke up again, night had fallen. The ranch's defenders were still tending to their wounds. Cartmill and every member of the crew had suffered at least minor scratches and scrapes. The most seriously injured man seemed to be Sanchez, who had taken the bullet in the leg when he was covering Evan's retreat to the house. The deep gash on Evan's head was probably the second most serious wound. He was lucky it had glanced off his skull, rather than penetrating and killing him.

He had always known Texans were hard-headed. This time, it had come in handy.

Evan sat up in bed while Penelope fed him from a bowl of Melinda's stew. His head still ached fiercely, but the food gave him strength and made him feel better. After supper, Cartmill came into the room and sat down in a cane-bottomed, ladderback chair. The left sleeve of the Englishman's shirt had been cut off, and a bandage was wrapped tightly around his forearm where an Apache bullet had dug a furrow.

Cartmill got Evan's pipe going, then lit his own. "They hit us as we were trying to get some of those longhorns moving back toward the house," said Cartmill. "I believe Melinda told you that we're running a bit low on beef."

Evan nodded. "She said you figured the Apaches wouldn't hit you again so soon."

"That assumption seemed reasonable to me, and to Pablo as well. They've never raided so closely together before. Always in the past, days or weeks or sometimes even months would go by after we'd beaten off an attack. Pablo says they return to their strongholds higher in the mountains to lick their wounds every time they suffer a defeat."

"That old war chief Nicholas is getting tired of butting his head against a stone wall," Evan said. "He figured you wouldn't be expecting him and his boys, so he decided to hit you again, harder than ever before."

Cartmill nodded. "That's exactly what happened. For a man who claims not to be an Indian fighter, Evan, you seem to understand them quite well."

"It's just common sense."

"Be that as it may, I'm glad you're here. We'll stand a better chance of fighting them off when they come again."

Evan hesitated. He had never intended to stay at the Cartmill ranch for any length of time. Now that he had found Billy and Penelope, what he really wanted to do was take them and move on, so that they could catch up to Frank and Suellen Wilson and find Rockly.

But that was impossible now. He had joined the fight on Cartmill's side, and to the Apaches that meant he was just as much the enemy as the Englishman and his crew of *vaqueros*. It would be suicide to try to reach Fort Davis or to re-trace the trail to the stage line. The Apaches would be on them instantly and would wipe them out.

No, Evan thought, for better or worse, his destiny—and that of his children—was tied firmly to the Cartmills.

After a few moments of silence while Evan

brooded on the situation, Cartmill asked, "What do you think Nicholas will do now?"

"How many men did he lose today?"

"It's difficult to say, because the Apaches took their dead and wounded with them." Cartmill puffed on his pipe and thought about the question. "I'd say at least a dozen killed, perhaps twice that many wounded."

"He suffered heavy losses, then."

"Pablo says we've depleted the number of warriors in the band by quite a bit over the past year of skirmishes."

Evan leaned back against the pillows propped up behind his back and rubbed his temples, trying to ease the ache in them. He said, "I don't reckon anybody gets to be a war chief by being a fool. Maybe he can starve you out, but it's going to take a long time."

"A long time indeed," Cartmill agreed.

"In the meantime, he's got the army to worry about, and more settlers moving into these parts all the time. Seems to me the smart thing would be for him to do like Pablo said: head across the border into the Mexican mountains and live out the rest of his life there, where nobody'll bother him and his people."

"We can only pray that you and Pablo are right, my friend," Cartmill said fervently.

Excited shouting somewhere in the house woke Evan the next morning. Even though he couldn't make out the words, he could hear the fear in the voices, and he knew he had to get out of bed and see what was wrong. His pants and shirt were on a chair in the corner, so he threw back the blanket covering him, swung his legs out of bed, and stood up.

The world seemed to stop itself, reverse its course, and spin crazily backward, out of control, for several seconds. Evan's hand shot out and grabbed the headboard of the bed to steady him. His stomach rolled nauseatingly. His fingers tightened their grip on the headboard, and he forced himself to breathe slowly and deeply. Gradually, the world righted itself, but he waited a minute longer before he trusted himself to walk.

The pain in his head had subsided to a dull ache, and other than the dizziness, that seemed to be all that was wrong with him. The spinning and the unsteadiness were going away, too, and he felt himself growing stronger. He still had to move carefully as he drew on the clothes, but within a few minutes he was dressed and walking down the corridor leading to the front of the house, the Henry rifle he had found in his room clutched tightly in his hands.

The shouting had stopped, but he still heard voices. As he came into the big main room, he saw Dinah, Billy, and Penelope waiting by the door with Melinda Cartmill. All four of them were armed with rifles. Evan glanced to right and left, up and down the hallway that fronted the house. *Vaqueros* were stationed at each of the rifle slits, ready to start firing if need be. What drew most of Evan's attention, however, was the big front door of the house, which stood open at the moment. Morning sunlight framed it brilliantly, and Evan had to squint and blink as he waited for his eyes to adjust to what was going on outside. Through narrowed eyelids, he saw Clive Cartmill standing in front of the *hacienda*, Henry repeater tucked under his arm, facing a short, stocky Apache wearing a colorful headband, a blousey shirt, and white trousers such as Mexican farmers wore. Cartmill and the Apache were speaking intently in Spanish. Evan couldn't understand enough of what they were saying for the conversation to make any sense.

Melinda noticed him and hissed, "Mr. Littleton! You shouldn't be up!"

Evan walked across the room, making an effort to keep his pace calm and deliberate, mainly so that he wouldn't fall down. "What's going on out there?" he asked in a half whisper.

"Nicholas himself has come under a flag of truce to speak to Clive. I believe Pablo called it a parley."

Evan glanced at the old Apache. Nicholas's face was seamed and cracked like the leather of an old saddle, and it was about the same color. But his dark eyes were as alert as the eyes of a much younger man. Evan hoped Cartmill was being mighty careful about what he was saying.

"Are you all right, Daddy?" asked Dinah, casting worried glances back and forth between Evan and the rendezvous going on outside the *hacienda*.

"I'm fine, honey," he assured her. "Told you this old skull of mine was as hard as a rock, and now I'm proving it. Still got a mite of a headache, but I don't reckon I'm too addle-pated." He looked at Billy, who stood a little stiffly because of the bandages wrapped around his torso under his shirt. "How are you doing?"

"I'll live," Billy said curtly.

Evan held back a sigh. Billy was still mad at him. Well, so be it. With a bunch of Apaches right outside the door, hurt feelings didn't mean a whole lot at the moment. There would be time to hash things out with Billy later—if they were lucky.

Evan couldn't see any of the Apaches except Nicholas, but he felt confident there were plenty of other warriors close by, ready to strike if there was any treachery or if their chief gave them the sign to attack. Nicholas didn't look upset, though. In fact, as Evan watched, the chief extended his hand and shook, white man fashion, with Cartmill. The Englishman smiled and nodded, both men exchanged another spate of rapid Spanish, then Nicholas backed away and left Cartmill standing there. The Apache chief turned and began walking off toward the creek, carrying with him the branch on which a bit of white rag was tied. The makeshift flag was responsible for the truce.

Cartmill waited until Nicholas was a good distance off, then turned and came into the house. He was grinning broadly, and his voice was exuberant as he announced, "It's over!"

"What's over, darling?" asked Melinda.

"The hostilities! Nicholas has agreed to have peace with us and all the other settlers. He's made this agreement as well with the commander of the fort."

Pablo appeared from somewhere, and Evan wondered briefly where the hatchet-faced *segundo* had been. Someplace where he could draw a bead on Nicholas, Evan would have been willing to wager. "Do you trust that . . . that Apache, *patron*?" asked Pablo.

Cartmill nodded. "I believe I do. He said that he and his people were moving across the Rio Grande, just as you suggested they might. He said that too many of his band's young men have lost their lives in a foolish quest, and it is time to end it. He promised that none of his people would raid us again. We shook hands on the agreement before he left."

Pablo drew a deep breath and still looked somewhat dubious, but he said, "Whatever his faults, Nicholas is a man of his word. If he says the Apaches will not raid, they will not raid."

Melinda exclaimed in relief. "Then it really *is* over!" She lowered her rifle and went into her husband's arms. "Oh, Clive! We can live a normal life again now."

He patted her on the back and nodded. "Yes. We're finally going to be able to make a success of the ranch, darling. It's what we've dreamed of . . ."

For a second, Evan thought about pointing out that Cartmill and even Pablo had been wrong about the behavior of the Apaches before, as recently as yesterday, in fact. But he kept his mouth shut, not wanting to ruin this pleasant moment for the English couple.

Pablo moved over beside Evan and said in a

low voice, "*Señor* Cartmill has not told you the most important thing Nicholas said."

Evan glanced over at the Mexican ranch foreman. "What might that be?"

"Nicholas said he and his people were going across the border for the winter, and that there would be no more raids on the ranches in Limpia Canyon." Pablo smiled thinly, but there was no humor in the expression. "That much will be true—as far as it goes. But Nicholas said nothing about what will happen when spring comes again to this land."

Evan caught his breath. Pablo was right. The wily old chief had left himself a loophole. The Mulehead would be safe enough for the winter . . . but come spring it was liable to be a different story.

Either way it wasn't going to affect him, Evan told himself. By the time that spring came again to the Davis Mountains, he figured that he and his kids would be long gone from these parts.

Because he still had one more child to find before his family was finally reunited . . .

16

Evan sat in the dining room of Clive Cartmill's *hacienda* and tried to keep a tight rein on his temper. "They're my children," he said, "and I'd just as soon have them with me."

"Well, of course you'd feel that way, Evan," said Melinda Cartmill from where she sat at her husband's left hand. "But we're just trying to suggest a reasonable alternative to what you had in mind."

"What I had in mind was finding my boy, Rockly."

"You can still do that," Cartmill pointed out. "And when you have, you can come back here and pick up the other children."

Evan took a deep breath. Nothing was ever easy in life, he told himself. At least it hadn't been in his experience.

Ten days had passed since the Apache war chief Nicholas had visited the Mulehead and declared a truce with Cartmill. During that time, Evan had rested and recovered his strength. The wound where the bullet had grazed his head was practically healed now, leaving behind a scar that ran across his temple and into his hair. The pounding headaches had gone away after four or five days. All in all, the good meals and the time spent sleeping in a real bed had improved Evan's condition so much that he was beginning to be afraid he would go soft if he stayed around here much longer.

And there was still Rockly to find, too . . .

But when he had announced this morning that he was ready to move on and take Dinah, Billy, and Penelope with him, the Cartmills had balked. Evan had known he was in for trouble as soon as he saw Melinda's eyes go wide with dismay at the prospect of the children leaving the ranch.

"It makes perfect sense," Melinda went on as she and her husband, along with Evan and the children, sat around the long, heavy dining room table and tried to come to an agreement. "You don't really know where your search is going to lead you or how long it will take. Wouldn't it be easier if you could go about it knowing that the children are safe here with us?"

"They weren't very safe when those Apaches were raiding the place all the time," Evan said with ill grace, knowing he was upsetting these people who had been so kind to him, but not knowing how to avoid it.

"That threat has passed," said Cartmill. "Nicholas and his men will not bother us in the future."

"What about other Indians?"

"The army is getting control of the situation. Soon Limpia Canyon will be as safe as . . . as the streets of London!"

Evan wasn't sure how safe that was, not knowing one blessed thing about London except that it was in England, but he had to concede—grudgingly—that Cartmill was probably right about the danger from Indians. Until next spring, when Nicholas and his Apaches might take a notion to come back from Mexico, it was unlikely there would be any more raids. Maybe, with any luck, there wouldn't even be any trouble then.

For all their talk about being reasonable and logical, though, Evan knew why Cartmill and Melinda were really putting up an argument about him taking the children with him. For more than a year, they had cared for Billy and Penelope as if the youngsters were their own, and in the time since he and Dinah had arrived here, the older girl had become quite close to the Cartmills, too. Cartmill had admitted to Evan that he and his wife couldn't have any children of their own. Now, they didn't want to turn loose of *his* kids.

"I reckon what you say makes sense," Evan said with a sigh. "But I'm their father, and they ought to be with me."

Billy spoke up. "Nobody's asked us how *we* feel about it."

"It's as much our business as anybody else's," added Dinah in her usual headstrong manner.

Evan turned toward his children and frowned. "Well? What is it you want to do?"

"I'd just as soon stay here," Billy declared without hesitation.

Dinah, despite her determination to be a part of this decision, looked unsure of what she wanted. Not so Penelope, who said, "I want to stay with Billy, wherever that is."

Evan pressed the issue with his eldest daughter, looking straight at Dinah and asking, "What about you?"

Dinah glanced at Cartmill and Melinda, then turned back to Evan and said, "It *does* make more sense for us to stay here. You can travel faster without us and find Rockly that much sooner. Then, we'll all be together again, just like—"

She stopped abruptly and caught her lip between her teeth. Evan knew what she had been about to say: *just like before.* But it wouldn't be, no matter what they did today. It could never be the same again, because Lynette was gone, and Thad, and their farm was in the hands of the Yankees.

Suddenly, thinking about all the pain his children had endured already, Evan was seized with the desire not to cause them any more. He nodded and said, "All right."

The abruptness of it took the others by surprise. Cartmill said uncertainly, "You mean—"

"I mean all of you are right. The best thing would be for the kids to stay here while I go looking for Rockly. I'll need to be traveling pretty fast, since it won't be long before winter sets in."

"That's right," said Cartmill, looking relieved. "From what the other settlers in the area tell me, we don't get a great deal of snow and terribly cold weather in these parts, but conditions *are* rather undependable. Heading on to El Paso right away is probably the best thing you can do."

Evan summoned up a grin. "Reckon you'd sell me one of those Henry rifles? I've gotten a mite attached to 'em."

"Sell one to you? No . . . but you're more than welcome to take one, and all the ammunition you can carry, in return for everything you did for us during those final skirmishes with the Apaches."

Evan didn't like the idea of charity, but he supposed Cartmill had a point. And since he didn't have two coins to rub together in his pocket, he was willing to accept the offer. Earning any money was something that had eluded him during the past weeks. There simply hadn't been any time to look for a job after that short-lived, disastrous attempt in Brady.

He nodded and said, "Much obliged."

"And you'll take plenty of supplies with you," Melinda said. "Now that we've fattened you up some, I don't want you getting skinny again."

Evan tried not to grin. His stomach was just about as flat and hard as a washboard, no matter how much he ate—and lately that had been quite a bit, because Melinda was a good cook.

He pushed back from the table. "No point in wasting time. I'll get ready to ride and leave today."

"So soon?" Dinah said. Clearly, she was torn between wanting to stay with the Cartmills and her desire to be with her father. Now that things were settled, Evan didn't want them getting stirred up again, so he nodded emphatically.

"That's right. I want to get to El Paso and find your brother."

Cartmill said, "You know, I recall Frank Wilson telling me once that his father was some sort of important man in El Paso. That might help you locate Frank." The Englishman smiled. "Of course, Frank could be a bit . . . blustery . . . at times, so you may have to take anything he told me with a grain of salt."

Evan stood up. "Liked to stretch the truth a mite, did he?"

"Oh, I wouldn't call him a liar. But I got the impression that what other people thought of him was very important to Frank, so he may have embellished the facts of his background somewhat."

Evan didn't care who Frank Wilson's father was; all he was interested in was finding the couple and getting his son back from them.

Cartmill lent a hand as Evan began gathering his gear for the trip. The owner of the Mulehead wasn't content with giving Evan one of the Henry rifles. Cartmill insisted that he take an extra horse to give the dun some rest, a sheepskin coat to keep out the chill winds of approaching winter, *aparejos* full of provisions and ammunition, not only for the Henry but for the Colt as well, and a couple of bottles of wine from Cartmill's fledgling vineyard. "You may need to put a little in your coffee on the really cold nights," he told Evan with a grin.

When Evan went to saddle the dun, he found that Pablo had already taken care of that chore.

The *segundo* led the rangy animal out of a corral and gave the reins to Evan, saying, "Are you sure you want to ride this beast, *señor*? He bites."

"His disposition's a mite lacking," admitted Evan, "but there's not an ounce of quit in him."

Pablo nodded in understanding. Out here on the frontier, a man didn't ask his horse to be a pleasant companion, just to get the job done.

Melinda and the children came out of the sprawling adobe house, and as Evan glanced at them, he thought—not for the first time—that he was soon going to have to stop regarding them as children at all. They had grown up quickly. He wondered if he would find that Rockly was the same way, mature beyond his years.

Dinah and Penelope weren't so mature that they didn't have the sheen of tears in their eyes as they hugged him goodbye, however. He held each of them tightly for a long moment, touched their hair awkwardly with his knobby, work-roughened fingers, smelled the clean fragrance of each of them. "I'll be back for you," he whispered to each of them in turn. "And don't you ever forget that I love you."

Then he turned to Billy, ready to sweep the boy into his arms for a hug, stopping when he sensed Billy's uneasiness. There was still some resentment lodged inside the youngster, thought Evan, and sooner or later it was going to have to come out, else it would sit in there and fester like a boil. But for now they were both going to have to live with what was between them.

"I'll be seeing you, son," Evan settled for

saying as he thrust out his hand. Billy hesitated, then took it, squeezing hard. Evan returned the grip and added, "You look after your sisters."

"We'll be all right," Billy said. "We're getting used to watching you ride off, I reckon."

Evan's jaw tightened. That was downright unfair: Billy had wanted to stay here on the Mulehead, yet now he sounded as if he held it against his father because Evan was leaving.

Nobody had ever said that raising kids was fair, Evan reminded himself, nor could he expect Billy to make sense all the time. Nobody human ever achieved that goal. Most folks, in fact, usually didn't make a lick of sense in their actions . . . himself included.

Evan shook hands with Cartmill and Pablo, got a hug from Melinda, then reached out to each of his children one last time, letting his hand brush one of theirs, squeezing a shoulder, touching an arm. They were real, they were alive and healthy, and he was going to carry that knowledge away from here with him, guard it as he would have his most precious possession.

Because that was just about the truth of it.

Then, before he could start bawling, too, he swung up into the saddle and rode away, looking back only once, and after that stubbornly keeping his eyes on the trail ahead.

17

Evan brought the dun to a halt at the top of a long, low ridge and looked across a miles-wide valley that opened up to the southwest. On the far side of the valley were mountains that he knew were in Mexico, because a strip of vegetation that was still green ran down the center of the valley, clearly marking the course of the Rio Grande.

Gentle slopes led up from the border river on both the Texas and the Mexico banks. Evan saw cultivated fields on both sides of the river as well. This far into West Texas, the winters were usually mild, the growing season long. A man could make a living from the soil here, as long as he was near the river and didn't have to depend on the sparse rains.

After everything he had seen and done, everything he had endured, Evan wasn't sure if he wanted to do that anymore. There were times when he wondered if he would ever be content to be a farmer again. That was really the only life he knew. If he didn't do that, what would he do?

That was a question which would have to be

answered later, he decided. As always, life didn't leave much leeway for pondering. He had a boy to find.

Almost a week had passed since he had left the Mulehead ranch in the Davis Mountains. In that time, he had ridden across some pretty country, some ugly country, and some pretty ugly country. No Indians had bothered him, and in fact he hadn't seen many people at all except in the widely scattered settlements. One day he had come across a mule train packing up silver from the mines in Mexico, and another time he had ridden for a while with a couple of cowboys who were headed for the town of Sierra Blanca to spend their monthly pay. Evan hadn't stayed in the town long; he found that it made him uneasy to have that many people around. It was liable to be a lot worse in El Paso, which was considerably bigger than Sierra Blanca. He would put up with whatever he had to, though, in order to find Rockly.

Noticing a small cluster of buildings between him and the river, Evan nudged the dun into motion again and rode toward the tiny village, leading the horse Clive Cartmill had given him. Most of the time, Evan had ridden the dun and used the other horse as a pack animal to carry his supplies. The dun had seemed to resent it when Evan swapped his saddle to the other mount, and became even more surly than usual, so Evan had let the horse have its way.

A glance at the sun told him it was around noon. A warm breeze blew from the south, across the river. That sheepskin coat had come in mighty handy the first few nights after leaving the Mulehead, but the closer Evan came to the border, the less he needed it. Today it felt more like spring than the closing days of autumn.

The village was a haphazard arrangement of buildings, many of them the adobe huts these farmers called *jacals*, with a few more substantial structures mixed in. If nothing else, thought Evan, this pilgrimage through West Texas had been an education of sorts. He might even wind up able to speak Spanish if he stayed out here long enough—at least the border lingo that passed for Spanish in these parts. He saw a building with the word CANTINA painted over its door, so he turned the dun toward it.

Two men came swaggering through the open door as Evan reached the building. They looked at him curiously as he swung down from the saddle and looped the reins of the dun and the pack horse over a hitch rack. Evan glanced at them, curious about them because they seemed to be interested in him, but he tried not to be as blatant about it as they were being. That was easier for him because he hadn't been drinking all morning, and evidently these men had.

They were white, dressed like cowboys only without the hard wear on their clothes which would have marked them as working hands. Their hats were pushed back on their heads, and they each wore a cocky grin. Evan noticed all that about them with a single glance.

Just as he noticed the gunbelts and the low-slung, tied-down holsters.

He tried not to let his mouth quirk in disgust as he recognized their breed. A couple of decades earlier, when folks had begun to talk about how fast he was with a gun and how good, there had been no such thing as gunfighters. He supposed he had been one of the first, although he hardly considered that anything to be proud of. Over the years, their numbers had grown. Shootists, pistoleers, whatever they wanted to call themselves . . . by and large, they were fakes, young men who postured and posed and cut notches in their guns when in reality they had never even drawn the weapons in anger, let alone killed anybody. The war had sort of disrupted the whole phenomenon, but from the looks of these two, it was coming back again.

But it had nothing to do with him, thought Evan. He didn't want any part of it—or of these men.

Except . . .

Maybe they could tell him something about Frank Wilson.

"Howdy, boys," he said with a nod, keeping his voice friendly. "Mind telling me what this place is?"

One of the men, who sported a long, wispy, pale mustache he had probably grown to make himself look older, jerked a thumb over his shoulder at the building. "You mean this cantina? Can't you read, mister?"

Mild, Evan told himself. Keep it mild. "Actually, I meant this town."

The other man laughed. "Wouldn't hardly call this a town. Ain't much more'n a wide place in the road. But they call it Acala."

Evan nodded. "Much obliged. I reckon this main trail here leads up to El Paso?"

The one with the mustache said, "You're just full o' questions, ain't you?"

Evan shrugged noncommittally and said, "It's my first time out here in these parts. Don't want to get lost."

"Follow the river and you won't. Road runs right along with it. El Paso's forty or fifty miles on ahead."

"Appreciate it." Evan nodded again and started to turn toward the door of the cantina. He stopped and added, seemingly as if it had just occurred to him, "Either of you boys happen to know a fella named Frank Wilson? His father's supposed to be some sort of important man out here in West Texas."

The questions got more of a reaction than he had ever expected. Both men tensed, and the one with the mustache asked, "This man Wilson a friend of yours?"

"Never met him," Evan replied honestly, hoping he hadn't accidentally run into a couple of Wilson's enemies.

"You will," said the other one, and then he reached for his gun.

Evan saw what was happening, but for a second his mind refused to comprehend it. This young gunman was actually throwing down on him, and a glance at the one with the mustache told Evan that *he* was going for his gun, too. Instinct took over, sending Evan's hand darting toward the butt of the Colt on his hip.

He was too late. The two men were fast, faster than he had expected them to be. They didn't shoot him, though. As Evan's gun cleared leather, the man closest to him slashed at his head with the long barrel of a Remington revolver.

At the same time the other man, the one with the mustache, stepped closer and grabbed Evan's gun, jerking it out of his hand. Evan staggered from the blow to the head, which sent blinding pain exploding through his skull even though the barrel of the Remington had struck him only glancingly. The bullet graze he had suffered during the Apache attack on the Mulehead was recent enough so that his head was still tender, he supposed. He didn't have a chance to ponder it because one of the men shoved him hard in the back, sending him stumbling forward, right into a hard fist that buried itself in his stomach.

He went to his knees, cursing himself for being so stupid. The two young men were much tougher than he had first given them credit for being. In fact, they were handling him as if they were veteran hardcases and he was nothing more than a green kid.

Anger swept through him. He had no idea what connection these men had with Frank Wilson, but clearly there was one, because Evan's mention of Wilson's name was what had set them off. He would find out, though, if he had to beat it out of them.

His hat had been knocked off by the pistol-whipping. One of the men grabbed Evan's graying hair and used it to jerk his head upright. "Listen here, old man—" he began.

"No, *you listen!*" Evan roared as he clubbed his hands together and brought them up as hard as he could. The man with the mustache was standing directly in front of him, legs spraddled, holding Evan's hair. That position made it easy for Evan to slam his clubbed fists into his groin. The man howled in pain and leaped back, releasing Evan's hair.

Evan used the momentum of the blow to help him surge to his feet. He whipped around as the other man jerked up his gun and yelped, "You son of—"

The back of Evan's right hand cracked across his mouth, silencing the epithet and knocking him back a step. Evan followed, boring in with a straight, hard left that crashed into the man's midsection. Evan got hold of the man's Remington and twisted, wrenching it out of the young gunnie's hand and maybe even breaking his wrist in the process. "You picked on the wrong old man!" Evan grated as he punched the man in the face again. The man went over backward, sitting down hard. He slumped to the side, eyes glazed.

Evan spun around, hoping he hadn't neglected the other one for too long. The man was struggling to stay upright, tottering around as he held one hand pressed tightly to his injured groin. In the other hand, however, was his gun, and he was trying mightily to lift the weapon and point it toward Evan. His pain-twisted features glared their hatred at the older man.

Lifting the Remington he had taken away from the other man, Evan eared back the hammer and said, "Better put it down, boy. I got no hankerin' to kill you."

A new voice said, "You won't be killing anybody, mister. If there's killing to be done, I'll do it."

Evan looked toward the cantina, saw a man standing just outside the doorway with several other men behind him. The man who had spoken was medium-sized, with gray hair under a hat that Evan recognized immediately: a Confederate cavalry officer's hat, plume and all, the feather looking vaguely ridiculous here in this dusty border village. There was nothing ridiculous about the LeMat revolver in the man's hand, which was pointing straight at Evan. He had seen officers during the war carrying the so-called grapeshot revolver; the guns had an extra barrel underneath their regular barrel which fired a shotgun shell, and at this range, the man could blow Evan apart with the weapon. The men looming behind the newcomer were all armed as well, and they didn't look happy.

For a second, Evan studied the man with the LeMat. He wore a fringed buckskin jacket, whipcord trousers, and high-topped boots. The boots and the hat were the only things that looked to be Confederate cavalry issue, but the man held himself with the unmistakable air of one accustomed to command. Evan figured he was really an ex-officer.

"All right, Major," he said, making a guess at the rank. Carefully, he lowered the hammer of the Remington and let the barrel sag toward the ground, but he didn't drop the gun. "Looks like you've got me outnumbered."

"It's Colonel," the man said crisply. "Colonel Randolph Dawson. Why are you attacking my men?"

Evan gestured at the two youngsters who had jumped him with no warning. "These gunnies are part of your outfit, Colonel? I would've reckoned you could do better."

There was a flash of anger in Dawson's gray eyes, and for a second Evan thought the man was going to squeeze the trigger on that LeMat. Dawson stepped forward a couple of paces, and the glance he threw toward the two young men was withering. "Perhaps you're right, my friend," he said to Evan, gaining control of himself again. "In these troubled times, however, an officer is forced to make do with whatever recruits are available to him." To the two gunmen, he snapped, "On your feet, Clegg! You, too, Billings!"

The colonel's words lashed at the men. The one with the mustache gulped and managed to say, "I . . . I'm already up, Colonel—"

Dawson had already turned away, ignoring him. To Evan he said, "Did you serve in the Late Unpleasantness, sir?"

Evan nodded. "I did my time and more, too much of it in a Yankee prison camp."

"I'm truly sorry. You've been through purgatory and back, then. Texan?"

"Yes, sir."

"I'm from Alabama, myself. Led a company of volunteers in the War for the Southern Confederacy. Now I find myself commanding a company of . . . irregulars."

Evan glanced at the men standing with the colonel. Some of them looked like ex-soldiers, their clothing and gear well cared for, their stance professional, ready for whatever might come. Others were more slovenly, and then there were the two youngsters who fancied themselves gunmen. Irregular was a good word to describe this bunch, all right.

"If you'd be interested in joining our ranks," Dawson went on, "I could always use another good man."

"Aw, Colonel, you can't do that!" protested the man with the mustache. "This fella hurt me! Shoot, after the way he hit me, I won't be able to—"

"I'm not interested in any of your romantic disadvantages, Mr. Clegg," snapped the colonel. "I've extended an offer of comradeship to this gentleman, and it's up to him to accept or deny it." He looked squarely at Evan. "What do you say, sir?"

"Afraid I'll have to pass, Colonel," said Evan. "I've got my own reasons for being here, so if it's all the same to you—"

"He wanted to know about Frank Wilson," interrupted the man Evan had knocked down earlier. Billings, his name was, Evan recalled.

Pointing a finger at Evan, Billings went on accusingly, "Asked if we'd ever heard of Wilson."

Colonel Dawson quirked a gray eyebrow. "Is that so?" he asked. "What's your business with Frank Wilson?"

Before Evan could answer that, a man came out of the cantina, stumbling a little on something that wasn't even there as far as Evan could see. He blinked rapidly, his eyes obviously unaccustomed to the bright sunshine outside after being in the dimness of the adobe building. After rubbing his knuckles across his eyes several times, he peered around in confusion and asked, "Did somebody call me? Thought I heard my name."

Dawson stepped aside and inclined his head toward Evan. "This gentleman was looking for you, Frank."

Evan's breath caught in his throat. *This* was Frank Wilson? The man was short and slender, clean-shaven, with a weak chin and watery eyes. Even though it was only the middle of the day, he was almost falling-down drunk. *This* sorry specimen was the man who had taken Rockly to raise?

And if Wilson was here with the Colonel and the rest of his bunch, then where was Rockly?

Wilson focused his bleary gaze on Evan, then said in a ragged voice, "Did they send you? Are you part of the gang?"

"I don't believe he's a Mexican, Frank," the colonel pointed out gently.

"Doesn't matter," Wilson said loudly with a

wave of his hand. "He's one of 'em, I know he is!" He clawed at the pearl-handled revolver holstered on his hip. "What've you done with 'em?" he screeched as he staggered toward Evan. "Where'd you take my wife and my boy?"

18

Shocked, horrified at the implications of Wilson's words, Evan could do nothing but stand there and stare at the man as Wilson fumbled to draw his gun. Colonel Dawson jerked his head at one of the other men with him, a tall, burly man with a neatly trimmed dark beard, and barked, "Sergeant!"

The bearded man stepped forward quickly and plucked Wilson's gun from its holster. Wilson snarled a curse. The bearded man's other hand came down hard on Wilson's shoulder and tightened, making Wilson gasp and stiffen. "Better do what the colonel says," advised the bearded man in a surprisingly gentle voice.

Wilson's head jerked in a nod. "A-all right!" he managed to say.

The sergeant released him and stepped back, taking Wilson's gun with him. His big hand almost swallowed up the pearl-handled revolver.

"Now," said Dawson, "I think the thing to do is to step inside out of this sun and have a drink while we discuss the situation. What do you say, sir?"

"All right," Evan managed to say, though his lips and tongue felt as dry as the sand beneath his feet.

"By the way, I don't believe I caught your name . . ."

"It's Littleton. Evan Littleton."

The name obviously meant nothing to Dawson, but Frank Wilson's eyes widened in surprise. The colonel said, "Pleased to meet you, Mr. Littleton. After you . . ."

Evan didn't like turning his back on these men, but he figured he was safe enough for the moment. Colonel Dawson was curious about him, and he wouldn't let his men get out of control again. As Evan stepped past Billings, he thrust the Remington out at the young man. "Here," he said. "Don't ever pull it on me again."

Then he strode into the cantina, the colonel falling in step beside him.

"That table there in the rear will do nicely," said Dawson, gesturing to indicate which one he meant. He turned and added, "Frank, you and the sergeant please join Mr. Littleton and me. The rest of you men may amuse yourselves, but please . . . no trouble."

"Yes, sir, Colonel," one of the group replied. They headed for the bar.

Evan supposed this was a typical bordertown cantina. The floor was swept, hard-packed dirt. There was a bar along one wall, a scattering of rickety tables and chairs. A beaded curtain hung over an arched doorway to the left of the bar. Behind the bar was a bald-headed Mexican in an apron that had perhaps once been white, a lot of years in the past. Dawson signaled to the man, who hurried out from behind the bar and brought a bottle and four glasses over to the table where Evan and the other men were sitting down.

When they had all settled into their chairs and the bartender had scurried back to his post, Dawson took a cigar from one of the pockets of the fringed jacket and stuck it in his mouth. He pried the cork out of the neck of the bottle and tipped some of the clear liquid inside into each glass. Frank Wilson grabbed eagerly for his. He kept shooting frightened glances toward Evan.

"Now, then, what's your business with our friend Frank, Mr. Littleton?" Dawson asked around the cheroot as he picked up his glass.

"He's got something that belongs to me," Evan said bluntly. "Or at least, he did."

Wilson had already thrown back his drink in one swallow, and now he licked his lips as if he desperately wanted more. He looked nervously at Evan.

It was all Evan could do not to lunge across the table, grab the man by the scruff of the neck, and start shaking him until he had the answers he wanted. Evidently Wilson was part of Dawson's group of "irregulars," however, so losing his temper like that would probably just get him slapped down by the massive sergeant, Evan warned himself. No matter how frustrated and impatient he was, he had to play this by Dawson's rules, whatever those might be.

But it was clear from what Wilson had said outside that something had happened to Rockly. Someone had taken the boy, along with Wilson's wife. That knowledge made a cold ball of fear grow in Evan's stomach.

Colonel Dawson looked at Wilson and said, "What about it, Frank? Do you know what Mr. Littleton's talking about?"

Wilson wiped the back of his hand across his mouth before saying, "He . . . he's crazy. I never saw him before."

"That's true enough," said Evan. "But you and your wife took in my youngest boy after my wife died. That was up close to Richland Springs. Remember, Wilson?"

While Wilson stammered meaninglessly, the colonel's eyes narrowed in suspicion. Dawson silenced him by saying coldly, "I thought you told us that boy was yours, Frank."

"Well, he is," insisted Wilson. "Practically, anyway."

Evan snorted in disgust and contempt. "Rockly's mine, and nothing you can say will change that. Now, I want to know what happened to him." The hard tone of menace in Evan's voice was plain for everyone at the table to hear.

"We . . ." Wilson swallowed hard. "We cared for that boy like he was our own. I . . . I guess I got to thinking of him as ours."

"And you told your father, as well as me, that

the child was yours," said Dawson. "But he still wouldn't pay the ransom."

The words were like a knife in Evan's gut. He didn't want to plead, but he had to know what had happened to Rockly.

Dawson didn't drag out the misery. He turned to Evan and said, "Perhaps it would be best if I explained, Mr. Littleton, just as Frank here explained it to me. Is that agreeable?"

"As long as *somebody* tells me the truth—and soon."

Relieved that he wasn't going to have to explain, Wilson reached for the bottle of liquor. He didn't bother with the glass this time. He put the bottle to his lips and tilted it up, letting the fiery stuff gurgle down his throat.

Dawson watched him for a moment with distaste, then turned back to Evan. "Mr. Wilson was on his way to El Paso with his wife and what we all assumed was their child. Their wagon was stopped and they were held up by a gang of bandits who had come across the border to raid. Mr. Wilson told the bandits that his father is a wealthy man and promised to pay them anything they wanted if only they would not kill him. The bandits agreed. However, they took Mrs. Wilson and young Rockly with them to insure that Frank would keep his pledge."

Evan looked at Wilson for a long moment, never hating anyone more in his life than now. For a man to barter for his own life with an innocent woman and child. . . !

Dawson must have seen plainly what Evan

was thinking. He said, "I assure you, Mr. Littleton, we share your dislike of Frank's choice of action. But he has since become one of us, and as a former Confederate, we will do our best to help him."

Evan forced his furious gaze away from Wilson and said, "I still don't understand. Mexican bandits kidnapped Wilson's wife and my child. How did you and your men get mixed up in this, Colonel?"

"Frank is something of a black sheep. Isn't that right, Frank?"

Wilson lowered the bottle, which was more than half-empty now. He belched but didn't say anything. His eyes were unfocused, and he seemed not to have heard the colonel's question.

"Ah, well," said Dawson, "clearly it's a good thing I'm telling this story and not our young friend here." He looked at Evan and resumed, "Frank's father owns a successful freight line that does business between El Paso and California along the old Butterfield route. As Frank said, he is quite wealthy. I've looked into the situation enough to know that that is true. Frank and his father have been estranged for several years, however, due to actions taken in Frank's youth that his father considered unsavory. It was Frank's intention to return to El Paso to heal the rift between himself and his father and demonstrate his newfound respectability by bringing along—"

"A wife and child," Evan finished for him. "Show his father that he was a family man now."

"Exactly." Dawson shook his head solemnly.

"Unfortunately, fate—in the form of those bandits—intervened, and when Frank did return to his father's house, he was not welcomed warmly."

Evan frowned, trying to control the fear he felt for Rockly so that he could follow this convoluted story and know what he had to deal with. "The old man didn't want to pay the ransom?"

"To put it bluntly, he didn't even believe that Frank *had* a wife and child." Dawson looked across the table. "How did you say he put it, Frank? That the whole thing was just another of your schemes to get your hands on his money so that you could spend it on liquor and gambling and fallen women?"

Wilson chuckled drunkenly. "F-fallen women!" he repeated. He hiccuped.

Both Dawson and the bearded sergeant grimaced in distaste. "Ah, well," said Dawson. "You can see the dilemma that faced our young friend, Mr. Littleton—though Frank was not our friend at the time, since we had not yet met him. However, we did shortly after that, and when he poured out his story to me in another establishment such as this one, I could not help but be moved by it. He was facing a terrible problem. He still is."

Evan nodded. "How does he get the prisoners back if his father won't pay the ransom." It wasn't a question.

"That's it in a nutshell, I'm afraid. It wasn't long before the answer occurred to me."

"What's that?" Evan asked, trying to keep the shakiness he was feeling out of his voice.

Dawson lifted his glass to his mouth and took a sip. Smiling over the glass at Evan, he said, "Why, we're going across the river into Mexico and taking those poor innocent captives out of there."

Evan took a deep breath. "That's what I was hoping you'd say. That offer to throw in with you still open?"

"The offer still stands," said Dawson.

"Then I'm going with you," Evan declared.

"Somehow," Dawson said slyly, "I thought you would, Mr. Littleton. I surely thought you would."

Evan was still so stunned by what he had learned in this sleepy little border village that he barely heard Dawson's invitation to join him for lunch. He accepted after a moment, and the colonel called out to the bartender to bring over some food. The sergeant stood up and wisely led Frank Wilson over to the bar. Wilson went willingly, since the bottle was now empty and there was more liquor to be had behind the bar. Evan was glad when Wilson was across the room, out of reach. His hands ached from the need to choke the life out of Wilson.

"Your self-control is admirable, my friend," commented Dawson around the unlit cheroot. "I imagine you want to kill Frank right about now."

Evan nodded curtly. "He's got it coming."

"Can't say as I blame you." Dawson seemed more relaxed now, less the stiff-postured officer. "But killing him wouldn't accomplish a thing, and we may even need him later on, once we've located the woman and the boy."

"His name is Rockly," Evan said harshly.

"Yes, of course. I remember you saying that." Dawson studied Evan for a long moment, a shrewd expression on his face. "Were you by chance an officer, Mr. Littleton?"

"Enlisted man," Evan said with a shake of his head. "Never made it above corporal, and that for just a week or so before the Yankees took me prisoner."

"I have a feeling that if you had not been captured, if you had fought on for the full duration of the war, there would have been some field promotions. I believe you would have been a captain, at least, by the time it was all over."

"Never had any interest in giving orders or being in charge. Just wanted to do what was right and get through it alive."

"Ah, but no one gets through it alive, so to speak, not in the end. Death is the ultimate victor."

Evan looked straight at the colonel. "A man can die without losing."

Dawson shrugged.

The discussion was interrupted then by the arrival of the bartender, who brought a couple of platters full of beans, tortillas, and tamales out of the cantina's back room. He carried them over to the table and set them down in front of Evan and Dawson. Dawson dropped a coin on the table, and the bartender scooped it up almost before it had a chance to rattle.

"It's a good thing you came along when you

did," Dawson said as he motioned for Evan to dig in. "We're gathering our supplies, and we'll be heading across the border tomorrow. I already have scouts on the other side of the river trying to locate the bandits responsible for capturing Mrs. Wilson and Rockly."

"You really think you can find 'em?"

"Of course. My cavalry unit never had any trouble locating the enemy during the war. It's all a matter of proper reconnaissance."

Evan hoped the colonel was right, but he didn't share Dawson's level of confidence. Tracking down a gang of Mexican *bandidos* was a lot different than engaging a bunch of Yankees who were blundering around, hundreds of miles from their home.

The food was surprisingly good, although the peppers cooked in the beans and the tamales were so hot that they made Evan gasp for breath a few times. He was glad the bartender also brought over a couple of buckets of beer, so that he was able to put out the fire in his mouth. The beer didn't help the blaze in his belly much, though.

He glanced at the bar. Wilson was slumped over it, snoring. Evan's jaw tightened. When this was all over, he promised himself, he had a score to settle with Frank Wilson.

While they were eating, Dawson said, "I must admit to a bit of curiosity over your *lack* of curiosity, Mr. Littleton. Don't you want to know how our little group got together?"

Evan shrugged. "Everybody's got to be somewhere. Figured you came out here after the war was over because there wasn't much left for you back where you came from."

The colonel sighed, and for a second Evan caught a glimpse of hate and pain in his eyes. "Not much left," he said. "Nothing left would be closer to the truth. The Yankees took everything . . ." He gave a little shake of his head. "But it wasn't strictly personal concerns that led the sergeant and me and some of the men who had fought with us to head west, picking up some new friends who shared our ideals along the way. No, sir. We are on a mission, a sacred mission for the Confederacy."

"There's not any more Confederacy," Evan pointed out.

Dawson touched the breast of his buckskin jacket. "There is in here, Mr. Littleton. In our heart of hearts, the South was never defeated. I have the greatest respect for General Lee, but I do not accept his capitulation at Appomattox. The war still rages."

Evan frowned. During the train ride to Atlanta, and during the long walk after he was released from Union custody, he had heard talk about how some of the Confederate officers were planning to turn renegade and continue the war by any means possible. It appeared that Colonel Randolph Dawson was one of those men. But what could he do to strike back at the North way out here in West Texas?

Then the answer came to him, and he said, "You're going to collect a reward from Wilson's father when you bring back the woman and the boy, aren't you?"

Dawson grinned. "Quite astute of you, Mr. Littleton. Once Frank's dear papa sees that Frank was telling the truth, I'm sure he will be grateful enough to reward us properly. Fighting a war *does* require funds, unfortunately. Idealism alone just isn't sufficient."

"And if Wilson's father doesn't go along with that idea?"

"Well, then, we shall be disappointed, of course. But insuring the safety of an innocent woman and child does provide its own reward in a sense of satisfaction at a job well done."

"Then you'll turn the prisoners over to Wilson either way?"

"Certainly. We're Southern gentlemen, Evan . . . may I call you Evan? . . . not Yankee barbarians. I promise you, our real motivation for venturing across the border is to rescue Frank's wife and your boy. Nothing else really matters."

Evan wished he could believe the colonel. He wanted to think that Dawson was telling the truth.

But he was still very glad that he was going to be traveling along with these men when they crossed the Rio Grande in search of his son and Frank Wilson's wife.

19

Evan quickly saw that although Colonel Randolph Dawson was in command of this group of former Confederates, it was the sergeant who actually did most of the work. The burly, bearded ex-noncom kept the men in line, saw that their horses were cared for and the supplies for the trip across the border were carefully packed on mules, and gave the actual order to move out the next morning as the men left Acala and headed for the river, some half a mile distant.

Evan had spent the night before in the Confederate camp just outside the village. The men had pitched tents and built campfires as if they were back in Alabama or Georgia, rather than the valley of the Rio Grande in far West Texas. Evan had shared a tent with a couple of men who were a far cry from the swaggering gunnies called Billings and Clegg. His tentmates had been members of Colonel Dawson's company during the war, and they still maintained military discipline.

Billings and Clegg were in camp, too, and

several times during the evening Evan had caught them looking at him with hatred in their eyes. He had made them look bad, and the desire for vengeance was strong in them.

He would have to keep an eye on those two, Evan told himself, if he didn't want a bullet in the back before they returned from Mexico.

The Rio Grande hardly looked impressive enough to live up to its name, nor to be the boundary between two nations. The stream was shallow and not too wide. The horses splashed across it easily, and just like that, Evan was in another country for the first time. Didn't really seem to make much difference, he mused. The ground was still dry and hard and dusty, except where irrigation ditches had been dug from the river, and the mesquite trees were just as scrubby as those on the Texas side, the dried bean pods rattling together as a soft wind blew.

"We'll rendezvous with our scouts tonight in a village about eight miles from here," Dawson explained as he rode alongside Evan. He had motioned for Evan to take this position of honor with him as they rode in front of the other men. The sergeant was directly behind them, then the other men trailed out, following in a rough formation.

"What about the Mexican authorities?" asked Evan. "They may not take it kindly that a bunch of Americans are riding around loose in their country."

"This area is patrolled only by scattered troops of *rurales* who care more for the bribes they collect from roving gangs of bandits than they do for actually enforcing any sort of law and order," Dawson said disdainfully. "Lone travelers or smaller groups might be well advised to avoid them, but they won't bother such a large, well-armed group as ourselves."

Evan hoped the colonel was right. They would have their hands full enough just finding the bandits who had kidnapped Rockly and Suellen Wilson, without having to worry about fighting off Mexican troops.

The only people they saw during the day were farmers working in the fields along the river or walking alongside carts being pulled by burros as they got farther away from the Rio Grande. The *peons*, who were all barefooted and who all wore similar white shirts and trousers and broad-brimmed straw *sombreros*, kept their eyes downcast as the horsemen rode by, not even wanting to acknowledge the existence of these strangers. If the *rurales* were anything like the Yankee State Police, Evan could understand that feeling. For common folks, it was always better not to get involved with the authorities, especially when those authorities were both brutal and corrupt.

Given the time of year it was, the sun seemed awfully hot as it rose to its zenith above them. Evan supposed that was because of how far south they were. But there was snow on the caps of some of the mountains that rose in front of them; up there it would be cold all year round, he thought.

The bandits had strongholds in those mountains, he recalled Dawson saying. Evan hoped—maybe even prayed a little bit—that wherever Rockly was, the boy was warm and dry and safe.

But even if that was the case, sooner or later Rockly's luck would run out. The bandits might get tired of waiting for a ransom that never came and decide to kill their captives just to simplify matters.

And it was possible, thought Evan in his bleaker moments, that Rockly was already dead, had in fact been killed soon after his capture.

If that was the case, he would have his vengeance, he vowed. He would see each and every one of those bandits dead and burning in hell if it took the rest of his life.

The terrain gradually sloped up, away from the river and its broad valley. By midafternoon, Evan, Dawson, and the others were riding through hillier country. The ground was still sandy, but there were more outcroppings of red and brown rock. Scrubby mesquites had been replaced by even scrubbier cactus plants. There were still cultivated fields here and there, next to isolated *jacals*, but the fields were small and not very productive. This far from the river, it would be hard to scratch a living from the ground, but that didn't stop people from trying. These little patches of land were all they had.

A little later, the buildings of a village came into sight, and Evan knew that must be where Dawson planned to meet the scouts he had sent ahead to search for the bandits. As they drew closer, Evan saw that the village consisted primarily of a mission with a bell tower, a couple of cantinas, and a few other squat adobe buildings. A handful of shacks huddled nearby in the shade of some withered trees.

"If my intelligence reports are correct—and I have no reason to suspect otherwise—this is the village of Dominguez," said Dawson. "Our scouts should arrive here tonight, if in fact they aren't in the village already."

There were only a few people to be seen as Evan, the colonel, and the rest of the men rode into Dominguez. "Where is everybody?" asked the sergeant.

"*Siesta* time," Evan said, remembering the custom from his days in South Texas. He summoned up a grin from somewhere. "It can last all afternoon, if you work it right."

The sergeant snorted. "These people could make more of themselves if they worked a little harder."

Evan didn't say anything, but he figured that the sergeant, who was likely from Alabama the same as Colonel Dawson, had never experienced summer in this region. He would be singing a different tune if he knew how hot it could get around here from May to September. It was warm enough today to bring a sweat to a man's brow, and winter was just about within spitting distance.

There was a communal well dug next to the mission, and a couple of women were lowering buckets into it. As the newcomers rode past, Clegg called out to them, "Hey, *señoritas*, you're mighty pretty. What say you come see me after a while?"

The women wore long skirts and shawls with hoods that came up and shaded their faces, so it was difficult to tell just how pretty they really were. They turned away, hunching their shoulders slightly and doing their best to ignore the strange Americans. With a frown, Dawson turned in his saddle and said quietly, "That'll be enough of that behavior, Sergeant."

"Yes, sir," barked the sergeant. He turned his head to speak to Clegg, and his voice was anything but soft as he said, "Shut up, Clegg! Show these people some respect."

"But, Sarge, they're just Mexicans."

"I gave you an order, mister."

Evan glanced back, saw Clegg's face harden with anger at the rebuke. Clegg didn't say anything except a muttered, "Yes, sir."

What he had told Dawson the day before was true, thought Evan. Men like Clegg and Billings didn't really have any place with these others. But as Dawson had said, a commander had to make do with the forces available to him. Evan didn't hold out much hope for the eventual success of the colonel's mission if he had to depend on gunnies like those two, however.

Truth to tell, Evan thought as he dismounted along with the others, he didn't figure Dawson's campaign against the Union had much of a chance anyway. The war was over; it made no sense to keep fighting it. Refusing to admit defeat was one thing. Being a pure, dumb-blasted fool was another.

Evan wasn't going to say as much to the colonel, though, not while his hopes of rescuing Rockly and the Wilson woman were riding squarely on the shoulders of Dawson and his men. There was no way Evan could get them out of the hands of the bandits without help. For now, he would just have to put up with annoyances such as Clegg and Billings.

The colonel was on his way into one of the cantinas, trailed by Evan and the other Americans, when a short, plump man in a black broadcloth suit, a limp white shirt, and a string tie came hurrying up to them. The man even had shoes on his feet, but no socks. "*Señores*," he said, "welcome to our village. I am the *alcalde* . . . how you say, the mayor . . . and if there is anything I can do for you—"

"We're just here to meet someone, Your Honor," Dawson said with a smile. "We aren't looking for trouble."

"No, *señor*, of course not. I did not mean to imply that you were. If there is anything we of this humble village can do for you—"

"Just some drinks and food," said Dawson, "and perhaps a place to stay tonight."

"*Si, naturalamente*. This cantina is the best between here and Mexico City. It is owned by my brother, who will treat you most fairly."

Evan felt like spitting on the ground. The eagerness of this man to please left a bad taste in his mouth. Clearly, Dominguez was a poor place. The *alcalde* hoped that these strangers would leave some gold here to fatten his pockets and the pockets of a select few others, including his cantina-owning brother.

Dawson was a diplomat as well as a soldier. He smiled and nodded at the mayor of Dominguez and traded compliments with the man as the sergeant ushered all the other members of the group into the cantina. The eyes of the skinny bartender fairly lit up as he saw the men filing into the dim, shadowy interior of the place.

Most of the newcomers headed straight for the bar and called for tequila or *cerveza*. Evan didn't feel much like joining them. He might be part of the group on a temporary basis, but he wasn't really one of them.

Besides, Frank Wilson was at the bar, standing next to Clegg and Billings, and Evan had been careful to keep his distance from the man all day. Being around Wilson was a sore trial for his self-control.

Evan settled down at one of the tables, and the sergeant joined him, somewhat to Evan's surprise. The sergeant hadn't seemed overly friendly to him so far, but to be fair about it, neither had the man been hostile to him. When you came right down to it, the sergeant didn't seem to have much in the way of feelings except for devotion to Colonel Dawson and an eagerness to follow the colonel's commands.

No, there was one other thing, Evan realized as he watched the sergeant glance toward Frank Wilson and then grimace slightly. The man shared Evan's distaste for Wilson.

At the bar, Clegg and Billings were laughing and talking loudly to each other as they stood flanking Wilson, who took no part in the conversation. Instead, Wilson used both hands to pick up the glass the bartender placed in front of him. He lifted it to his lips and gulped down the drink greedily. All day long, he had appeared pale, washed-out, sick. Now, for the first time, some color came back into his face, and he smiled as he replaced the glass on the bar and asked for another drink.

"I hate to see any man in a shape like that," the sergeant said in a low voice, so that only Evan could hear. "Such a waste."

"I never met Wilson before yesterday," said Evan, "but I'd be willing to bet there wasn't much there to start with."

"You're probably right." The sergeant looked across the table at Evan. "Are you going to kill him when this is all over?"

For a moment, Evan didn't answer, then he said honestly, "I don't know."

Before either of them could say anything else, the colonel came into the cantina, having finally shaken free of the *alcalde*. He came directly to the table shared by Evan and the sergeant and sat down without being asked to join them. "Fetch a bottle, Sergeant," he said.

"Yes, sir."

While the sergeant went over to the bar, Dawson looked at Evan and said, "You must be getting rather anxious."

"Nervous as a long-tailed cat on a porch full of rocking chairs, my daddy used to say."

Dawson chuckled. "I know the feeling. I've experienced it before battle many times, and I see no shame in admitting that. True bravery is going ahead despite your fears."

Evan didn't want to debate philosophy with the man. He said, "Those scouts of yours aren't in town yet, are they?"

"The *alcalde* assures me that no white men have arrived in Dominguez other than ourselves. But as I told you, the rendezvous was not planned until tonight at the earliest. The possibility exists that we may have to wait here several days for my men to return."

Evan sighed. The prospect of such a delay didn't sit well with him.

"Patience, my friend, patience. Once we know exactly where the stronghold of the bandits is located, then we'll be able to proceed with a plan of attack."

"I thought you figured to slip in there, grab the prisoners, and slip back out again."

"That would be ideal. This is, however, not a perfect world. We must be prepared for any contingency."

Evan had never cared for the few strategy sessions he had been in on back during the war, before his capture by the Yankees. His brain had never been able to wrap itself around the sort of tactics that military commanders usually favored. To him, the simplest solution had always been the best one.

"That's your department, Colonel, not mine," he said now, adding silently, *As long as you don't do anything that's liable to get my boy killed.*

The sergeant returned to the table with a bottle of tequila, and it was followed soon after by platters of food brought by a serving girl. She wore a long red skirt that swirled around her bare feet as they brushed across the dirt floor and a white blouse that left her shoulders and the upper half of her bosom bare. To no one's surprise, especially Evan's, the girl's arrival brought hoots of approval from Clegg, Billings, and several of the other men. Evan looked at her, saw that she was about Dinah's age, and felt a pang of loneliness. He missed his children and hoped they were all right back there on Clive Cartmill's ranch in the Davis Mountains.

There was nothing to do but eat, drink, and wait, so that was what Evan did. The colonel talked quite a bit, stories about the war and about his life as an overseer on a plantation in Alabama before the war. Evan was surprised to discover that Dawson hadn't *owned* a plantation himself; usually it was the wealthy planters who had wound up as officers in the Confederate army. Some of the Rebel officers had been in the Union army, and others had been cadets at West Point before hearing the call that summoned them back to their homeland; but as always, wealth and privilege had played a part in who received promotions, just as it did in countless other situations.

Night settled down over the village. The day's ride hadn't been a particularly hard one, but Evan was tired anyway. Yet, he was too keyed up to sleep, so he sat in the cantina with Dawson and the sergeant. Some of the other men continued to drink, while others drifted off in search of female companionship. Eventually, since there was an adobe wall close behind him, Evan leaned his chair back and tilted his hat down over his eyes, half dozing.

He must have been more tired than he thought, because as he came awake suddenly he realized he had been sound asleep for an unknown time. He was alone at the table. A glance around the room showed him that a few of the men from the colonel's troop of irregulars were still in the cantina, including Frank Wilson, who was passed out with his head lying on one of the other tables. Colonel Dawson and the sergeant stood in the open doorway with the *alcalde*. The colonel was talking in low voices with the village official, and after a moment they stepped outside, where two more men, shadowy figures in the darkness, joined them. Evan could hear none of the conversation. He stood up and moved toward the doorway. Those strangers had to be the scouts Dawson had sent out looking for the bandits.

Before Evan could reach the door, one of the newcomers nodded and said, "Right, Colonel." He and his companion turned and walked quickly to the hitch racks where the horses were tied. They began unsaddling two of the mounts. Evan watched them, suddenly wishing he could see them better in the thick shadows. There was something familiar about one of the men . . .

Dawson turned to him and said, "There you are, Evan. I didn't want to wake you, you seemed to be sleeping so soundly. The scouts have reported in, just as I expected."

"Did they find out where the bandits are hiding?" Evan asked tensely.

"Of course they did. The bandits have a hideout some fifteen miles south of here in the mountains. With some hard riding tomorrow, we can reach the area by nightfall and get ready for our raid on their camp. Then, as soon as the captives are freed, we'll make a dash for the border."

Evan felt a surge of impatience. "Why don't we start down there tonight?"

"No point in pushing the men or the horses until we have to," said the colonel. "We'll have to wait until well after midnight before we can make our move against the bandit stronghold anyway. I want utter blackness when we launch our raid, so the moon has to have set."

Evan grimaced and rubbed a hand across his face. Dawson's words made sense, but waiting was hard, mighty hard, especially now that he knew his son was probably only fifteen miles away.

The scouts had swapped saddles on a pair of horses, trading their own mounts for fresh animals. They swung up into their saddles and snapped brisk salutes at the colonel, then turned the horses and rode out of Dominguez, heading south. Evan asked, "Where are they going?"

"Just to keep an eye on the bandit camp," said Dawson. "That way, if the situation changes, they'll be able to warn us before we go riding into trouble."

Evan nodded. That was a smart move on the colonel's part.

Dawson clapped a hand on Evan's shoulder and steered him back into the cantina. "Be patient, my friend," he said as he took a cigar from his jacket pocket. "Soon you'll be together again with your young lad."

Evan sighed and nodded. Finding Rockly couldn't come soon enough to suit him.

In the distance, he heard the hoofbeats of the scouts' horses fading into the Mexican night.

20

E van woke to the feel of a gun barrel being pressed to his temple. Somewhere nearby, he heard a startled exclamation and then the ugly sound of something hard hitting flesh and bone.

"Do not move, *señor*, or I will be forced to splatter your brains all over the floor of this mission, and that would be a sacrilege."

The voice was harsh and heavily accented, and the smell of peppers and unwashed flesh filled Evan's nostrils as the man knelt beside him and held the gun to his head. Evan's eyelids jerked open as he fought to control the impulse to sit up and reach for his gun. Giving in to that impulse would just get him killed. Movement of *any* sort might make the man pull the trigger, so Evan lay as still as possible, motionless except for his eyes and the rapid rise and fall of his chest.

"Ah, that is wise, *señor*," said the gunman. "You know that I will kill you if you cause any trouble."

"I'm not here to cause trouble," Evan said, although that wasn't strictly true, he supposed.

The man kneeling beside him was a Mexican. A *sombrero* decorated with embroidered beadwork was strapped tightly to his head. Bandoliers of filled ammunition loops crisscrossed his chest over the short jacket he wore. The gun in his hand was a Walker Colt, its cylinder etched with a portrait of Texas Rangers fighting Indians. The Mexican must have taken it off a dead Ranger, Evan thought, somewhat irrelevantly; that was the only way he could have gotten one of those specially made revolvers.

"I am Augustin Morales," said the man. "These are my *compadres*."

Evan glanced to the side and saw that half a dozen other Mexicans dressed and armed like Morales had come into the mission and were holding their guns on Evan's companions. Colonel Dawson and the sergeant were both sitting up in their bedrolls, glaring angrily at the Mexicans. Blood oozed from a long gash on the sergeant's forehead, and Evan guessed that the sound he had heard as he was being jolted from sleep had been one of the raiders pistol-whipping the sergeant.

"I'm in command of this patrol, Morales," the colonel said sharply. "If you have business with us, you need to speak to me."

Morales grinned down at Evan and inclined his head toward Dawson. "This one, he is full of himself, no? I guess I will have to go talk with him. You be good, and my men will not shoot you."

"Can I sit up?" asked Evan.

Morales shrugged and nodded. "Do not bother reaching for your gun. It is no longer there."

Sure enough, Evan saw when he glanced at the coiled shell belt beside him, the holster was empty. As Morales straightened, Evan saw his Colt tucked behind the Mexican's broad leather belt.

Slowly, Evan sat up and looked around. All the men sleeping in the church had been taken by surprise. The colonel had left a guard outside the night before when part of the group had bedded down here. Evan wondered what had happened to the man, but even as he asked himself that question, the probable answer came to him. More than likely, the unlucky sentry was lying outside somewhere, his throat cut.

Morales sauntered over to stand in front of Dawson. "What is your name, *jefe*?" The scorn in his voice made the colonel flush brick red with anger.

"I'm Colonel Randolph Dawson of the Confederate Army," he snapped. "It may interest you to know, Morales, that your government has offered asylum to me and my men."

"And it may interest you to know, Colonel, that I have nothing to do with any government. They leave me alone, and I leave them alone." Morales struck his chest lightly with a clenched fist. "I am a law unto myself."

"You are a bandit, sir, a bandit and a kidnapper. Where are the prisoners you've been holding illegally?"

Evan's heart sank. As soon as he had woken up good and looked around, he had been afraid that these Mexicans were the same men who had taken Rockly and Wilson's wife. Now he had it confirmed for him as Morales spat on the floor and asked, "Where is the ransom we were to be paid? Well, *Colonel* Dawson?"

"I never agreed to pay you any ransom. That was Frank Wilson." Dawson's tone made it clear just how little he respected Wilson.

"I care nothing for that," Morales shot back. "All I want is the money that was promised me. Then the woman and the *muchacho* shall go free."

Evan's spirits lifted a little. Morales had indicated that Rockly was still alive, as well as Suellen Wilson. However, Evan knew better than to place too much faith in anything the bandit leader said. Evan was going to have to see his son with his own eyes before he would truly believe that Rockly was all right.

Dawson ignored Morales' question about the ransom money and said, "Where are the rest of my men?"

"You want to see them?" asked Morales. "Very well. Come along." He gestured curtly with the barrel of the revolver he held.

All of the Mexicans stepped back as Evan, Dawson, the sergeant, and the other Americans got to their feet. Several of the bandits held rifles, and the others had all drawn their pistols. Dawson and the rest of his group had been disarmed, just like Evan. Under the circumstances, they had no choice but to file out of the mission. They were covered closely by the bandits, and there was nothing they could do except cooperate—for the moment.

But sooner or later, they would have a chance,

Evan told himself, and when that time came, they would have to seize the moment without hesitation. It wouldn't come again, more than likely.

Evan had known it was morning because of the sunlight slanting in through the narrow, stained-glass windows of the mission. Now, as he and the other men stepped outside, he squinted against the brightness of day. They were herded like cattle toward the well, where another group of men waited. Evan saw Frank Wilson, Clegg, and Billings among them, all three of them looking nervous and scared. They were being covered by another half-dozen Mexicans, the rest of the gang led by Morales. Clearly, the bandit leader had planned well, striking early in the morning while the Americans were still asleep. It was equally clear that Morales had known where to find all of the men he was after, which meant that he must have had help.

The pudgy little *alcalde* of Dominguez came hurrying up to Morales, practically bowing and scraping as he did so, plainly afraid of the bandit chieftain. "Was the information I gave you sufficient, *Señor* Morales?" the *alcalde* asked anxiously.

"It was *muy bueno, mi amigo*," replied Morales with a grin. "You did well to send a rider to me when these strangers arrived in your village. I am so grateful that my men and I shall protect you and your people from any marauders who might come this way in the future."

Evan knew that Morales was promising he and

his own gang wouldn't raid the village again, at least not for a while. The *alcalde* was so grateful that he was hopping back and forth from one foot to the other, practically dancing with joy and relief.

So it had been a trap almost right from the start. The mayor had sent a rider to warn Morales yesterday afternoon as the Americans were approaching the village, Evan reasoned. Then Morales and his men had ridden all night in order to be in position early this morning to capture the group of Americans in a combination of quick strikes. Dawson had been clearly outclassed as a tactician this time, and Evan could see that knowledge gnawing on the colonel. Dawson looked furious.

How they had been caught didn't really matter to Evan. All he cared about was his son, and he didn't see Rockly anywhere. Had Morales left him and the Wilson woman back in the outlaw stronghold? Something about that possibility didn't seem right to Evan. Morales had asked Dawson about the ransom, indicating that the bandit hadn't completely given up on getting the money Frank Wilson had promised him. If Morales thought it was possible that the Americans who had ridden into Dominguez had brought the ransom with them, wouldn't he have brought the prisoners with him so that he could complete the swap? Unless, of course, the prisoners really were dead and Morales had never had any intention of returning them safely, ransom or no ransom. Unfortunately, that was just as possible as any other explanation, Evan thought grimly.

The uncertainty was driving him mad. He stepped forward, ignoring the rifle and pistol barrels that swung menacingly toward him, and said in a loud voice, "Morales."

The bandit leader turned toward him and grinned. "Ah, my friend from inside the mission. Something about you struck me as dangerous, *amigo*, which is why I chose to awaken you personally. What do you want?"

"The boy you're holding," Evan said. "He's not Wilson's son. He's mine."

Morales didn't bother concealing his surprise. "But that one said the *muchacho* was his," he said with a contemptuous gesture toward Frank Wilson. "When he was pleading for his life, he offered us his wife and son."

"Wilson may have claimed the boy, but I'm his father," said Evan. "Bring him out here and I'll prove it."

It was a gamble, but it paid off. Morales turned and spoke sharply in Spanish to one of his men, who hurried off. Hoping against hope, Evan waited to see what was going to happen. The man Morales had dispatched on the errand vanished into one of the cantinas. A few moments later, he reappeared, prodding two figures in front of him.

Evan's heart practically stopped in his chest. One of the figures was a little boy around eight years old, with reddish-brown hair and a freckled face. Evan called, "Rockly!"

The boy had been trudging along in front of

the Mexican, eyes downcast, feet scuffing the dirt. At the sound of Evan's voice, his head jerked up, and even at this distance, Evan could see his eyes widen in surprise. The boy cried, "Pa!" and dashed forward.

One of the bandits moved to stop him, but Morales motioned the man back. Rockly ran across the little plaza that separated the mission and the well from the cantinas and the other buildings. Evan stepped forward to meet him and scooped the little boy up in his arms. Rockly's arms went around Evan's neck and hugged him tightly. Evan felt his son's tears on his cheek.

"Are . . . are you a ghost?" asked Rockly in a whisper.

"I'm no ghost," Evan told him. "I'm real, son." He could barely choke out the words.

"You came for me," Rockly said. "I dreamed you would, Pa, but I never really thought—" A fresh round of sobs shook him.

"It's all right, son." Evan patted Rockly's back, stroked his hair. "It's all right now. I'm here for you."

Morales came over to them, frowning in thought. "The boy is yours, there is no doubt of that," he said. "Which leaves me with a bit of a problem, *señor*. You do not look like a man who can pay a ransom, for yourself or your son."

"I'm about as far from rich as you can get," admitted Evan.

"The woman, she is your wife?"

Evan glanced at Suellen Wilson. She was blond and probably would be pretty under other circumstances, but now her hair was tangled and windblown, her eyes were red and puffy from crying, and there was an ugly bruise on her jaw. Her once-fancy traveling gown was dirty, torn, and disheveled. Obviously, she had been treated pretty rough by the bandits, and Evan felt sorry for her. Her choice of a husband hadn't worked out very well for her.

"No, she's not my wife," he told Morales. "She's really married to Wilson."

"Then she is worth a great deal more to me than you and the boy, no?" Morales lifted his gun.

For one terrifying second, Evan thought Morales was going to shoot them down right here and now. He tensed, ready to shove Rockly to the side and make a probably futile leap for the bandit leader. But then Morales eased down the hammer of the gun and holstered it. Evan started to breathe again.

"What are we going to do with you?" Morales asked, as much to himself as to Evan. "It is a long walk to the border, especially for a child. Take your son and your horse, *amigo*, and leave this place."

Evan could scarcely believe his ears. Morales was letting him go, and more important than that, allowing him to take Rockly with him.

But they weren't the only ones in trouble here, and again somewhat to his disbelief, Evan heard himself asking, "What about the colonel and the other men? What about Wilson and his wife?"

The face of the bandit leader hardened. "These

men came armed to a village that is under my protection. For all I know, they are American invaders."

"That's insane," said Dawson hotly. "I told you, the Mexican government has extended the hand of friendship to members of the Confederacy."

"And I told you that I recognize no government, especially that of a French dog such as Maximilian!" Morales reached for his gun again. "Wilson and the woman will live—for now. Perhaps his father can still be persuaded to pay the ransom. But as for the rest of you . . ."

Morales lifted his gun and pointed it straight at Dawson.

Evan stood tensely to one side. Morales planned to execute Dawson, the sergeant, and the other men. How could Evan turn his back on them, even though it meant saving his own son? But how could he place Rockly in further danger by trying to help the colonel?

The next instant, the decision was taken out of Evan's hands by the whipcrack of a rifle shot. Morales' head jerked back so sharply that the tightly strapped *sombrero* fell off. Blood welled from the hole in his forehead as he swayed back and forth for a second before falling over backward.

Evan was wheeling away from Morales before the echo of the shot even began to die away. He saw the puff of powdersmoke coming from the bell tower of the mission. Another shot rang out, then another and another, coming so quickly that they had to be from a repeater. Somebody up there in the tower was making a Henry rifle do everything except sing and dance.

Nor was the rifleman in the bell tower alone. More shots came from one of the cantinas. Carrying Rockly clutched tightly to his chest, Evan sprinted for the nearest cover, which happened to be the low stone wall around the well. Several of the bandits had already fallen, driven off their feet by the lead thrown by the hidden riflemen. Fighting broke out all around Evan as Dawson's men took advantage of the opportunity to jump their captors. Blood and confusion were suddenly everywhere.

Evan circled the well, dropped to his knees, and placed Rockly against the stone wall. "Stay here," Evan told the boy, and he hoped Rockly understood the seriousness of the command. Rockly seemed to; his eyes were big with fear, but he was able to nod calmly.

On hands and knees, Evan moved around the well. One of the Mexicans tumbled to the ground beside him, the man's head flopping limply on his neck. Evan saw the crimson flood pumping from the man's throat where a bullet had torn through it. The bandit's right arm was outstretched toward Evan, and lying loosely in the hand, as if being offered to Evan as a present, was a gun. Evan reached out, snatched the weapon from the dead fingers of its former owner.

Instinct sent him rolling to the side as one of the bandits loomed over him. The Mexican's face was contorted with rage as he fired the pistol in his hand. The slug thudded into the hard ground where Evan had been an instant before. Then Evan was triggering the gun in his hand, feeling it buck back against his palm as his shot tore into the bandit's abdomen and angled up sharply through the man's body. The Mexican screamed and stumbled a few steps, his gun blasting harmlessly into the ground again as his finger contracted involuntarily, before he collapsed.

Evan rolled again and scrambled up onto one knee. The fusillade from the hidden riflemen had stopped, probably because they had emptied their Henrys and were reloading. But they had already done a lot of damage, and Dawson's men had done more when they jumped the bandits. Evan saw the sergeant with his hands tight around the necks of two Mexicans as he smashed their heads together. Not far away, Colonel Dawson stood coolly with a liberated revolver in his hand. He took deliberate aim at the black-suited figure of the *alcalde* of Dominguez as the man tried to run away. Dawson fired, and the mayor was thrown forward by the impact of the bullet as it struck him in the back, bored through his body, and burst out his chest in a spray of blood. The *alcalde* flopped onto his face, dead before he hit the ground.

Seeing no immediate threat, Evan got to his feet and hurried around the well. Rockly was right where Evan had left him, watching the dying battle with wide, staring eyes. Evan crouched beside him and asked, "You all right, son?"

Rockly looked up and nodded. He reached out and took hold of Evan's free arm, clutching it tightly. "Is . . . is it almost over?" he asked.

"Almost," replied Evan.

As a matter of fact, only a few of the bandits were still on their feet. The others were sprawled on the ground, motionless and bloody, around the well and in the plaza. As Evan and Rockly watched, more shots rang out from the bell tower, and the remaining bandits went spinning off their feet.

"Now it's over," Evan told his son.

Several of the Americans were down, too, including Frank Wilson, who clutched a bloody thigh and sobbed uncontrollably. At least Wilson was alive, thought Evan. The other men who had fallen weren't that lucky. All of them were dead, along with the bandits who had been led by Augustin Morales.

Colonel Dawson was alive and apparently unharmed, however, as he strode toward the well. "Were you hit, Evan?" he asked as he came up to them.

Evan shook his head. "Not even a scratch, Colonel, and the boy's all right, too. We were mighty lucky."

"Yes, we were." Dawson turned his head. "Sergeant—report!"

The sergeant was moving among the bodies of the bandits. He had a gun in his hand, and as he stopped beside one of the Mexicans who was still moaning faintly and moving around a little, he pointed it at the man's head and fired. The wounded bandit jerked and then lay still.

"All the enemy are dead, Colonel," said the sergeant. "We've won the day."

"Casualties?"

"Three of our men killed, five wounded, none seriously except for Wilson—and he'll live, I reckon, if we patch up that hole in his leg."

"See to it," ordered the colonel. He looked around. "What about Mrs. Wilson?"

Evan had been wondering the same thing himself. He glanced around and saw Suellen Wilson huddled at the base of one of the small trees near the well. At first he thought she had been wounded, but then he saw that she had wrapped her arms around the trunk of the tree, closed her eyes, and was still holding on for dear life. Her lips were moving, and Evan figured she was praying. He didn't see any blood on her.

Dawson walked over to her, bent down, and touched her lightly on the shoulder. Suellen jerked and clutched the tree even tighter.

"It's all right, Mrs. Wilson," Dawson told her gently. "Your troubles are over. The Mexicans are all dead, and you're among friends."

Gradually, Dawson's quietly spoken words penetrated the woman's stunned brain, and she opened her eyes. Smiling, Dawson helped her to her feet. She began to sob as she buried her face against his chest. Looking slightly uncomfortable, the colonel peeled her away from him and handed her over to the sergeant, who looked even more daunted by the task of comforting a weeping woman. The sergeant was not one to refuse a command, however, even one such as this. He put a brawny arm around Suellen's shoulders and led her away.

Dawson came back over to Evan, who stood with a hand on Rockly's shoulder. "I told you, Evan, I like to be prepared for any contingency," the colonel said.

Evan frowned. "Looked to me like you were as surprised as any of us when those bandits jumped us this morning," he said bluntly.

"Indeed. But two of my men weren't surprised, and their actions—which I had prepared them to take—turned the tide of victory for us."

"The scouts," said Evan, realizing now who the hidden riflemen had to have been.

"Precisely. They must have seen what the bandits were up to last night and managed to get into position in time to launch the first attack before it was too late." Dawson nodded toward the cantina. "Here comes one of them now, and I'm sure the other one is climbing down from that bell tower."

Evan saw the scout who had come in through the back of the cantina and caught the bandits in a crossfire being greeted by his friends. He was a slender, bearded man, and he grinned sheepishly as several of the other Americans slapped him on the back and congratulated him.

More shouts of acclamation made Evan turn his head toward the mission. He saw the young man who emerged from the big adobe building, Henry rifle canted back over his right shoulder. The second scout was tall and rangy, and his hat was pushed back on a thatch of shaggy black hair. Not for the first time today, Evan's heart seemed to stop beating. Looking at the young man was like looking into a mirror and seeing twenty years fall away.

The second scout was his son Thad. Thad, who had followed his father off to war and died . . .

21

But like his father, who was also supposed to have died in the war, Thad was still alive. *Alive!*

Coming after everything else that had happened, not only today but also all the traveling and danger since he had first discovered what had happened to his family, the sudden knowledge that his oldest son was not dead after all was almost too much for Evan to comprehend. Sure that his eyes were playing tricks on him, he rubbed them hard with his knuckles and blinked away the moisture that had sprung into them. The tears came right back, though, because standing before him was undoubtedly Thad, and the young man seemed every bit as shocked as Evan was.

"Pa?" he asked in a strained, husky whisper.

"Son," Evan said. He stepped toward Thad, his arms outstretched.

He wasn't ready for the punch that exploded in his face.

Thad's fist caught him flush on the jaw and

sent him reeling backward. Evan tripped and sat down hard. Bright lights flashed in his brain, and he was shaking his head groggily as Rockly rushed past him, yelling, "Doggone you, Thad, you hit Pa!"

Thad grabbed his little brother and held him off as Rockly swung wildly at him, flailing with his fists. "Rockly!" exclaimed Thad, evidently almost as surprised to see his brother here in this formerly sleepy little Mexican village as he had been to come face to face with his father. "Rockly, what are you doin' here?"

Rockly stopped flailing and gaped up at Thad, who, until moments earlier, he had thought was dead along with Evan. "Thad," Rockly said, and the sound was almost a moan.

Dropping the rifle he still held, Thad pulled Rockly into his arms, lifting the little boy off his feet. He was laughing and crying at the same time.

Which was the same thing Evan felt like doing. He sat there on the hard ground and rubbed his aching jaw and watched as his sons began to whoop in excitement and pound each other on the back. At least Thad hadn't greeted his little brother with a clout in the jaw, Evan thought ruefully.

"Excuse me," said Colonel Dawson from behind Evan, "but what in blazes is going on here?"

Evan looked back up over his shoulder at the colonel. "Those are my boys," he said. He started to climb to his feet.

Dawson took hold of his arm and helped him. "You mean one of my scouts—*and* one of the prisoners we came here to rescue—are both your sons?"

Evan laughed hollowly. "The trail takes some mighty strange turns sometimes, don't it?"

"Thaddeus," Dawson said sharply, "come over here."

Thad swung Rockly one last time, then set the boy on the ground. He picked up his rifle, then with one hand on Rockly's shoulder, came over to face Evan and Dawson. "Yes, sir?" he said to the colonel.

"First of all, good work on that ambush," Dawson said gruffly. "You and Carter saved our bacon, that's for certain. Now, what's this about you being this man's son? And why did you never tell me that your last name is Littleton?"

Thad looked hard at Evan. "I reckon he's my pa, all right, and by the time I met up with you and the boys, Colonel, I didn't care if I ever heard my last name again or not."

"Why'd you hit me?" asked Evan.

"That was for not bein' dead," snapped Thad. "You put us all through a heap of misery, mournin' you. And Ma might not have died if she hadn't thought you'd gone on without her."

A sharp pain touched Evan deep inside. "You're not telling me anything I haven't told myself a hundred times in the last couple of months, boy. But you don't believe I let all of you think I was dead on purpose, do you?"

"Well . . ." Thad frowned. "I reckon not. What happened to you, anyway?"

"The Yankees captured me, took me up north,

and threw me in a prison camp. Didn't get released until after the war was over, and then it was a mighty long walk back to Texas."

"Oh, Lord," breathed Thad. "We got word that you were dead, Pa. I . . . I felt like I had to go and pay the Yankees back for what they'd done to you."

"But we heard that *you* were dead, too, Thad," Rockly put in. "The Yankees didn't kill you?"

Thad dropped to one knee in front of Rockly. "Nope, they sure didn't," he said with a grin. "I'm right here, big as life and twice as ugly." He glanced up. "Sort of like Pa."

"What happened to you after the war was over?" asked Evan.

Thad patted Rockly on the shoulder again, then stood to face his father. "I had a horse, so I got home faster'n you did. Wasn't nothing or nobody waiting there for me when I did, though. I found Ma's grave on that hill overlooking the place. The cabin was empty, abandoned, and I didn't know what to make of it."

"Couple of carpetbagger brothers are squatting on the farm now," Evan said. "Must've been before they got hold of it when you were there."

"Must have," agreed Thad. "I rode into Richland Springs and asked old man Conyers in the general store what'd happened. He said Ma had died of a fever and the rest of the kids had been split up amongst anybody who would take them in. None of 'em were around town anymore." Thad shook his head and grimaced bitterly. "I didn't see any reason to stay myself, so I rode on. I . . . I was hurtin', Pa. I just wanted to get away from there, put some ground behind me, maybe see some new places."

"And the lad wound up falling in with us and becoming one of my scouts," finished Colonel Dawson. "An incredible story," he added with a shake of his head, "but such is life. As you put it, Evan, the trail takes some strange turns indeed."

Thad rubbed the back of his hand across his mouth, looked down at the ground, and said, "Pa, I guess I'm sorry I busted you in the jaw. I was just so mad there for a minute . . . but I reckon you and I were just about in the same shape, each of us figurin' the other one was dead."

"That's all right, son," Evan said with a grin. He worked his jaw back and forth. "Just don't do it again."

"I won't." Thad looked up. "What about the rest of the family? Where's Dinah, and Billy and Penelope, and little Fulton?"

Evan glanced around at the bodies lying sprawled in the sun and said, "That's a long story, Thad. Why don't we go inside the mission, and I'll tell you all about it."

By midmorning, Evan and Thad and Rockly had finished catching up with each other about the events of the past few years. While they were talking, Dawson's men took care of the burying that needed to be done. Morales and the other bandits, along with the *alcalde*, were tossed into a gully on the edge of the village, but the three members of Dawson's group who had fallen were given Christian burials in the little graveyard behind the mission. It bothered Evan a little to hear the sergeant's report on how the other corpses had been disposed of, but Dawson seemed satisfied. When Evan thought about the terror the bandits had caused for Rockly and Suellen Wilson, he didn't feel quite as bad about their ultimate fate.

Thad looked down at the table where he and his father and brother were sitting and said, "I ought to be ashamed of myself. I should have gone looking for the others, just like you did, Pa. I should have tried to get the family back together."

Evan shrugged. "You're not a daddy, Thad. Makes sense you wouldn't feel the same way I do. And you were just back from a war that was mighty hard on everybody. But I reckon you would've gotten around to looking for the others sooner or later, once you'd thought about it some more."

"I'd like to think so, anyway," Thad said.

"What are we going to do now?" asked Rockly.

Evan grinned at the little boy. "Why, we're going home, that's what we're going to do. Or at least back to the Mulehead ranch, in the Davis Mountains. That's where Dinah and Billy and Penelope are."

"What about Fulton?"

"We'll fetch him, too, don't you worry." Evan was sitting between his sons, and he reached out and put a hand on each boy's shoulder.

"We'll all be together again." At that moment, all the hardships he had endured were more than worth it.

So he should have known it couldn't last, he told himself later.

Across the room, Frank Wilson sat at one of the tables, pale-faced and groaning as one of Dawson's men wrapped a bandage around his wounded leg. The bandit lead had gone clean through his thigh, leaving behind a good-sized hole and a lot of spilled blood. Wilson would be all right, if the wound didn't fester, and Dawson's man had guarded against that by drenching the bullet hole in tequila before patching it up. When the fiery liquor splashed on his raw flesh, Wilson had let out a howl that would have done justice to a lovesick coyote.

Suellen sat beside him, her face blank, her eyes vacant. Between moans, Wilson was talking to her, trying to beg her forgiveness, but so far she was ignoring him. Evan couldn't much blame her. What Wilson had done had been unforgivable.

Colonel Dawson strode in from outside, holding a pair of gloves in his right hand and slapping them against his left palm. The sergeant trailed him. Dawson went to the table where Wilson and Suellen were sitting and asked, "How are you doing, Frank?"

"It hurts awful bad, Colonel, awful bad!" Wilson replied. "I never knew it hurt so bad to get shot."

"Count your blessings, Frank," said Dawson as he switched the gloves to his left hand. "You made it this long without picking up a bullet hole. Of course, now you've got two."

Wilson looked up at him. "Don't you mean one? Unless you're talking about one where the bullet went in and one where it came out. I guess that would make—"

"I mean one in your leg and one in your head," the colonel told him.

Wilson frowned and began, "There's no hole—"

That was all he got out before Dawson drew his pistol and shot him in the head.

The sudden blast took everybody by surprise except the sergeant, who must have known what Dawson was planning to do. Across the room, Rockly jumped and so did Thad. Evan controlled his own reaction a little better, but he couldn't stop his hand from moving toward the butt of his gun. He stopped as the sergeant swung toward him. The burly ex-noncom had already drawn his pistol, and the muzzle centered on Evan's chest.

The Rebel who had been patching up Wilson's injury let out a curse and sprang backward. Suellen flinched and closed her eyes for a second. Even Frank Wilson looked surprised by the black-rimmed hole that had suddenly appeared in his temple—but only for a moment, and then, as a trickle of blood welled from the wound, he slid down in his chair and slumped to the floor underneath the table.

Colonel Dawson holstered his revolver and smiled. "There," he said as he turned toward the table where a stunned Evan, Thad, and Rockly sat. "That's taken care of."

Suellen opened her eyes, leaned back in her chair, and looked underneath the table. "Frank . . . ?" she said in a quavery voice.

Dawson sauntered across the room. "Wilson had it coming to him," he said. "He was a man with no courage, no honor."

Evan found his voice. "You shot him down in cold blood."

"Would you hesitate before stepping on a rat or a snake? Frank Wilson was even less than that."

"He was a human being!" exclaimed Thad.

"Barely." The colonel shrugged. "At any rate, what's done is done. Now there remains the question of what to do next."

Evan's jaw tightened as he realized what Dawson planned. "You're still going to try to sell the woman back to Wilson's father, aren't you? You never intended to turn her loose."

Dawson shook his head. "I very much doubt if Frank's father would pay much—if anything—for a daughter-in-law he's never even met. But with poor Frank dead, killed by those brutal *bandidos* as he tried to rescue his wife and child, well, then, all Frank's father will have left of the boy is his grandson." Dawson reached out and ruffled the reddish-brown hair on Rockly's head. "I think the old man will pay handsomely for this little lad."

Rockly jerked away from Dawson. "I ain't his little lad!" he cried. "I ain't a Wilson! I'm Rockly Littleton, and you can't make me say anything else!"

Dawson arched an eyebrow and asked, "Not even to save the lives of your father and brother?"

"Colonel, you can't do this—" Thad began.

"He can do anything he wants," Evan cut in, his voice low and taut. "He's got the whip hand, son, and what he wants is money. Maybe he cared once about the Confederacy, but he don't anymore. Now he's nothing but a bandit, just like Morales and his men."

Dawson's features flushed with anger. Beside and slightly behind him, the sergeant remained impassive. As Dawson's fingers tightened on the pair of gloves he still carried, he said, "I need you and Thad alive so that the boy will cooperate, Evan, otherwise you might pay for that uncalled-for comment."

Evan put his hands flat on the table and got ready to heave himself to his feet. "You might as well get ready to kill me, then, Colonel, because you're not getting any of my sons."

"Sergeant—" Dawson backed up a step and spoke sharply.

Evan was halfway up from the table, unsure what was going to happen next but caught in the grip of a rage that would no longer be denied. He had come too far, been through too much, to give up Rockly now, just so Dawson could pass him off as Frank Wilson's son and collect a ransom. His hand flashed toward the gun on his hip, even as Thad kicked away from the table in the other direction and started to bring up the Henry rifle in his hands.

That was when Suellen Wilson came out from under the table where her dead husband lay, Wilson's pearl-handled revolver clutched tightly in her hand. She screamed, "You killed him!" as she began to jerk the trigger. "You killed Frank!"

The roar of the shots filled the low-ceilinged room. Colonel Randolph Dawson's eyes opened wide in shock and pain as the bullets slammed into his back. He came up on his toes as Suellen emptied the revolver into him, then crashed forward, face down on the table where Evan and Thad and Rockly had been sitting.

Evan and Thad were both on their feet, and Rockly had leaped away from the table into a nearby corner, where he stood with his back pressed against the adobe wall of the cantina. Evan had his Colt in his fist, and he had it trained on the sergeant, who stood staring at the bloody corpse of Colonel Dawson sprawled on the table. Thad was covering the other men in the room, moving the barrel of the Henry back and forth slightly to take them all in.

Suellen Wilson still held the pearl-handled revolver outstretched in front of her, her grip rock-steady. "You killed Frank," she said again to Dawson, who could no longer hear her. A shudder ran through her, and she lowered the empty pistol so that it pointed toward the floor. "*I* wanted to kill him."

Evan took a deep breath. His heart was pounding heavily in his chest. "There's been enough killing," he said, the words directed toward the sergeant, who still seemed stunned by the colonel's sudden death. Evan went on, "Nobody else dies. I'm taking my boys and the woman, and we're riding out of here."

Slowly, the sergeant lifted his gaze from Dawson's body and looked straight at Evan. "Go," he said. "Nobody's going to stop you."

Evan blinked in surprise.

"I never believed in holding anybody for ransom," rumbled the sergeant. "I'd have followed the colonel right into Hades, but he's dead now. It's over."

"That's making sense," Evan said. He wasn't going to put his complete trust in the sergeant just yet, however. Keeping the Colt lined up on the big man, he said, "Thad, get your brother and the lady and move on out of here. Rockly, can you saddle us some horses?"

"Yes, sir!" The boy sounded excited to have such a task given to him.

"Go on, then. Get moving."

Thad lowered his rifle and went over to Suellen Wilson. "Come on, ma'am," he said gently. "We've got to be leavin'."

"Yes," she said. "I want to go home."

Cautiously, watchfully, Thad ushered his brother and Suellen out of the cantina. Evan backed toward the arched doorway, still covering the sergeant.

He squinted as he emerged into the sun. For a moment, he realized what a good target he made for the men in the cantina, silhouetted like that against the midday brightness. Then the sergeant stepped out of the adobe building as well, hands held well away from his gun. Evidently he had meant the safe conduct he had promised Evan.

But the sergeant didn't speak for everyone in

the group. A shout of "Hey! What's goin' on over there?" came from across the plaza. Evan's head jerked around and he saw Billings and Clegg walking swiftly toward him, their expressions a mixture of anger and puzzlement. The mission was behind them, the bell tower where Thad had ambushed the bandits looming above them.

"Back off," Evan warned, starting to swing around toward them.

"Stop right there, you two!" called the sergeant. "Mr. Littleton and his sons are leaving with Mrs. Wilson, and I don't want anyone interfering with them."

"Where's the colonel?" demanded Billings.

"The colonel's dead," the sergeant replied, a slight catch in his voice. "What he planned is over."

"Like blazes!" yelled Clegg. "He promised us a big payoff for that kid, and we're gettin' it one way or another!"

His hand stabbed toward his gun as he and Billings suddenly veered apart. Billings drew, too, cursing as he slid his Colt from leather with blinding speed.

"Thad!" Evan called as he threw himself to the side and jerked up his gun.

Thad must have known what was about to happen, because from the corner of his eye Evan saw the young man shove Rockly and Suellen Wilson out of the line of fire behind the horses Rockly had saddled. He brought the Henry up one-handed and fired his first shot that way before grabbing the rifle with his other hand to steady it against his hip. He kept firing from that position, blasting shot after shot as fast as he could work the Henry's lever.

Evan's Colt was roaring as well. He thumbed off three shots in little more than the space of a heartbeat, tracking Billings with the gun barrel. Billings got a shot off, but it went high and wild as Evan's slugs ripped into his chest, spinning him around. To his right, Clegg managed to fire twice before the shots from Thad's rifle stitched across his torso, leaving bloodstains that blossomed like crimson flowers. He staggered back, tried to raise the gun in his hand, and went to his knees instead. The gun blasted, kicking up dust in front of him as he pitched forward.

Silence fell along with Billings and Clegg.

Evan looked over at his oldest son and saw the red stain on Thad's shirt. "Thad!" Evan cried raggedly as he started toward the young man.

"It's all right, Pa," Thad told him as he pressed a hand to his side. "Just . . . nicked me . . . that's all . . ."

His eyes rolled up in his head and his knees gave way as Evan reached him. Evan caught him, still holding the Colt as he gathered Thad to him. He turned, shouting, "I need some help here! Blast it, I need some help!"

The sergeant was there then, taking hold of Thad and lowering him to the ground, and despite the gentleness of his actions, his voice was hoarse with rage as he shouted, "Anybody else who bothers these folks will answer to me!"

Rockly came running, trailed by Suellen

Wilson. While Rockly grabbed hold of Evan's leg, Suellen dropped to her knees beside Thad. Her eyes were alive again, and she seemed to have regained some of her strength. "Let me help," she murmured as the sergeant tore away Thad's shirt.

Evan breathed a sigh of relief as he saw the furrow the slug had plowed in Thad's side. The crease was a deep one, messy but nothing more. He sighed again, reached down and rested his hand on Rockly's shoulder.

The sergeant looked up and said, "Looks like it'll be a little longer than you expected before you get home, Mr. Littleton. But I reckon you'll get there."

"We will," Evan vowed.

And wondered just where home really was.

22

Six weeks later, Evan and Thad reined in atop the hill overlooking the farm that had once been their home. Evan was riding a big blood bay stallion and leading the rangy dun, which he intended to return to Andrew Brackett. A powdering of white dusted the landscape, and the cold wind that had brought the first snow of the season a few days earlier still blew from the north. Evan was grateful for the warmth of the sheepskin coat he wore as he and Thad swung down from their saddles and stood solemnly in front of the massive stone that marked the final resting place of Lynette Littleton.

"Well, I did it, Lynette," said Evan as the wind rustled the bare branches of the oaks above their heads. "Found all the kids, safe and sound, even Thad. Soon as we pick up Fulton and head back out to West Texas, we'll all be together again, just like you would have wanted. I'm just sorry we can't . . . stay here with you."

"I don't reckon she minds about that, Pa,"

murmured Thad. "Like you said, Ma would rather that the rest of us be together again."

Evan nodded, feeling the chill of the tears that ran down his leathery cheeks. He was unashamed of the tears; he was leaving something very important behind here in Central Texas. But he had no choice in the matter. The future was out there waiting, and for the sake of his family, that was the direction he had to face from now on.

In some ways, the decision had been an easy one to make. Evan had known that despite whatever good memories he had of this place, he would never again be content to be a farmer. The dangers he had faced during the long search for his children had touched something wild inside him, a part of his being that he had thought successfully buried many years earlier. Now he knew he needed a challenge again.

And establishing a ranch in the wilds of the Davis Mountains would be just such a challenge. There was plenty of unclaimed land out there for the taking—and the holding—including a magnificent valley not far from Clive Cartmill's spread. The Cartmills would make fine neighbors, but when you came right down to it, it would be up to Evan and his children to carve whatever legacy they could out of that rugged land.

He was looking forward to every minute of it.

"I reckon we'd better be going," he said after he and Thad had spent a few minutes of silence by the grave. "We've still got to fetch your little brother, and it's a long ride back to the mountains."

They turned toward the horses, then stopped as they both saw the riders approaching the farm below. Even at this distance, Evan recognized the long dusters, the broad-brimmed black hats.

"Those are State Police, aren't they?" asked Thad, sounding a little nervous. He knew about Evan's earlier run-ins with the carpetbagger lawmen.

Evan nodded grimly. "Could even be the same bunch I tangled with the day I first found your little brother at the ferry. I got the feeling they patrolled regular-like in these parts."

"Well, let's just ride on around the farm and head on over to Brackett's and Russell's. We came here to get Fulton, Pa, not to hunt up more trouble."

Evan glanced sharply at his oldest son. "You think I go hunting for trouble?"

"Maybe not, but it's got a way of finding you, especially lately."

Evan couldn't argue about that. Most folks might go along for years without having any exceptional runs of luck, either good or bad. But in the past few months, it had seemed that everywhere Evan had turned, he had run into some sort of twist of fate. He'd had about enough of it to last him a lifetime.

He rubbed his jaw, stubbled with beard after several days of hard riding. "I don't like leaving anything unfinished," he said quietly.

"I don't like those carpetbaggers any more'n you do, Pa, but hating 'em doesn't do any good. You said so yourself."

That was true, too. After seeing how Colonel Dawson's devotion to the defeated Confederacy had grown into something warped and evil, Evan had known it was time to stop fighting a war that was long over. Eventually, the carpetbaggers would leave Texas; he felt certain of that. But until that day came, it made sense to try to get along with them, rather than fighting them. That was what he had told his children.

Of course, it didn't hurt that the family was going to be settling in West Texas, where the Yankee presence was almost nonexistent. That had played a part in Evan's decision to stay in the Davis Mountains, too.

But as he stood there and watched the black-hatted riders stop at the double cabin and dismount, he felt an irresistible pull, a need to put a finish to this matter. He wasn't sure if he could live with himself if he rode away now and left this last confrontation undone.

"You go on to Brackett's," he said abruptly to Thad as he put his foot in the stirrup and grasped the saddlehorn. "I'll be there directly, then we'll ride over to the ferry."

Thad snorted. "Not hardly! I know what you're up to, Pa. You're going down there to have it out with those Yankees who stole the farm, aren't you?"

Evan stepped up into the saddle and looked down at his son. "Do as I tell you," he said harshly. "Go get Fulton."

"No, sir," said Thad with a shake of his head. "I'm not going to ride off and let you get yourself killed. Not by yourself, anyway."

Evan wanted to argue, but he sensed it wouldn't do any good. A part of him wanted to give in and ride around the farm, like Thad wanted, but that wasn't possible, either. So he sighed and said, "You let me do the talking, boy. And if there's any trouble, you stay out of it. I want you to swear that—" he glanced toward the stone grave marker, "—on your mother's grave."

"Blast it, Pa, that's not—"

"Swear it!"

Thad grimaced. "All right, all right. I swear on Ma's grave that if there's any trouble, I'll stay out of it. There. Is that what you wanted?"

Evan grinned humorlessly and said, "I reckon it'll do. Come on." He turned his mount and rode down the slope toward the cabin. After a second, Thad mounted up and followed, taking the reins of the dun and leading it.

Evan didn't stop until he was about fifty feet from the cabin. As he reined in, he drew a Henry rifle from its saddle boot and rested it across the saddle in front of him. Lifting his voice, he called, "Hello, the cabin!"

The sight of the place made a pang of regret go through him. Smoke curled up from the chimney on the right-hand part of the cabin. The place looked very much like it had during the years he had lived here with his wife and family . . . but now there was something alien about it, due no doubt to the knowledge that there were near-strangers in there, and Yankee carpetbaggers, to boot. Even though Evan knew he could no longer live here, the presence of the Yankees seemed *wrong*.

The door of the right-hand side opened, and a man stepped out into the dogtrot. He wore a woolen shirt and carried a rifle, and Evan recognized him as Abner Crane, one of the men who now claimed to own the farm. Crane's eyes widened in surprise, and Evan knew the carpetbagger had recognized him.

"Howdy," Evan said. "Remember me?"

"How could I forget you?" asked Crane. "There was a lot of gunfire the day you visited here before."

"None of it from me," said Evan. "It was those State Police who were doing the shooting." He glanced at the horses tied up at the hitching post. "Where are they?"

A couple of duster-clad figures stepped around the corner of the cabin. "Right here, Littleton!" one of them called. Both men had leveled Colts in their fists.

Evan sat very still, making no move toward his gun to give them an excuse to start the ball. He hoped Thad would follow his lead. "I didn't come here looking for a fight," he said.

The third lawman appeared at the other corner of the cabin. They must have heard him coming, thought Evan, and slipped out a window to prepare this reception for him.

The third man was holding a pistol, too, and he eared back the hammer with a loud click as he asked, "Then what are you doing here, Littleton? And who's that with you, another outlaw?"

Evan drew a deep breath and held tightly to

his temper. "This is my son Thaddeus," he said, "which ought to tell you that I don't want any shooting. I wouldn't bring my boy into the middle of a gunfight, now would I?"

Maybe Thad wouldn't say anything about that fracas below the border with Billings and Clegg. The bullet crease in his side was fully healed now, but he would always carry the scar. Evan hoped he wouldn't ever have any more bullet scars.

The burly, bearded Crane brother appeared in the dogtrot beside Abner. Lucius, that was his name, recalled Evan. He might not have remembered had not the events of that day been etched in his brain by their poignancy.

The State Police were familiar, too. As Evan had suspected, they were the same trio he had first encountered at Russell's ferry, where he had stopped them from roughing up the old man. Later that day they had found him up on the hill beside Lynette's grave and had tried to bring him down with their rifles, chasing him a good ways to the west before giving up. The man who stood alone at the far corner of the cabin was the one who held the strongest grudge, the one who had wanted to try to gun him down at the ferry, even though Evan had had the drop on them. Now the tables were turned.

"I don't care why you're here, Littleton," the man said. "You're a wanted outlaw, part of the Stubbs gang. We could take you in for trial . . . or string you up right here and now."

"Wait a minute, Mike," said Abner Crane. "The

way I heard it, Littleton helped save a rancher and his family out west of here when the Stubbs gang raided their place. I don't think he was one of the outlaws."

"Stay out of this, Abner! This is State Police business. Littleton helped Harry Stubbs escape from the gallows in Brady, and there ain't any doubt about *that*!"

"I had to ride out of that livery barn or get gunned by Stubbs' *segundo*," Evan said harshly, using the Spanish word he had picked up in West Texas without thinking. "That doesn't make me one of the outlaws."

"I say different," grated the Yankee star packer. "And I've got a rope on my saddle just waiting for your neck, mister."

"Pa," Thad said nervously.

Before Evan could say or do anything, Abner Crane swung toward the lawman and snapped, "Not here, Mike!"

Evan was taken by surprise, but the carpetbagger called Mike was just as shocked by the vehemence of Abner's statement. "What in blazes are you talking about?" demanded Mike.

"You're not going to lynch anybody on this farm," Abner said stubbornly. "I won't allow it."

Lucius stepped forward, following his brother's lead. "Neither will I," he rumbled.

"Blast it! This is as much my place as it is yours! Or did you forget that . . . *brother*?" The final word dripped with scorn, and it took Evan by surprise, too. But then he remembered Abner saying that he and his brothers had taken over the farm for the taxes that were owed on it. Evan had never wondered until now who the third brother was—and now he knew.

Abner strode toward Mike, shaking his head angrily. Evan flicked a glance at the other two State Policemen. They looked confused and uncertain about what to do, and he figured that they wouldn't do anything without orders from Crane, who was clearly the leader of their patrol. He looked back at Abner, who was stepping up to Mike.

"Watch it!" exclaimed Mike. "You're getting in the line of fire, Abner!"

"There's not going to be any gunfire," Abner declared. He reached up, grabbed hold of Mike's gun barrel, and shoved the weapon down. "You know the way people around here feel about us, Mike. They think of Lucius and me as interlopers, Yankees who came down here after the war and stole what didn't belong to us." He glanced at Evan, then went on, "And maybe they've got a point. But we've worked this land now. We're part of it, and it's part of us. We're going to stay, and by God, we're going to be good neighbors if anybody will let us!" He took a deep breath. "We're Texans now, Lucius and me. That's the way we want it."

"You're crazy!" exclaimed Mike. "You start sticking up for Rebs like this, and you'll get yourself arrested for sedition, Abner."

"The war's over, Mike," Abner Crane said quietly. "At least, it is if you'll let it be over." His voice was persuasive as he added, "Put your gun up. Forget about fighting."

For a long moment, Mike hesitated. Then,

glaring at his brother, he lowered the hammer of the Colt and jammed the gun back in its holster. The other two State Policemen followed suit. "All right," Mike said grudgingly. "There won't be any gunplay."

Evan relaxed slightly, and Abner smiled and said, "There. Now don't you feel better?"

"I will," said Mike, "as soon as I've beaten that Reb to death with my bare hands!"

He leaped without warning toward Evan, reaching up to grab the sheepskin coat. Evan wasn't completely taken by surprise, but Mike's action was so unexpected that he didn't have time to get ready for it. Almost before he knew what was happening, Mike had hauled him out of the bay's saddle, and both men hit the ground hard. Evan's hat flew off, and the breath was jarred out of his body by the impact.

"Mike!" he vaguely heard Abner shout. "Stop it!" At the same time, there was the unmistakable ratcheting of a Henry's lever being worked, and Thad cried, "Hold it, gents! I'll drop the first one who touches a gun!"

Evan was too busy to worry overmuch about what else was going on. Mike Crane's fist slammed into his jaw, rocking his head to the side and making stars dance behind his eyes. Evan grabbed hold of Crane's coat and heaved the man to the side, at the same time shaking his head in an attempt to clear some of the cobwebs from it. Crane rolled away, and Evan pushed himself to his hands and knees, still a little groggy. Crane caught himself and lashed out with a booted foot. Evan saw it coming, grabbed it before Crane could drive the heel into his face. He heaved again, and this time as Crane was forced back, Evan went after him.

It was bare knuckles, tooth and nail, all-out fighting as dust rose around the two struggling figures in the small yard in front of the cabin. Evan blocked punches, threw some of his own, absorbed his share of punishment. After a few moments, he was able to shove Crane away again, and he took advantage of the respite to scramble back to his feet. His chest heaved as he gulped air into his lungs, and the pounding of his pulse in his head was like a series of hammer blows against his skull. For a second, Evan thought about stepping forward and kicking Crane as the carpetbagger lawman floundered around on hands and knees, trying to get up. That was what Crane would have done had their positions been reversed, Evan knew.

But it wasn't the way he had lived his life and fought his fights, and he was too blamed old to change now. He stepped back, set himself, and waited for Crane's charge. It came as soon as Crane was back on his feet.

Lowering his head like a bull, Crane drove forward, bellowing out his rage like a bull, too. Evan met him with a hard right that straightened him up, followed the blow with a left that snapped Crane's head around. The lawman was a brawler, and he shrugged off the pain before Evan could press his advantage. His fist caught Evan on the breastbone and rocked him back.

They stood there, almost toe to toe, slugging back and forth, drops of blood flying through the air around their heads each time a punch landed. It was brutal, with nothing fancy or artistic about it. The man who could withstand the most punishment was the man who would be left standing on his feet when the battle was over.

Time meant nothing. They might have been there a minute or an hour when Evan sunk his left fist deep in Crane's belly. The carpetbagger grunted and leaned forward, hugging himself momentarily against the pain. That left his jaw in perfect position for the roundhouse right that Evan threw with all of his remaining strength behind it.

The sound was like the blade of an ax striking a stump. Crane straightened and stumbled back a couple of steps, then his feet went out from under him. He fell sideways, bouncing a little on the hard ground when he landed. He was so motionless that he might have been dead, if not for the rasp of breath in his throat.

Evan swayed but stayed on his feet. He blinked blood out of his eyes, then lifted his hand and blearily studied it. Knotted and swelling, with a busted knuckle or two for sure. It would be a while before he could handle a gun again.

But it had felt so good to give that Yankee what he had coming to him!

Mike Crane wasn't the only Yankee around here, Evan was reminded a second later when Abner said, "That was some fight. Mike will be hurting for a week."

"He . . . ain't the only one," Evan managed to say.

Abner tucked his rifle under his arm and walked over to face the other two State Policemen. "Lucius and I will tend to our brother," he said. "The two of you had best go on with your patrol."

One of them gestured at the bloody figure slumped on the ground. "We can't leave without Mike," he protested.

"Of course you can. In fact, you'll be neglecting your duty if you don't. I'm certain you wouldn't want me to report that to your Captain McNelly in Austin."

The lawmen did some grumbling, but within a matter of moments, both of them had mounted up and ridden away from the cabin. Evan suspected they were secretly relieved that they hadn't had to try to arrest him and Thad. The young man had been ready to do some damage with that Henry rifle he still held in his hands.

Briskly, Abner went on, "Lucius, will you see to Mike while I speak with our visitors here?"

"Yeah, I reckon," said Lucius, already beginning to sound a little like a Texan. "He's not going to be happy when he wakes up."

"He hasn't been happy since we were all children, and I'm not sure he ever was then," said Abner. He turned to Evan and went on, "That hand's going to be mighty sore for a while."

"Yep."

Abner grinned. "But I imagine you thought it was worth it."

Evan returned the grin. "Yep. You're a hard man to figure out, Crane."

"Because I'm a Yankee, you mean, and yet I'm not unsympathetic to the problems of the people here in Texas?"

Remembering Colonel Randolph Dawson, Evan said, "I reckon there's good folks—and lowdown snakes—in just about every kind of people, whether they be Yankees or Rebs or anything in between."

"As I said before, I'm content now just to be a Texan, my friend, . . . Now, I'd suggest that for your own good, you conclude whatever business you have around here rather quickly and head west again."

"That's what I figure to do, all right," agreed Evan.

Abner frowned slightly. "Why *did* you ride down here? You could have avoided this farm."

Evan drew a deep breath and stuck out his hand. "Maybe so I could do this."

Abner took the hand, being careful of the broken knuckles.

Evan turned away a moment later and picked up his hat, then swung up onto the bay. He and Thad turned their horses, and as they rode off, Abner Crane called after them, "Have a safe trip home!"

Evan lifted a hand in a wave without looking back. He thought about his children: the son here beside him, the one waiting up ahead at the ferry, the two girls and the two boys who had been left behind in the Davis Mountains. . . . He and Thad were still getting used to the idea that someone they had believed dead was still alive;

Billy still harbored some resentment toward both of them, but things had been getting a little easier by the time Evan and Thad had left the Mulehead; Dinah and Penelope were thrilled to have not only their daddy but their big brother back; Rockly and Fulton had both been so young when Evan left for the war that he felt he was going to have to get to know both of them all over again, but he was looking forward to that opportunity. All in all, he was sure they would have their share of fusses and squabbles, just like any other family, but they would be together and they would never stop loving each other. The future held hope again. Once Evan had wondered where home really was, but now he knew the answer to that question.

Home was where folks loved each other, and were loved right back.

ABOUT THE AUTHOR

A professional author for more than twenty years, JAMES REASONER has written dozens of novels, many of them Westerns and historical sagas, including the *Wind River* series and *The Wilderness Road* for HarperPaperbacks. He is married to popular mystery and Western novelist L. J. Washburn.